KHUSHWANT SINGl
much the most widely read columnist in India today. ~~~ ~~~~ ~~~~y
columns are reproduced by over 50 journals in India and abroad.

With 62 books to his credit, Khushwant Singh first shot into
fame with his award-winning bestseller *Train to Pakistan*
(1955), which powerfully depicted the mass hysteria and senseless
communal violence that followed the 1947 partition of the country.
This novel was followed by *I Shall Not Hear the Nightingale* (1959),
a short-story collection *A Bride for the Sahib* (1967), and the nonfiction collection *Good People, Bad People* (1977).

Over the years he has lectured and written extensively on history, culture, and philosophy. In 1966, he published a two-volume
History of the Sikhs, which now, fully updated, is still considered the
most authoritative writing on the subject. His two recent bestsellers
include *Delhi—a novel* and *Need for a New Religion in India and
other Essays*.

ROHINI SINGH has already compiled and edited four anthologies of
Khushwant Singh's writings. She has authored a number of cookery
books published in India and the UK as well as the bestseller *Party
Games for All Ages*.

Also by Khushwant Singh
in UBSPD

**Need for a New Religion in India
and Other Essays**

Edited by Rohini Singh

Sex, Scotch & Scholarship

Khushwant Singh
selected writings

Compiled & Edited by
Rohini Singh

 **UBSPD**
UBS Publishers' Distributors Ltd.
New Delhi • Bombay • Bangalore • Madras
Calcutta • Patna • Kanpur • London

UBS Publishers' Distributors Ltd.
5 Ansari Road, New Delhi-110 002
Bombay Bangalore Madras
Calcutta Patna Kanpur London

© Text KHUSHWANT SINGH 1992
© Introduction, selection, and arrangement ROHINI SINGH

First Published   1992
First Reprint   1992
Second Reprint   1992
Third Reprint   1993
Fourth Reprint   1993

ISBN   81-85674-50-7

Jacket Design : UBS Art Studio
Cover Photo: Sondeep Shankar

Lasertypeset by ADR Enterprises, G-51, Saket, New Delhi-110 017.
Printed at Rajkamal Electric Press, B-35/9, G. T. Karnal Road
Industrial Area, Delhi-110 033

for
anita shourie
the fairest and bravest of women

Contents

Introduction

T his is the fifth anthology of Khushwant Singh's writings
that I have had the pleasure of compiling. I seem to be getting more efficient at the job. In all the earlier ones, it devolved
upon me to preface the collection with a short biographical piece
on the author, tracing his rise from being an academic failure to
one of the most widely-read and highest-selling authors in India
today. This time I have deftly absolved myself of this task by
inspiring Khushwant himself to write an expansive, autobiogra-
phical piece. It is the first in this book, written in his characteristi-
cally candid, forthright style, with the eye to detail that is his
forté. It makes satisfying reading, being as it is perhaps one of
the most 'complete' and accurate self-portraits he has ever made.
As he turns the telescope on himself, he tells you what his alarm
clock says to wake him up, the kind of tea he drinks, the strictly
regimented daily routine he follows as well as the lesser-known
details of his early childhood and later years as he struggled to
establish himself as a writer.

A few words about this anthology. The earlier selections
of writings were usually confined to a limited number of topics.
Unlike them, in this collection, an attempt has been made to not
only bring out the quality of Khushwant Singh's writing, in his
own opinion, comparable to R K Narayan, Mulk Raj Anand,
Manohar Mulgaonkar, Ruth Jhabvala, Nayantara Sahgal and Anita
Desai, but also to highlight its depth and diversity which, as it
happens, is closely interlinked to the author's experiences
and interests over the years. This selection mirrors these concerns.

Khushwant Singh started life by practising law then switched
to diplomacy which he gave up after a few years to turn to serious

writing. Along the way, he taught Comparative Religions at Princeton, Swarthmore and Hawaii, translated the Sikhs' prayer, *Japji,* as also researched and wrote a two-volume *History of the Sikhs,* considered one of the most authoritative works on the subject. His interest in religion was aroused early in life. Though born into a highly religious, God-fearing family, he began to question the value of rituals and the need to conform to Khalsa traditions while in college. In his own words, "I decided, however, to go along with them rather than create trouble for myself. I took pains to understand the prayers I had been reciting.... Meanwhile, at St. Stephen's College, I attended Bible classes. Although the emphasis was on the New Testament, and the life of Jesus Christ, it was the language of the Old Testament, particularly the Psalms, the Song of Solomon and the Book of Job that I found myself drawn to. Later, while working on the Sikh scriptures, I found so many references to the *Vedas, Upanishads* and the epics, the *Ramayana* and the *Mahabharata* including the Geeta, that I decided to study them to better understand the meaning of my own *Gurubaani.*" Two translations, taken from the book, *Hymns of Guru Nanak,* are included here. "Interest in religion," he continues, "also made me read whatever I could on Jainism, Buddhism and later developments in Hinduism. Islam was the last religion I turned to, largely to free myself of anti-Muslim prejudices which had been instilled into me as a child. By the time I was 40, no religion evoked much enthusiasm in my mind." Expectedly, Khushwant's views on religion are unconventional. He is a self-professed agnostic, and has consistently lectured as well as pleaded in print for a rationalisation of religions, shorn of unnecessary rituals and customs. You will find four short pieces here, mirroring his attitude.

Another of his pet passions has been a study of nature. As he explains in the preface to his book, *Nature Watch,* it all began many summers ago while he was spending a holiday with his English friends, the Wints, in Oxford. Their three-year-old daughter, who was an avid collector of wild flowers, was his first teacher and the one who kindled an interest in natural phenomena, which has endured to this day. Over the years, Khushwant has given talks on the subject on All India Radio as well as done a highly-rated television serial, *The World of Nature* for Doordarshan. For this anthology, I have selected one chapter, May, from *Nature Watch*, a book patterned after the traditional *Baramasi* of the Indian poets and in Khushwant's own words, "one of the most precious books" he has written.

Khushwant Singh is a widely travelled man and insists that he has seen all that is worth seeing: cathedrals, temples, pagodas, mosques, palaces and picture galleries, deserted cities, pyramids, the Sphinx, sea-sized lakes, lofty mountain ranges, waterfalls, subterranean grottoes lit by myriads of glowworms, ballets, theatres, music halls, strip-tease joints. He is quick to point out that he has rarely had to pay for his travel or hospitality. His hosts, however, I am sure, have felt amply compensated by accounts of his trips published in his syndicated columns and carried by over 50 newspapers in all the major regional languages of the country.

What makes Khushwant's travelogues special is his total lack of inhibition. He tells it all as he saw it, missing out nothing, whether it was a rebuffed pass at a girl, a joke at his expense or a lecherous intention that came to nothing. He quotes the local poetry, describes the local cuisine, art, customs and culture. Perhaps more than in any facet of his writing, his travelogues highlight one of his unique gifts—the ability to laugh at himself. It comes through in the pieces selected for this book. Only one could be called an exception—the piece on Pakistan, the country of his birth and one to which he has always felt obsessively attached, to the point of being dubbed "a Pakistani agent." The piece selected for this anthology in which he returns to Hadali, his birth-place, is unashamedly emotional.

Another two pieces about which you could say the same thing are the two speeches included here, made in Parliament: one a tribute to Mrs Indira Gandhi on her death and the other focussing on the situation in Punjab, a subject on which Khushwant has been perhaps the most vocal Sikh, arguing for a more balanced and humane approach to a problem that has now become a thorn in the body politic of the nation. Though he has written extensively and regularly on the subject for Indian and foreign newspapers—a piece on Khalistan is included here—the time at which his voice was perhaps heard the loudest was during his years as a Member of Parliament. He documented his experiences in the Rajya Sabha in his typically acerbic style, lampooning many of his fellow-parliamentarians. The piece, written for *Sunday* is included here.

Lampooning people, in any case, is Khushwant's speciality. Not the tiniest quirk or mannerism escapes his attention and he is faithful in recording it to the minutest detail. I am sure many of his caricatures have irked and annoyed but they have certainly had the ring of truth and whether or not one admits it, it is certainly one of the parts of his writings that are most enjoyable, the more malicious, the better. You will find a small variety here.

You will also enjoy reading three pithy commentaries on life in India—on sex, humour and poverty. On a different plane, are two brilliant short stories, taken from a collection comprising thirty two. It was a difficult choice to make and I finally settled for one with an earthy, rural flavour while the other sketches, tongue-in-cheek, a westernised Indian gentleman, his rustic wife and their totally alien attitudes. If you haven't read it already, I will not ruin it by telling you the ending.

Over the years Khushwant has done a number of translations from Urdu and Punjabi to English. Though Allama Iqbal's *Shikwa* and *Jawab-e-Shikwa* are perhaps the better known, for this anthology, I have selected a masterfully written extract from *Umrao Jaan Ada* by Mirza Mohammad Hadi Ruswa which Khushwant translated along with M.A. Husaini.

Khushwant is exceptionally easy to work with, quick to accept suggestions and take decisions. While sifting through the material for this collection I came across this letter written to Mr Lewis Bergman, the editor of an American magazine, *Across the Board*. Khushwant writes: "I enclose my piece as required. It needed a hell of a lot of research and writing. Take any liberties with it you like." It is precisely this attitude that has made it such a pleasure to edit and compile this anthology of writings.

New Delhi   — Rohini Singh

LOOKING BACK

"Looking into the depths of one's own eyes can reveal the naked truth. The naked truth about oneself can be very ugly ..."

On Myself

"**N**aana, are you really a womaniser?" my sixteen-year-old granddaughter asked me one morning. My wife (her *naani*) and my daughter (her mother) were present.

How does a 77-year-old grandfather answer so direct a question put to him by his teenaged grandchild? "Of course I am!" I replied. "Don't you see all the pretty women who come to see me: Saadia, Kamna, Jayalalitha, Syeda, Prema, Kumkum, Mrinal, Masooma?"

"That's not the same thing," she replied looking very knowledgable.

What had provoked the question was an incident that took place in her English class at school. They had a new teacher who did not know much about her students parentage and my granddaughter had in any case never told anyone about me! Only her closest friend, who sat next to her in class, knew about our relationship. The lesson that morning was my short story *The Portrait of a Lady* about my grandmother. The teacher thought it best to tell her students something about its author before she dealt with his work. She told them that the writer of the story was the worst stereotype of a Sardarji's image in the popular mind: loud-mouthed, aggressive, a philanderer, drunkard and womaniser. The girls took it down in their notebooks. My granddaughter and her friend giggled merrily. By the next morning, the teacher had discovered that one of her students was my granddaughter. She adopted a different tone. She lauded my virtues as a writer of great sensibility concise in the use of words, etc., etc. My granddaughter and her friend had more reason to giggle as they sensed their teacher painfully trying to make up for the *faux pas* she had committed the day earlier.

I cannot blame the teacher too much because that is my popular image: of a drunkard and a womaniser. I can't even blame people who visualise me inebriated, with my arms round well-stacked bosomy women. I am chiefly responsible for painting myself in those lurid colours. Unfortunately, it is not a true portrayal. I am not a drunkard; I have never been drunk even once in the over fifty years I have been drinking. And though some women have come into my life as they do in the lives of most men, I have never made unwelcome passes at them, nor been snubbed or slapped for taking undue liberties with any. As a matter of fact, though I am nothing to look at, it is women who have sought my company more than I have sought their's. I am a good listener and very liberal with my compliments. These two traits account for the limited popularity I enjoy with the opposite sex.

My daily routine which has varied over the years, with my whereabouts and my preoccupations at the time has been much the same for the last ten years that I have been living in Delhi. I get up between 4 and 5 a.m. It is usually closer to 4 a.m. and never beyond five as two alarm clocks make sure I sleep no more. One is the conventional type which goes off with an ear-splitting explosion of metal striking metal. The second is a Japanese speaking clock which starts with a short musical piece followed by a Jap speaking Ameringish "Good morning! It is five 'o' clock. Time to get up." Five minutes later, it comes on again to remind me: "It is five minutes after five. Time for you to get going." And five minutes after that yet another reminder: "It is now ten minutes after five. Please hurry!"

I do. I go into my study, switch on the kettle, get milk out of the fridge, a packet of Ginseng from a pewter box. I fill a platter with chilled milk and dilute it with hot water; I make two mugs of tea for my security guards (I've had them for over five years) and one with Ginseng for myself. As I open my front door, a dozen cats of different sizes and colours charge at me. I put the platter of milk on the floor—about six manage to get their heads in to sip; others stay at a respectful distance. I give mugs of tea to my guards and am rewarded by a copy of *The Hindustan Times* which is delivered to me free of charge around 4 a.m. because I edited it for three years (1980-83). I scan the headlines while I sip my Ginseng. I look up obituaries and In Memoriams on page 4 to find out which of my fellow citizens have left for their heavenly abodes. I switch on my transistor and listen to *Asa di var* from the Golden Temple or hymns on the national service while I change into my tennis clothes.

In summer, I am at the Gymkhana Club tennis courts at 6 a.m. (in winter it is 7 a.m.). My tennis has deteriorated with time. I no longer play it with the vigour I did some years ago; my sporting companions suffer me because I am their best supplier of imported tennis balls. I now rarely play more than one set. Back home, I have a quick shower—I believe in taking a cold shower on the coldest of days as a preventer of colds—and get down to reading other papers while I have my breakfast of two toasts and tea. About the only time I waste is solving crossword puzzles. Then I get down to my reading and writing. I have to fight off telephone calls and visitors. Sometimes I simply put the phone off the hook and tell my security guards to tell visitors I am not at home. I never see anyone who has not made a prior appointment. This is not snobbery but self-preservation. To me, time is sacred. And fleeting. There is so much to read, write, see and do. And so little time left to fit it all in.

I have a very light lunch—a bowl of soup or yoghurt, germinated cereals or *thayeer saadam* followed by half-an-hour of siesta. Then back to reading and writing and fighting off the telephone. I receive an average of between 10-20 letters a day and make it a point to answer every one. Often, it is no more than a line or two on a post card. I regard not answering letters gross discourtesy. Dealing with correspondence wastes a lot of my time as there are quite a few people who write very long letters and far too frequently. They write in English, Hindi, Urdu and Punjabi. I often receive abusive letters as well as love-letters from girls I have never met.

I take a couple of hours' break to go for a swim in the Golf Club open-air pool. They let me in before others and I usually have it all to myself to do 30-40 lengths. I do not enjoy it any more than I do my tennis but feel I must persist in taking exercise to keep myself fit for mental work: *mens sana in corpore sano* —A healthy mind needs a healthy body. I always take a book with me to read after I've had my swim. I have to dodge people who want to talk to me.

Comes the evening and I look forward to my Scotch. After all that exercise and frugal meals, I feel it warming its way down my entrails. Left to myself, I would like to drink alone while listening to music or watching T.V. But I am rarely left alone, and usually have quite a *mehfil* to drink with me. I rarely go to cocktail receptions given by Delhi's diplomatic community, except when my stock of Scotch is low and then too, for just long enough to take my quota of three large Scotches and get back home.

Many stories of my rudeness have been circulated. They are true. I prescribe the time for my drink and dinner and walk out if my host does not observe it. In my own home, I have dinner parties at least twice a week. I make sure my guests arrive on time. And ask them to leave before 9 p.m. They do. And are quite happy to have an early evening. I watch the English news on Doordarshan and take a crossword puzzle to put me to sleep. I also have a collection of books on dirty jokes by my bedside which I dip into before my siesta and night's sleep. By now I know almost all the jokes there are in the world. I enjoy dirty jokes.

Now consider how much time I have to indulge in drinking or womanising! My drinking never lasts more than 40 minutes. And as I have said before, not once in my life have I been drunk: high, yes; garrulous, yes; amorous, yes. But never out of control, staggering or talking bullshit. I have even less time to indulge in women. And when I have, as when I am in Bombay, Calcutta, Madras, Hyderabad or abroad, I have a gunman with a bayonet fixed on his rifle outside my hotel door. That can dampen the ardour of any Casanova and turn any nymphomaniac frigid.

The picture of my present-day life would be incomplete if I did not tell you something about my wife. Most people who don't know me or my family are under the impression that she doesn't exist or is tucked away in some village like the wives of many of our *netas*. This is a grievous error as my wife is quite a formidable character who rules the home with as firm a hand as Indira Gandhi ruled India. Unlike the mod girls of today who bob their hair, wear T-shirts, jeans and speak *chi chi* Hindish but when it comes to being married, tamely surrender their right to choose husbands to their parents, my wife made her own choice over fifty years ago.

I soon learnt that I could not take my wife for granted. If she did not like any of my friends, she told them so on their faces in no uncertain terms. She is a stronger woman than any I have known. Her mother was very upset when she discovered she drank whisky. One evening she stormed into the room, picked up her glass and threw it on the marble floor. The glass did not break but slithered across the floor, spilling its contents. My wife quickly picked it up and refilled it. "I am an adult and a married woman. You have no right to dictate to me," she told her mother. When her mother was down with cancer, she asked her to promise that she would say her prayers regularly. Despite my pleas to say "yes" to her dying mother, she refused to do so. "I will not make a promise that I know I will not keep." She nursed her mother for many months, sitting with her head in her lap and pressing it all through the nights. She was with her when she died. She took her bath and went to the coffee house to have her breakfast. When some friends asked her about her mother's health she replied, "She is okay". She then came home and told the servants that she would not   receive any visitors who came to condole with her. She did not shed a tear. She did not go to her mother's funeral or any   religious ceremonies that followed. On the other hand, when our dog Simba (he was really a member of the family) fell ill, she sat all night stroking him. When he died at the ripe old age of 14, (90 by human reckoning) she was heartbroken.

The rigid discipline of time maintained in our home is entirely due to her. I have only recently taught myself how to speed the departure of long-winded visitors. She has always given them the short-shrift. No one drops in on us without prior warning. If any relation breezes in, in the morning, she ignores their presence and continues with her housework and decides the menus for the day. We eat the most gourmet food—French, Chinese, Italian, South Indian and occasionally Punjabi. She has two shelves full of cookery books which she consults before discussing it with our cook Chandan, who has been with us for over 30 years, or she continues to teach the servants' children and help them with their homework. We don't accept lunch or tea invitations nor invite people for them. When we have people for dinner, no matter who they are, Cabinet Ministers, Ambassadors or whoever, they are reminded to be punctual and told that we do not expect our guests to stay after 9 p.m. Once the German Ambassador and his wife came over. The meal was finished at 8.30 p.m. Liqueurs were served. It was 8.45 p.m. The Ambassador took out his cigar and asked my wife, "I know, Mrs Singh, that you like your guests to leave before 9 p.m. but can I have my cigar before we go?" My wife promptly replied, "I am sure Mr Ambassador, you will enjoy it more in your car." He laughed and stood up "I get it." And departed without any rancour.

I have a lot of pretty girls visiting me. They are dead scared of my wife and know that they have to be on her right side to keep dropping in. All of them take good care never to offend her.

Why do so few people know about my wife? She is allergic to photographers and pressmen. All you have to do is take out your camera, tape recorder or pen and she will order you out of the house. The allergy runs in the females of the family. My daughter and granddaughter react the same way.

I may sound like a virtuous old man rather than the dirty old one of the popular image. Neither is true. That this should happen to me at a time when I should be regarded as a respected senior citizen, a venerable scholar needs to be explained. I will go back to my childhood.

Where I was born I know. When I was born remains a conjecture. I was born in a tiny hamlet called Hadali, lost in the sand dunes of the Thar Desert. It was seven miles west of the river Jhelum and about forty miles south of the Khewra Salt Mine range. I recall very little of my village days except the endless wastes of sand on which we played on moonlit nights. My parents had migrated to Delhi taking my elder brother with them. I was left in the care of my grandmother. It was she who took me to the school attached to the village temple. And while I was taught the letters of the Gurmukhi alphabet, she read the holy scripture, *Granth Sahib*. Our classes ended before noon. She would take me back home. We were followed by hordes of pi-dogs because she always brought left-over bread to give them. In the afternoon she plied her spinning wheel as she murmured *Sukhmani*, the psalm of peace. In the evening almost the entire village turned out of their homes. After being milked, buffaloes were driven to the pond to wallow. Women formed groups to find sheltered spots where they could defecate and gossip. Boys made their own groups to do the same. Since there was no water at hand we devised our own means of cleaning ourselves and having fun at the same time. We sat in a line and at a given signal, propelled ourselves forward by our hands as fast as we could. By the end of the race our bottoms were cleaned and dried, and also full of desert sand. The game was known as *gheesee*—the bottom-wiping race.

We ate our supper before sunset. On moonlit nights I was allowed to go out to play with the other boys. These were the happiest memories of my childhood. There were others which continue to disturb my sleep to this day. Our village was largely populated by Muslims. They were big, brawny men, well over six feet tall and proud of their martial traditions. We Sikhs and Hindus were tradesmen or moneylenders. Muslims relied on us for their supplies of tea, salt, spices, vegetables, and ready cash. They were usually indebted to us. If we refused to give them credit or became too insistent on being repaid, they thought nothing of instigating gangs of dacoits to teach us a lesson. Once a Sikh family had a wedding and needed money to give their daughter a suitable dowry. They pestered their debtors. One night a gang of dacoits raided their home, killed three men, took all their cash and jewellery, and abducted the bride as well. The nearest police station was more than nineteen miles away. Most of the police were also Muslims. No arrests were made. Neither the money nor the bride was found. She was converted to Islam and married off to a young Muslim soldier. Such periodic experiences kept us in dread of our Muslim neighbours.

When I was five-years-old, my parents sent for us. By then I had a baby brother. My parents had rented a small shack near where my father had taken contracts for the building of a new capital of India, New Delhi. My grandmother and I shared one bedroom, so there was no break in our friendship. My elder brother and I were put in a newly opened school known as the Modern. Unlike other schools in northern India, the Modern was co-educational: there were five girls among thirty boys. The principal and majority of the teachers, including two English, were women. Besides the usual courses of study, we were also taught music, painting, and carpentry. It was a nationalist school; leaders like Mahatma Gandhi, Pandit Nehru, and Sarojini Naidu were invited to address us.

It was in my third year at school that I discovered when

approximately I was born. In Hadali there were no such things as registers of births and deaths. Since my father was away in Delhi when I was born, he did not put it in his diary as he had done in the cases of my elder brother and younger brother and two others that came after him. When he had to fill out my school admission form, for reasons unknown he put down my date of birth as 2 February 1915. Other children at Modern School came from westernised families and celebrated birthdays. I found I was the loser, as I had to take presents wherever I was invited. So I decided to have my own birthday party. I had a birthday cake with seven candles and lots of eats and fizzy drinks. Boys and girls turned up carrying gifts. It was then that my grandmother asked me, "What is all this fuss about?"

"I am having my seventh birthday party," I replied.

"You are a silly boy!" she snapped. "You were not born in the winter. It was summer. Sometime after the beginning of the World War." She was not sure of the date but mentioned the month by the Indian calendar—*budroo. Budroo* corresponds to July-August. All I know about my nativity is that I am a Leo. I later decided to fix my date of birth at 15 August 1915—India became an independent country on 15 August 1947.

Most people say that their school days were the happiest of their lives—carefree and full of fun. Mine certainly were neither carefree nor packed with laughter. I dreaded school and often bunked it by pretending to be sick and spending hours at a wayside clinic. I was neither good at studies nor at games. I barely scraped through my yearly exams and was often punished. Although our school proclaimed that it had abolished corporal punishment, I was often caned. I was scared to death of the lady principal, who often smacked my knuckles with a foot ruler. The nine years at Modern School gave me examphobia which I have not overcome to this day. My anxiety dreams usually take the form of finding myself in an examination hall without being able to answer a single question on the test paper. I wake up sweating round the neck. I was glad when my school days were over. I passed my matriculation examination in 1930.

The carefree years of my life began and ended with my eight years at different colleges. I first joined St. Stephen's College in Delhi. It was run by the Cambridge Mission and regarded amongst the best in northern India. By then my father's contracting business had prospered and we were living in a large double-storeyed house with three acres of lawn, a fruit and vegetable garden, and a tennis court. My father had two cars and hordes of servants. My elder brother and I were given motorcycles to ride to college, which was almost five miles from our home. Even in the large house with over a dozen bedrooms, I continued to share mine with my grandmother. By then there had been two further additions to the family, a sister and another brother, making us five in all.

There were five boys at St. Stephen's with motorcycles, all Sikhs. Indian colleges had borrowed a very unhealthy institution from British universities known as ragging. New entrants, known as "first-year fools," were subjected to a lot of rough horseplay, ranging from standing up on the bench and announcing, "I am a first-year bloody fool," to being taken into hostel rooms and stripped naked. Some were forced to masturbate; the more effeminate were kissed; there were occasions when they were buggered. Fortunately, I was spared this ordeal, as after being admitted I went down with typhoid. I had several relapses and had to miss the entire first term. By the time I began attending classes, the baiting season was over. Besides, my having a motorcycle made most of my would-be baiters settle for a ride on the pillion.

My two years at St. Stephen's were very happy but in no way distinguished. I continued to be as poor a student as I was a player of tennis and hockey, on which I wasted more time than I did on my textbooks. I did however attend Bible classes, which were optional, and got to savour the language of the Old and New Testaments. The Old Testament became my favourite reading—not because of its moral precepts but because of its sonorous language. I also made friends who have stayed friends throughout my life. The one who came into my life in more ways than one was E N Mangat Rai, from a Christian family. He was the brightest student in my class and walked away with more prizes than anyone else every year. He subsequently made the coveted Indian Civil Service, did his probation at Keble College, Oxford, and rose to the seniormost posts in government service. He was a great and persuasive talker. Also an agnostic. It took me many years to shed his way of thinking. He moulded the minds of many of his contemporaries.

I scraped through my intermediate exam largely because, having been taught by English women, I knew the language better than most other Indians, who usually started with the alphabet at the age of twelve. This gave me a head start over others answering questions on history, logic, and economics. However, at the end of two years, I decided to shift to Lahore, where I intended to settle down later. I chose to join the Government College, then the most prestigious in the country. For my interview I was accompanied by my uncle, who, in his time, had captained the college hockey team, and was then a member of the Punjab Legislative Council. In Government College, family connections and influence mattered more than scholarship. When I was admitted to the third year, my cousin joined the first year. For a time we lived with my newly married uncle and his second wife. She was not very kind to her stepson. We moved to the college hostel, where we shared a room. I brought my motorcycle from Delhi and, being the only one to have such a vehicle, was accepted by the elite of the student body, consisting of boys from princely or landed families. By then vastly exaggerated stories of my father's wealth had begun to circulate. He was said to own half the new city of Delhi. That assured me of special consideration by my professors and fellow students.

I did no better in Government College than I had done at St. Stephen's. The only difference was that I did a little better at games, and after strenuous practice made it onto the college swimming team. I also put my name down for the annual college debate. It came as a pleasant surprise to me that instead of being hooted, as most speakers were, I was heard with rapt attention, my jokes evoked a lot of laughter, and I got away with the first prize, the only one I ever won in any university.

Although Government College was known for its prowess at sports—it always had four to five players in the Indian Olympic hockey team and several in its track-and-field events—it also had several distinguished men of letters. On the staff was Ahmed Shah Bokhari, the best after-dinner speaker in English that I have heard, who also wrote very witty Urdu prose. With him were two other Urdu writers, Tahseer and Imtiaz Ali Taj. They translated English classics into Urdu. Their rendering of *Figaro* and Shakespeare's *Mids''mmer Night's Dream* were better enacted on the Lahore stage than anything I saw later. At the same time we had Faiz Ahmed Faiz, who had just taken his master's degree but was often seen in college. His poems were being widely published, and most critics conceded that Faiz would soon blaze a new trail in Urdu poetry—which in fact he did.

There were other contemporaries at college whose latent powers blossomed in their later years. Most of them made it to the top in the film world in Bombay. They included actors Balraj Sahni and Dev Anand, actress Kamini Kaushal, and directors B R Chopra and Chetan Anand.

I passed my Bachelor of Arts examination in the third division. With my poor academic record I had little prospect of making it into Oxford or Cambridge. Of the London colleges, where I would be admitted, I opted for King's College, for no other reason than its regal name, in preference to University College, the School of Economics, or the School of Oriental Studies. In any case, all I wanted to do in England was to qualify for the bar. This in years past required no more than dining at the Inns of Court for three years and paying a fee which gave you licence to practise law in any high court.

In the summer of 1934 I left Delhi by train for Bombay. Hundreds of my father's friends and distant relations came to see me off at the railway station. In those times going abroad was a rare adventure for Indians. I was loaded with garlands as if I were going out to conquer the world. My elder brother and his wife were sent with me to see me safely on board my ship.

My first sea voyage was on the Italian boat *Conte Rosso*. Most of the economy class was taken up by Indian students. I was given the lower berth in a cabin for six. It was monsoon time. Lunch was announced as the boat pulled out of the harbour. By the time soup was served, the boat began to rock and roll. The dining room emptied and we ran back to our cabins. For the next five days the ship reeked of vomit. I only left my berth to rush to and back from the bathroom and let the cabin steward make my bed. Huge waves washed over the decks; the boat groaned and shuddered as if it was about to break into pieces. It was only when we got to Aden that the sea became calm.

Aden was not a great change. All the shops were owned by Indians. The only Arabs we saw were pedlars or beggars. Thereafter, began the pleasanter part of our voyage. A placid Red Sea; at sunset dolphins by the hundreds doing cartwheels as far as the eye could see; moonlit nights heavy with the fragrance of the desert.

We entered the Suez Canal. The more enterprising went off to visit the pyramids and reboard the ship at Port Said. One boy who was in my class in Government College and had been there had told us of nude shows and brothels stocked with young whores from distant parts of the world. And how little it cost to be laid. Much as I yearned to savour joys of the flesh, I was far too scared to risk such a venture. Like me, another two boys made a virtue of timidity and we spent our time walking along the seafront to the statue of Ferdinand de Lesseps, the engineer who designed the canal, and wandered round Simon Arzt, the largest department store in the east. We took sly glances at dirty picture postcards which were stuck in front of our noses by insistent pedlars. By the evening the other boys came on board and we eagerly heard of their adventures. For most of them it was their first experience of sex. The brothels were almost entirely furnished with Arab or Negro women, fat and middle-aged. At eighteen, boys are not choosy about who they lose their virginity to. It was easy money for brothel keepers, as these over-excited young men had shot their seed having barely touched their targets. They were now apprehensive about the outcome. Every day they examined their organs to see if there were any signs of venereal disease.

From Port Said to Venice, where our sea journey terminated, the only topic was this first encounter, gone over and over again in great and varying detail.

After spending a day in Venice, I took the boat train to London. My first encounter with sex awaited me.

While at Government College I had been corresponding with a lady teacher of the Modern School. She was only a few years older than me. Our correspondence had gradually got more and more amorous, and once when in Delhi I had gone to see her in her room and kissed her passionately in the moonlight. She had reprimanded me, but thereafter her letters to me were even friendlier than before. She was in London doing some kind of advanced course in teacher's training. My fears of getting lost in London were lessened by the knowledge that she was there. She was there at Victoria Station to receive me and had booked me a room in a *pension* on Gower Street run by an Italian. We hired a cab to take us to our destination.

I had not seen her since I had taken liberties with her and was unsure of how she would treat me. My doubts were soon dispelled. No sooner was the taxi in motion then she turned my face towards her and glued her lips to mine. It continued all the way to the *pension*. I was in a frantic state of excitement by the time we paid off the cab driver. She helped me with my luggage to the third floor of the *pension*. No sooner had the Italian patron turned his back to us than she bolted the door and we tumbled on the bed kissing each other with wild abandon. I got bolder with my advances. She withdrew. Seeing the protrusion in my trousers, she tapped it with her finger and

said, "Not sex; only love." It was no use. I tore her blouse and
sari off her. She protested, "No, no. I have no protection. We
must get contraceptives before we do that." Even that was no
use. I tried to lunge into her and came into her thighs. A strong
feeling of shame, guilt, and revulsion came over me.

She cleaned herself as best as she could with a dry towel
and again lay beside me. She said she had forgiven me because
she loved me. And again began to kiss me. This time I found
her mouth malodorous and was very reluctant to return her
kisses. But eighteen is an age of physical compulsions. I was
roused again. And once again savagely went for her bosom and
then for her middle. This time she held me back and took the
discharge in her hands.

The dinner gong came to my rescue. I refused to take her
back to my room and walked her down to the tube station. For
the next three days I avoided her by keeping away from the
pension till late hours of the night. In her frustration she went
off on a sightseeing tour of the country with one of her other
students who happened to be there. He was more adept at the
game than I, and she returned at peace with herself.

The sexual Pandora's box had been opened wide—and
along with it fear of sex. In my letters to my friends who
wanted to know of my exploits with white girls, I created all
kinds of fantasies about my conquests. For the first time I sat
with girls in class, played tennis, badminton, and squash with
them, saw couples copulating in parks—so it did not take
much for me to fantasize about them. My mind was more pre-
occupied with girls than with Roman law and jurisprudence.
However, I managed to pass my tests.

My first year in England made me fall in love with the
country and the people. I moved out of Gower Street to an
English boardinghouse in Streatham. I was the only Indian
among four women, including two young nurses, and two
elderly men. Spent my Christmas in a Quaker hostel in Buckinghamshire, where the Penn brothers are buried. I learnt to
sing Christmas carols and made many friends. Although there
were several Indians at college, I was fortunate enough to

befriend English boys who took me home for weekends. It exploded the myth that the English regard their homes as their castles. And that English women are frigid. Both the nurses in my boardinghouse and the sisters of some friends were more than willing to extend their favours to me. I was too unsure of myself and never went beyond kissing and cuddling them. One after the other, they dropped me in favour of more aggressive paramours.

I came home again for my summer vacation travelling on the Italian *Lloyd Trestino*. I continued bragging of my exploits with English girls. This was perhaps my earliest foray into the world of fiction.

Back in England I decided to move out into the country. Through an introduction from an English friend whose father was one of the founders of the garden-city movement, I moved to Welwyn Garden City (Hertfordshire). He found me a room with a retired professor, F S Marvin, who had written many books. His little cottage was at the end of a lane with the Sherrards Park woods on one side and the rolling country on the other. It took me an hour by train and bus to get to college but it was well worthwhile. I became a part of the Welwyn Garden community; I played tennis, hockey, badminton, and squash for it, travelled with the same group of men and women on the train, and made close friends who continue to keep in touch with me to this day. Above all it was the walks in the woods ablaze with azaleas and rhododendrons and loud with bird song which made me fall deeper in love with everything English.

It was during my stay in Welwyn Garden that I ran into a girl, Kaval Malik, who had been with me at Modern School. She had always been a good-looking, light-skinned girl and a bit of a tomboy, playing hockey and soccer with the boys. When I left school she was still a gawky girl, a couple of years my junior. I lost track of her when I moved to Lahore. When I ran into her in England she had blossomed into a beauty and was much sought after by many boys I knew, some from India's richest families. Her parents were orthodox Sikhs and determined to marry her off to a Sikh boy in the Civil Service. They stood in awe of the Indian Civil Service, as her uncle, who had made it, was worshipped as a hero. They were negotiating with parents of Sikh boys sitting for competitive exams. Meeting the girl now grown into a young lady caused me anguish, as I fell desperately in love with her and also felt that I stood little chance of winning her. Besides other obstacles, there was the fact that her father was a senior engineer in the Public Works Department, while mine was a builder who had to get contracts from the PWD (Public Works Department). Besides, I was studying law, and lawyers, being a dime a dozen, were poorly rated in the marriage market. Her parents thought well of me, as a year earlier they had visited me in my lodgings. Her mother had found the Sikh prayer book under my pillow and had been deeply impressed. I met them again in the Lake District. They were staying in a fancy hotel at Bowness; I in a lodging house at Windermere. I rowed up seven miles to have breakfast with them. I knew they would agree to their daughter marrying me if they could not find a better Sikh proposal.

My best chance was to bypass the parents and approach the girl directly. Christmas vacation was near and she had nowhere to go. I suggested that she come to the Quaker hostel in Buckinghamshire. She wrote to her parents to seek their permission. To my utter surprise, they agreed that she could go. I began courting her as soon as the train left London. And continued paying court throughout our fortnight's stay with the Quakers. On our way back to London, I asked her if I could ask my parents to approach hers with the proposal. She nodded her head.

Our engagement was announced a few days later. It caused a lot of heart-burning amongst her many suitors. A particularly ardent one, whose sister was married to my fiancee's brother, said very acidly, "the bank balance won." By that time my father was known to be a man of considerable wealth. Though most of them envied me, the only one to try to dissuade me from marrying the girl was my closest friend,

E N Mangat Rai, who, at the time, had a poor opinion of her. He was later to fall deeply in love with her and almost succeeded in wrecking our marriage.

It took me a year more than prescribed for the course to take my bachelor of law degree, and I became a Barrister-at-Law of the Inner Temple. In the meantime I had sat for the Indian Civil Service exam. Rating my chances as negligible I had not taken one paper. When the results were declared, I discovered to my great surprise that I had just missed getting in. I was the only candidate, English or Indian, to be given full marks in the *Viva voce*. I must have impressed the interview board more than the examiners of my papers.

I returned home by sea in the summer of 1939. There was talk of war breaking out. By the time I reached Delhi, German armies had been launched on their conquest of neighbouring countries.

In October 1939 I got married. It was a grand affair. My wife's father was by then Chief Engineer of the PWD, the first Indian to rise to the position. My father was acknowledged as the biggest owner of real estate in Delhi. We lived in a large stone and marble mansion with over a dozen bedrooms, a teak-panelled library, and chandeliered sitting and dining rooms. My father also entertained politicians. At our wedding reception there were over fifteen hundred guests, including M A Jinnah, founding father of Pakistan. Champagne flowed like the river Jumna in flood. My wife received presents which, after fifty years of being given away, have not yet been exhausted. My father gave me a new car and rented an apartment and office space for me near the High Court at Lahore. After a short honeymoon at Mount Abu in Rajasthan, the two of us drove to Lahore in our new Ford.

My comparative affluence and family connections opened many doors for me in Lahore. I joined the two elite clubs of Lahore, including the Gymkhana, which rarely took Indians.

We were entertained in the homes of ministers, judges and senior lawyers. However, none of that brought me clients. I spent hours in my office and at the Bar Association, hearing cases being argued by eminent lawyers. For a while I worked as a junior to the top criminal lawyer, but for months did not have a brief to handle on my own. I took undefended murder cases for as little as sixteen rupees (under one U.S. dollar a day) and took up a part-time lecturer's job at the law college. I earned very little. I began to get bored with the law and turned to reading English poetry and classics, which I had ignored in my college days.

I spent the war years in Lahore. Although after some years I did pick up a little practice, it was never enough to maintain myself at the level I was accustomed to. My father was a very generous man. He bought me a large bungalow alongside the Lawrence Gardens, and twice replaced my old car with a new one. But it was common knowledge that I had a very small practice, and the best I could hope for was through my connections to be elevated to the bench. The one thing Lahore gave me was my friendship with Manzur Qadir, who was fast rising to the top of the legal profession. He was a man of incredible ability and integrity. Also, like me, an agnostic. He rose to be Pakistan's foreign minister and chief justice.

As the British decided to pull out of India, it became evident that India would be divided and Lahore would go to Pakistan. In 1946 savage killing of Hindus and Sikhs had begun in northwestern Punjab, and the violence gradually spread eastwards to Lahore and Amritsar. By the summer of 1947 it became clear that unless the rioting was somehow stopped, Hindus and Sikhs would have to get out of Pakistan. He even had word sent to me that I should stay on in Lahore, clearly hinting that he wanted some non-Muslims on the bench. But so fierce was the animosity between the communities that early in August 1947 I decided to leave Lahore till the violence subsided. I handed over possession of my house to Manzur Qadir for safe-keeping. I was never able to return to it as its owner. After some years I came to stay in it as a guest of the Qadir family.

Strange that, though I lost my home and livelihood, I heaved a sigh of relief that I had done with the law. I had begun to hate it and resolved never to return to it. In Delhi I applied for a job in the Ministry of External Affairs. They were looking for personnel to man their many newly opened embassies. Without as much as an interview I was appointed Information Officer in our High Commission in London. By October 1947 I was back in England, this time with my wife, our two new children, and two servants. I rented a cottage in Welwyn Garden City.

The High Commissioner at the time was Krishna Menon, an acerbic-tongued, prickly character who had been picked up by Pandit Nehru to be India's ambassador to Great Britain. My immediate boss was Sudhir Ghosh, who regarded himself as Mahatma Gandhi's personal envoy and a cut above Krishna Menon. The two clashed fiercely. Menon was supported by Prime Minister Nehru, Ghosh by the Home Minister, Sardar Patel who had charge of foreign publicity. The quarrel came to a head a few months after I had joined the office. Menon used me against Ghosh and had him sent back to India. Patel retaliated by transferring me to Ottawa. I had to pack up again and take the boat to New York *en route* to Ottawa.

In Ottawa my boss was my wife's uncle, H W Malik of the Indian Civil Service. He was a great golfer and a party man who disdained to mix with anyone except heads of state, ministers, and the rich. He spent more time on the golf course and at diplomatic receptions than in the office. In any event, there was very little for us to do. I began to write short stories, cultivate writers, poets and editors of literary journals. It was in Canada that my literary efforts first appeared in print in the Canadian Forum, *Saturday Night,* and *Harper's.* Although I soon fell out with my High Commissioner, I made deep and abiding friendships with many Canadians. I travelled across the length and breadth of the country, went skiing in winter, hiking in the Rockies in summer, and saw the autumn light maple forests on fire. Canada remains my favourite country.

Just as my relations with the High Commissioner were

reaching a breaking point, I received orders of transfer back to London. External publicity was taken over by the Prime Minister and at Menon's insistence I was brought back to London to take over as Press Attache and Public Relations Officer.

This time I first shared an apartment with the Trade Commissioner, A.S. Lal, then moved into a small house in Hendon, a northwestern suburb of London.

My second posting to London proved to be a turning point in my career. I soon tired of diplomatic life, which for me meant an endless succession of lunches, cocktail parties, and receptions. I kept an open house for journalists. Post-war England was short of booze. I had come back from Canada with several crates of premium scotch. My parties became very popular. Apart from eminent journalists like Kingsley Martin, Harold Evans, William Clarke, and David Astor, I entertained writers like C P Snow and Professor C E M Joad, the poets Auden, Louis MacNeice, and Dylan Thomas. My first collection of short stories, *The Mark of Vishnu*, largely based on my experiences in Lahore and Ottawa, was published by Saturn Press. It got very good notices—no doubt due to my cocktail-party contacts. I began to seriously think of taking up writing as a career. My relations with the High Commissioner, Krishna Menon, had begun to sour. He was unbelievably discourteous and surrounded himself with a horde of snivelling sycophants. I got caught between his ageing English mistress and a young Indian girl he was enamoured with. She worked as a clerk in his secretariat. He tried to belittle me by sending orders through her. Instead of asking for a transfer, I decided it was time I did what I wanted to with my life. I was approaching forty. If I wanted to become a writer, it had to be now or never. I decided to give up the perks of diplomatic life— invitations to Buckingham Palace, embassy receptions, as much diplomatic duty-free liquor as I wanted, a CD plate on my car. The now or never became now. I put in my resignation in 1951 to try to make myself a writer. "Nothing venture nothing have," I kept repeating to myself. I did not consult anyone, as by now there was little communication between my wife and me. I packed her off with our children and servants. The day they left, I sent in an application for leave that was due to me along with my resignation. Menon made a half-hearted attempt to dissuade me, saying he looked upon me as a friend. "You have no friends" were the last words I said to him before leaving India House for good.

I rented a basement apartment in Highgate and got down to work. I had come to the conclusion that in order to survive in the highly competitive world of writing, I had to specialise in some subject. I chose the study of my own people, the Sikhs. I translated the Sikhs' morning prayer, *Japji*, composed by the founder of Sikhism, Guru Nanak. It was published by Probsthain. I also wrote a short history of my community entitled *The Sikhs* which was published by Messrs Allen and Unwin. It was not much as a book of history, but my prediction that by the turn of the century the Sikhs would merge back into the Hindu fold roused a lot of controversy, and the book sold out.

However, none of the three books I had published so far had brought me much money. My total earnings from my first two books were under £500. Whatever I had saved in four years as a diplomat ran out and I decided to return home. I was back in Delhi by the summer of 1951, living in my father's house and on his bounty. Everyone thought I was a little mad to have given up a diplomatic career, and with my poor academic record I was hardly expected to succeed as a writer. I had to suffer barbed shafts from members of my family and friends. I decided to get away from this atmosphere. I went off to Bhopal in central India, where my father had an ice-cream factory, an orchard, and a house along the lake. I lived alone in the house, working mornings on a novel on the Partition of India. I watched the bird life on the lake and caught an occasional glimpse of the Nawab's maid-servants, divesting themselves of their burqas and peeling off their clothes to bathe in the water. Strip tease has always been my favourite voyeur sport. I took long walks through the forest and drank myself to sleep on rum and gin. In three months I had the draft of the novel *Mano Majra* ready and returned to Delhi.

My self-confidence was at a very low ebb. I was drawing money from my father's account; my wife was paying for our children's education. She saw more of Mangat Rai than was good for her reputation. Very reluctantly I took a job with All India Radio in charge of their English overseas programmes. I had very little to do, and the only positive aspect of the job was that I was able to befriend Nirad C Chaudhuri, who wrote scripts for us, and Ruth Prawar Jhabvala, who came occasionally to record talks.

I had not till then had my novel typed out. The American wife, Tatty, of an English diplomat, Walter Bell, agreed to type it for me. I decided to send it to Grove Press of New York, which had announced a thousand-dollar award for the best work of fiction from India. "But it's no damn good," said Tatty Bell to me, "you are wasting a lot of money on postage." Despite the damper I mailed my manuscript to New York using an assumed name, as Krishna Menon was one of the judges.

During my second year with All India Radio I happened to interview Dr Luther Evans, who was then Director General of UNESCO in Paris. We hit it off very well. A few weeks later I received an offer to take over as deputy head of its Mass Communication Division. Without any regret I resigned my radio job, leaving a note behind recommending that the post be abolished, as I had never had more than fifteen minutes of work in a day.

Once more I took my wife and two children and sailed for Europe. I was the only one in the party looking forward to the venture. We were in Paris for two years. My children learnt to speak French, my wife learnt to love French cuisine and wines, and once again I had very little to do besides writing letters, attending conferences and receptions in different parts of the world: Madrid, Montevideo, Geneva, London. For me the most pleasant part of my stay in Paris was the announcement that my novel had won the Grove Press award and been accepted by a number of European publishers, including Chatto and Windus (London) and Gallimard (France). It appeared under two titles, *Mano Majra* and *Train to Pakistan* (also *Dia Brucke am Satledsch* in German). It got undeservedly good reviews. I decided to quit my job. I found UNESCO full of petty intrigue and with more than the normal quota of the loonies found in all international organisations. I didn't have much problem picking a quarrel with a Norwegian who had been made my boss and handing in my resignation. As earlier in the diplomatic service, I sent my family back to India. I moved into a small cottage near Houdan and started working on my second novel. I finished the first draft in three months and sailed back to India.

I was still dependent on my father's generosity, and my children's education was still being paid for by my wife. And once again I had to take a job to prove to Delhi society that I was not a *nikhattoo*—an idler. For them writing could be a hobby, never a full-time occupation.

I became chief editor of *Yojana*, a new weekly in English and Hindi published by the Planning Commission. It gave me the opportunity of travelling all over India with a young photographer, T S Nagarajan. We visited dams, factories, mines, rural projects. I got to know my country better. I wrote about everything I saw. But no matter how I slogged, the journal did not pick up circulation. It was dismissed as government propaganda and distributed in the lackadaisical manner common to all governmental publications. I was also caught up in rivalries between senior officials and ministers of government. If I praised one, I annoyed six others. Fortunately for me, I ran into the talent scout of the Rockefeller Foundation. He had read my short book *The Sikhs* and asked me if I would care to do a more definitive work on the same subject. I jumped at the offer. I drew up a project report, got the Aligarh Muslim University (I deliberately chose a Muslim university to explode the theory of historic Sikh-Muslim animosity) to sponsor my application. It was immediately accepted and I put in my resignation as editor of *Yojana*.

I had made a very poor deal with the Rockefeller Foundation and soon discovered that I would be out of pocket for another three years. My son was then studying in King's College, Cambridge (paid for by my wife). We left our daughter in a convent in Mussoorie and flew to London. The first thing I wanted to do was to examine material on the Sikhs at the India Office Library.

The three months in London proved very fruitful. Apart from collecting material, I was able to complete a biography of Maharajah Ranjit Singh as well as a smaller book on the ten years of turmoil that followed his death and culminated in the annexation of the Sikh Kingdom by the British. Before I left London, both books were accepted by publishers. My wife returned to India, I proceeded to the United States and Canada to gather material on Sikh communities settled on the west coast, stretching from Vancouver to Southern California. Much of this material had remained untapped. By the time I returned home I had a clear idea what I would write. Fortunately for me, the English woman who had been my secretary at UNESCO, Yvonne Le Rougetel, agreed to come over and work for me for the pittance of five hundred rupees a month.

We slogged for many months. She typed and retyped what I had written several times. My fellowship was coming to an end. I asked for an extension of one year. It was turned down. I managed to finish the two volumes in four years. Both were later published by the Princeton and Oxford University Presses. At long last I came to be recognised as somewhat of an authority on the Sikhs. The *Encyclopaedia Britannica* asked me to write their items on Sikhism and Sikh history. The Spalding Trust of Oxford invited me to deliver a series of lectures on Sikhism. Princeton University invited me to teach comparative religion. By then several of my short stories and articles had appeared in American, British, and Indian journals. I was commissioned by the *New York Times* and the *Observer* (London) to write for them. These gave me an entry into serious journalism.

After a short stint at Princeton and Hawaii, I also taught Indian religions and contemporary Indian politics at Swarthmore College. These lectures were published under the title *Vision of India*. While teaching in America I learnt more about my country than I had known living in it. As a famous *Rababi* said, "I have learned much from my teacher, still more from my colleagues, but from my pupils more than from all of them." From a student who could barely pass his examination, I had become a Professor with several books to my credit. It was living in University campuses that set the pattern of my later life. I learnt to eat little, drink more and became a stickler for time. I had no illusions about my being a good teacher or a great writer. But I always managed to raise a laugh whenever I spoke. I am a born jester. And whatever rubbish I wrote, got published.

It was at Swarthmore that I was invited to take over the editorship of *The Illustrated Weekly of India* in Bombay. I had earlier been chosen by its last English editor, C.R. Mandy, to succeed him, but had declined the offer because of the grant from the Rockefeller Foundation. The editorship had gone to an Indian, A.S. Raman, who, though he Indianised the journal, also used it for blatant self-publicity. He was inordinately fond of the bottle and was fired for indiscipline.

It was on a warm autumn day in 1969, when Bombay is sultry and smelling of rotting fish, that I stepped out of the Delhi-Bombay Express at Victoria Station. My friends Gopi and Manna Gauba were there to receive me. Besides them and my son Rahul, I knew no one in the city. Rahul had vacated his room at the one-guest *pension* run by the young Parsi couple, the Jehangirs, and resigned his job with *The Times of India* to take over as editor of *Readers' Digest*. He did not wish to work under the same roof as his father. Sensible boy !

The Gaubas deposited me at the Jehangirs flat near Church Gate. I spent the afternoon acquainting myself with the neighbourhood and restaurants as the Jehangirs were to provide me only with breakfast. My room overlooked a spread of lawn on the other side of which stood the Raja Bai Tower with its clock, Bombay University and the High Court. It was a pleasant neighbourhood with many large shops and eateries both European and Indian. I was only a stone's throw away from the sea along Marine Drive and Nariman Point. My office was walking distance, about a couple of kilometres away past the Gymkhana Club. It faced Victoria Terminus.

Life soon fell into a routine. I got to my office an hour before anyone else. By the time others came I had done my day's work—editing articles and short stories, writing edits and captions and answering all the mail that remained unanswered—and was free for any advice my colleagues sought of me. It was not very hard work and more rewarding than I deserved. My months of lecturing on India and Indian religions at Swarthmore College and earlier at Princeton University stood me in good stead. I had known so little about my country till I was forced to teach myself about it to be able to teach my American students. What went for me went for the vast majority of my educated countrymen—they did not know how their next door neighours lived, what they ate, the gods they worshipped, the customs and rituals they followed. So I launched a series on the different sub-communities of India : Chitpavans, Vokkalingas, Lingayats, Aiyers, Aiyengers, Jats, Gujars, Memons, Khojas, Bohras and so on. The response was spectacular. Every copy of the journal sold out; the circulation began to shoot up. *The Weekly*, which was at the bottom of the list of *The Times of India* publications, came to top it with a wide margin. I became a cult figure in the world of Indian magazine journalism, admired by many, and envied and hated by my colleagues.

In Bombay my world was quite different from what it had been when I was living and teaching in the States and what it became after I was sacked from *The Weekly* and returned to Delhi. My social life was dominated by one family, the Zakarias. Fatma Zakaria, though junior to the other two assistant editors, became *de facto* my number two on the staff. Although she wrote very little herself, she was an excellent organiser and sub. Others who wrote much more like Bachi Kanga (later Karkaria), R G K, Raju Bharatan, M J Akbar, Jiggs Kalra and Bikram Vohra accepted her as a mother figure. Her domination did not end with office hours. She saw to it that I only mixed with people she approved of; if I wasn't dining out, I had to dine with her family. If I wanted to spend an evening alone, she sent my dinner to me. On Sundays and holidays I played tennis or went to swim with her sons, Arshad and Fareed. Wherever they went, I had to go. Since Rafiq was then Minister of Maharashtra government, I went to a lot of places. Pune, Matheran, Aurangabad, Nagpur and to lots of parties in Bombay. Their friends had to invite me. Faisal Essa, Consul General of Kuwait, Rajini Patel, the architect, Ibrahim Qadri, the Chudasamas. And many others. Virtually the only friends I made on my own were Ghafoor Noorani, the Palkhiwalas and Sorabjis. Also a few girls surreptitiously: Saryu Doshi, Devyani Chaubal, Nina Merchant, Nirmala Mathan. Also Trilochan and Bir Sahini and the Advanis who lived in the flat above me in Sentinel House in Colaba where I spent the last five years of my tenure with *The Illustrated Weekly*.

It is strange that it was in the nine years in Bombay that I acquired the unsavoury reputation I enjoy today. Nothing I did in office or outside merited it. During office hours, although I had to receive a variety of visitors, the regulars were mainly the cartoonists R K Laxman and Mario Miranda who designed the bulb logo in which I have remained imprisoned ever since. The only explanation I can offer is that it was my writing which earned me both popularity and ill fame. Being an agnostic, I wrote a lot against conventional religiosity and the cult of godmen. Being uninhibited I published pictures of semi-nude girls (always with a valid excuse). There were angry protests from some parents and educational institutions saying that the *Weekly* which had been a respectable family journal was no longer fit enough to be displayed in school libraries and drawing rooms. Some subscriptions were cancelled. Subscriptions formed a very small proportion of the journal's buyers: it depended largely on stall sales. They doubled, trebled, quadrupled till the circulation went up from under 80,000 when I had taken it on to over four lakhs by the time I was fired. I became the most widely read journalist, the most talked-of magazine editor, as well as a notorious iconoclast, a kind of *goonda*-scholar. I was sought after by politicians, industrialists and socialites. In 1975 I was honoured with the Padma Bhushan (Order of the Lotus) and by the Punjab government for a distinguished contribution to literature and journalism.

Why they sacked me is for the proprietors, Ashok Jain and his son Samir to say. I had been given two extensions. I expected to get a third one. Ashok Jain told me that this was not possible as Prime Minister Morarji Desai was unhappy with my continuing support for Indira Gandhi and her son Sanjay. I accepted the date of my departure and the induction of M V Kamath in my place. I hoped they would give me a farewell party and make a few speeches praising me. What I got instead came as an unpleasant surprise which has rankled in my mind ever since. A week or so before I was to hand over charge, I arrived in office and was handed over a letter asking me to quit immediately. I picked up my umbrella and walked out asking Fatma Zakaria to tell the staff what had happened. It later transpired that someone (probably one of my colleagues) had spread the rumour that I had written a nasty piece on the management as my last contribution. This was untrue. On the contrary, I had written a nostalgic piece bidding everyone a tearful farewell. This was published in many papers afterwards. The Jains or their faithful minions did not have the courtesy to admit that they had erred. Wealth and power make people arrogant and mannerless.

However, setbacks don't keep me down for too long. Within a few minutes of my return to my apartment in Colaba, I resumed work on my novel *Delhi*. And a couple of months later, I left Bombay for good. By now I had become something of a cult figure. I received many tempting offers from newspapers and magazine proprietors but chose to accept the editorship of Mrs Gandhi's *National Herald* without pay. It was a dead loss. The staff were usually on strike because they were not paid for months. Twice the police raided the office and took away documents hoping to implicate the manager in fraudulent deals. After six months I threw in the sponge and resigned to take over the editorship of *New Delhi*, a fortnightly magazine launched by the Ananda Bazar Group of Calcutta. This also proved abortive, as the magazine was printed in Calcutta and rarely appeared on time. By then Mrs Gandhi was back in power. Both she and her son Sanjay were beholden to me for the dogged support I had given them over the years. I was offered the choice of taking either a diplomatic assignment (High Commissioner in London) or membership in the Upper House of Parliament and editorship of *The Hindustan Times*. I chose the latter. In 1980 I became a Member of Parliament as well as editor of the largest circulating paper in the capital.

My six years in Parliament were very eventful. They coincided with troubles in the Punjab. Since Sikh members of the Opposition hardly ever opened their mouths, and later resigned, it fell upon me to put forward the Sikh point of view. I was usually the only discordant voice on controversial issues like the army's storming of the Golden Temple and the massacre of Sikhs that followed the assassination of Mrs Gandhi. Though a nominated member was expected to support the government, I invariably spoke and voted against it. Mrs Gandhi was very upset with me and saw to it that my three-year contract with the *Hindustan Times* was not renewed. However, the proprietor, K K Birla, though he gave in to Mrs Gandhi, asked me to continue writing my weekly column, "With Malice Towards One and All." The arrangement proved very beneficial to me as the column was picked up by almost fifty papers. My successor as editor, N C Menon, who did his best to get rid of me, had to suffer its appearing in the paper without his consent. He was later shifted to Washington as a subordinate to another editor.

I had few illusions that I would be given another term in Parliament. Despite President Zail Singh's efforts to have me renominated, Rajiv Gandhi refused to do so. By 1986 I retired fully to devote myself to free-lance journalism and writing. I am also consulting editor of Penguin India.

I am now seventy-seven—the evensong of my life. As I look back over the years, my only regret is that I wasted so much time studying and practising law—and on futile socialising. I could have written a lot more and perhaps produced some books that would be read fifty years from today.

I am not being falsely modest when I say that I really do not know how many books I have written. In 1989 I was at the Wilson Centre of the Smithsonian in Washington updating my two-Volume *History of The Sikhs*. A Pakistani working at the Library of Congress who got me books and journals I needed asked me about my publications. When I confessed I did not know, he said he could find out easily by feeding my name in the computer. He did. The next day he brought me a long sheet of paper with 58 titles to my credit. This includes some translations: Ruswa's *Umrao Jan Ada* which I did in collaboration with Mehdi Husaini, Amrita Pritam's *Pinjar* (The Skeleton) which I translated on a voyage from Bombay to London by a cargo boat in 21 days and Rajinder Singh Bedi's *Ik Chaadar Mailee See* (I Take This Woman). Iqbal's *Shikwa* and *Jawab-e-Shikwa* (Complaint and Answer) was done over a year-and-a-half while still an editor of *The Hindustan Times* and Member of Parliament. Since then I have had at least a dozen others published, including my third novel, *Delhi* which was written off and on spanning twenty years. It was published in 1990. Not too bad for a man who barely passed his school and college exams.

I have packed my latter years with a lot of activity. I have been round the world many times, staying in the best of hotels, without ever having to pay for my travel or hospitality. I have drunk several swimming pools of hard liquor and wine. I have known the affection of dozens of women of different nationalities and still manage to be surrounded by the prettiest girls in town, most of them younger than my children. I am working longer hours than ever before and making more money than I did as the highest paid editor in the country. I have reason to believe that I am more widely read than any other Indian journalist. I am recognised wherever I go in India, sought after by fans, pestered by autograph hunters. All this is vastly flattering to my ego.

I am also aware it will not last very long. My inkwell is fast drying up, and many of my readers find that I am getting progressively boring. I do not have the stamina to write another novel; many short stories remain half-written and I do not have the energy to finish them. I also have symptoms of old age creeping up on me: my hair is silver-white (I dye my beard), I have four false teeth and may soon need to replace all the others with dentures.

My memory, of which I was once very proud—I rarely needed to consult a telephone directory in Delhi, London, Paris or New York to ring up friends of olden times—is no longer the same. Now I often forget my own telephone number and may soon decline into senility. I have cataract developing in both my eyes. I suffer from serious headaches; I am slightly diabetic and have blood pressure problems. I also have an enlarged prostrate gland; at times it produces illusions of youth in the form of a massive erection; at others, it does not give me enough time to undo my flies to urinate. I will have to get it out soon; with it will go erections and fantasies of youth. Every day I swallow dozens of pills of different shapes and colours. I know that one setback—a fall on the tennis court, a bad cold, or a slip on the bathroom floor—and I will be into decrepit old age. How much longer do I have? My parents were long-lived; my father died at 90, a few minutes after having his scotch. My mother followed him eight years later when she was 94. Before she went into a coma, her last request made in a feeble, barely audible voice was "Wiskee". It was given to her. She threw it up and spoke no more. I hope when my time comes, I too will be able to raise my glass and take one for the long road.

I am now working on my autobiography. I give myself another four or five years of creative activity. I propose to devote them in recording whatever I can recollect of my past. I have not performed any great deeds that need being recorded for history. But I have been witness to many historical events, and as a journalist, met and interviewed characters who played decisive roles in these dramatic events. All I can say in my defence is that I have penned my impressions of people, places and events as objectively and as truthfully as I can. I am not an admirer of great people as the few I got to know at close quarters turned out to have feet of clay: they were pretentious, feckless, lying and utterly commonplace.

I have no pretensions of being a craftsman of letters. Having to meet deadlines did not allow me time to wait for inspiration, indulge in witty turns of phrase or polish up what I had written. Having met deadlines for the last forty years, I have lost the little I knew of writing good, scintillating prose. All said and done, my autobiography will be a child of aging loins. Do not expect too much from it: some gossip, some titillation, some tearing up of reputations, some amusements. That is the best I can offer. Take it or leave it. It will inevitably be the last book I will write.

How many of my books will be read 50 years after I am gone I have no idea. And, quite honestly, I would not give a damn.

FACTS OF LIFE

"The easiest and the best way of understanding India is to look upon it as a diamond necklace. Its races, religions, languages and cultures are like precious stones strung together: each stone has a brilliance of its own but is also linked to the others by a chain which can best be described as Indianness. As long as the chain remains strong, the necklace will remain intact. When someone snaps that chain, its precious stones will fall apart."

Sex in Indian Life

Many winters ago I happened to be travelling by a night train from Delhi to Bhopal. It was a fast express that made only a few halts at major stations. I found myself in a compartment of five berths: three below and two on the sides above. I had a lower berth, as did the other two passengers who were there before me. The upper berths were reserved in the names of a Professor and Mrs Saxena. Fifteen minutes before the train was due to leave, a party of men and women escorting a bride decked in an ornate sari drawn discreetly across her face, her arms loaded with ivory bangles stopped by our compartment, read the names on the panel and came in. They were dismayed to see the two berths reserved for them were separated by a 15 foot chasm of space. One of the party approached me and asked if I could take one of the upper berths to accommodate the newly married couple. I readily agreed and moved my bedding roll. Another passenger who had the middle berth also moved up on the other upper berth so that the bridal couple could be alongside each other. I heard one of the party stop the conductor guard and tell him to wake up the pair at a particular junction where the train was to make a brief three-minute halt at 3 a.m.

As the conductor guard blew his whistle and waved his green flag, the party took leave of the bridal pair with much embracing and sobbing. No sooner had the train cleared the lighted platform, the bride blew her nose and uncovered her face. She was a woman in the mid-twenties: pale-skinned, round-faced and wearing thick-lensed glasses. I couldn't see much of her figure but could guess that she would be forever fighting a losing battle against fat. Her groom looked a couple of years older than her ("professor" being a honorific for a junior lecturer) and, like his bride, was sallow faced, corpulent and bespectacled. From the snatches of conversation that I could hear (I was only four feet above them) I gathered that they were total strangers and their marriage had been arranged by relatives and through matrimonial columns of *The Hindustan Times*. They talked of their papajis and mummyjis. Then of their time in college (the halcyon days for most educated Indians) and of their friends: "like a brother to me" or "better than my own real sister." After a while the conversation began to flag; I saw the man's hand resting on his woman's on the window.

The lights were switched off leaving only a nightlight which bathed the compartment in blue. I could not see very much except when the train ran past brightly lit platforms of wayside railway stations.

The couple did not bother to use the middle berth vacated for them and decided to make themselves as comfortable as they could on a four-feet wide wooden plank. They ignored the presence of other passengers in the small compartment and were totally absorbed in getting to know each other. Such was their impatience that they did not find time to change into more comfortable clothes. They drew a quilt over themselves and were lost to the world.

The sari is both a very ornamental as well as a functional dress. Properly draped, it can accentuate the contours of the female form giving a special roundness to buttocks. A well-cut blouse worn with the sari elevates the bosom, and exposes the belly to below the navel. There is no other form of female attire which can both conceal physical shortcomings of the wearer as well as expose what deserves exposure. A fat woman looks less fat in a sari than she would in a dress and a thin woman looks more filled in. At the same time a sari is very functional. All a woman has to do when she wants to urinate or defecate is to lift it to her waist. When required to engage in a quick sexual intercourse, she needs to do no more than draw it up a little and open up her thighs. Apparently this was what Mrs Saxena was called upon to do. I heard a muffled cry "*Hai Ram*" escape her lips and realised that the marriage had been consummated.

The Saxenas did not get up to go to the bathroom to wash themselves but began a repeat performance. This time they were less impatient·and seemed to be getting more out of their efforts. More than once the quilt slipped off them and I caught a glimpse of the professor's heaving buttocks and his bride's bosoms which he had extricated out of her *choli*. Above the rattle and whish of the speeding train, I heard the girl's whimper and the man's exulting grunts. They had a third go at each other before peace descended on our compartment. It was then well past the hour of midnight. Thereafter it was only the wail of the engine tearing through the dark night and the snores of my elderly companions that occasionally disturbed our slumbers.

We were rudely disturbed by someone thumping on the door, slapping the window panes and yelling "Get up, get up. It is Sehore. The train will leave in another minute." It was the conductr f guard.

I pressed the switch and the compartment was flooded with light. A memorable sight it was! Professor Saxena fast asleep with his buttocks exposed; Mrs Saxena also fast asleep, her mouth wide, breasts bare, lying supine like a butterfly pinned down on a board. Her hair were scattered on her pillow. Their glasses lay on the floor.

Whatever embarrassment they felt was drowned in the hustle and bustle of getting off the train. We heaved out their beds and suitcases. The professor stumbled out on the cold platform adjusting his flies. She followed him covering her bared bosom with a flap of her sari. As the train began to move, she screamed: one of her earings was missing. The friendly guard brought the train to a halt. All of us went down on our knees scouring the floor. The errant earing was found wedged in a crevice of the seat. We resumed our journey.

"It is love", remarked one of my travelling companions

with great understanding. "They are newly married and this was their first night together. All should be forgiven to people in love."

"What kind of love?" I asked in a sarcastic tone. "A few hours ago they were complete strangers. They haven't the patience to wait till they get home and start having sex without as much as exchanging a word of affection. You call that love?"

"Well," he replied pondering over the episode. "They may not get another chance for some days. There will be his relatives: his mother, sisters, brothers. And lots of religious ceremonies. Youth is impatient and the body has its own demands. Let us say it is the beginning of love."

"It may be the beginning of another family but I don't see where love comes in," I remarked. "I can understand illiterate peasants coupling like the cattle they rear but I cannot understand two educated people: a lecturer in a college and a school teacher so totally lacking in sophistication or sense of privacy as to begin copulating in the presence of three strangers."

"You have foreign ideas" said the third man dismissing me. "Anyway, it is 3.30 in the morning. Lets get some sleep." He switched off the light and the argument.

The episode stayed in my mind because it vividly illustrated the pattern of the man-woman relationship that obtains among the vast majority of Indians. Love, as the word is understood in the West, is known only to a tiny minority of the very westernised living in the half-a-dozen big cities of India who prefer to speak English rather than Indian languages, read only English books, see only Western movies and even dream in English. For the rest, it is something they read about in poems or see on the screen but it is very rarely a personal experience. Arranged marriages are the accepted norm; "love" marriages a rarity. In arranged marriages the parties first make each others acquaintance physically through the naked exploration of each others bodies and it is only after some of the lust has been drained out of their systems that they get the chance to discover each others minds and personalities. It is only after lust begins to lose its potency and there is no clash of temperaments that the alliance may in later years develop bonds of companionship. But the chances of this happening are bleak. In most cases, they suffer each other till the end of their days.

I have no idea what became of the Saxenas whose nupital consummating I witnessed. It is likely that by now they have produced a small brood of Saxenas. He is probably a full professor teaching romantic poetry and occasionally penning a verse or two to some younger lady professor ("like a sister to me") or to some pig-tailed student ("like my own daughter"). Mrs Saxena probably tries to retain her husband's interest by dog-like devotion, prayer and charms brought from "holy" men. On the rare occasions when the professor mounts her, she has to fantasize about one of his younger colleagues ("exactly like a real brother to me") before she shudders in the throes of an orgasm with the name of God on her lips: "Hai Ram".

The Saxenas are luckier than most Indian couples because they live away from their families and are assured a certain amount of privacy. To most newly married Indian couples, the concept of privacy is as alien as that of love. They rarely get a room to themselves; the bride-wife sleeps with other women members of her husband's family; the husband shares his *charpoy* lined alongside his father's and brothers'. Occasionally, the mother-in-law, anxious to acquire a grandson will contrive a meeting between her son and his wife. The most common technique is to get her to take a tumbler of milk to the lad when other male members are elsewhere. The lad grabs the chance for the "quickie". Hardly ever do the couple get enough time for a prolonged and satisfying bout of intercourse. Most Indian men are not even aware that women also have orgasms; most Indian women share this ignorance because although they go from one pregnancy to another, they have no idea that sex can be pleasurable. This is a sad commentary on the people of a country which produced the most widely read treatise on the art of sex, *Kama Sutra* and elevated the act of sex to spiritual sublimity by explicit depictions on its temples.

Humour in Indian Life

Do we Indians have a sense of humour? I would answer the
question in one word. No. Sense of fun, yes. Laughter,
yes. Wit, sometimes. Sarcasm and irony, often. Sense of
humour, never. What passes for the Indian sense of humour is
no laughing matter. It may occasion a smile. More often it
makes you want to spit.

You may well ask, how do you differentiate between
laughter, wit, sarcasm, irony on the one side and sense of
humour on the other? I will reply, "Don't ask me for defini-
tions because the best I can do is to quote different dictionar-
ies. And that will not get us anywhere." James Thurber, who
was America's best known humorist of recent years defined
humour as "a kind of emotional chaos told calmly and quietly
in retrospect." Quite frankly, I don't understand what Thurber
was talking about. I much prefer the description of a humorist
as "a comedian who doesn't tell dirty stories." Even this is not
really satisfactory as I am often regarded as an Indian humorist
but I am no comedian and I tell a lot of dirty stories.

Humour is something very subtle and therefore eludes
precise definition. I don't recall who said that it was like kicking someone so courteously that he is happy about it since he
thinks it was the new fellow who got kicked. It is something
that makes you laugh at something which would make you
mad if it happened to you. The closest anyone can get to label-
ling a humorist was Hunt who described him as "one who
shows faults of human nature in such a way that we recognise
our failings and smile—and our neighbours' failings and

laugh." Humour is not hurtful. Humour is not hateful: on the contrary it is an anti-biotic against hate. That's as close as I can get to defining a sense of humour.

Now let me analyse why we as a nation are lacking in it. The first condition, the *sine qua non*—without which nothing humourous can be created, is our inability to laugh at ourselves. We take ourselves too seriously and are easily offended by those who do not share our self-esteem. Sometime or the other, everyone of us makes an ass of himself. But how rare it is to hear an Indian tell a joke about himself in which he is shown in a poor light! Let me give you a couple of instances of how seriously we take ourselves. This is a true story about a minister of government. You know what most of our ministers are like! No sooner they become powerful they lose all sense of proportion and get inflated with self-esteem. Well, this minister I am going to tell you about was an exception to the general rule of arrogance and exaggerated importance. I saw him sitting all by himself in a corner of a restaurant. I went up to him and invited him to join my friends. He graciously agreed to do so. I introduced him and added, "my friends were saying that of all the important people in this country, you are the only one who has not lost his head and retains his sense of modesty."

The minister blushed to the roots of his grey beard and replied: "*Hanji*, everyone says I am very modest. In school and college I never stood second in my class (in case you don't know, that is an Indianism for saying you were always tops) but I never gave up my modesty. I had the biggest legal practice in my district, but I never gave up my modesty. And now I am the youngest ever man to be made a full minister but I remain as modest as ever."

With great difficulty I kept myself from breaking out into guffaws of laughter. But I couldn't retain this gem, illustrative of our national character, in my belly for too long. I narrated the dialogue at many parties and also wrote about it saying that as a nation we were unable to stomach success and even a modest Indian was not happy unless he could prove himself to be the most modest man in the world. Needless to say all this got back to the minister. He never forgave me for making him out to be a bit of an ass. And once when I went to see him to ask for a favour, he dismissed me very curtly: "*Aap mera mazaak uratey rahtey hain*—you keep making fun of me."

The other anecdote, also true, is about a young and very bright student who had topped in every exam he took and ended with a scholarship at Oxford University where also he got a first class first. He became a kind of guru and gave sermons on the Vedanta. The main theme of the message he preached was that the source of all evil was *haumahain* I am, the ego which inflated into *ahamkara*—arrogance. And that unless you conquered this ego, you could not hope to better yourself. One day one of his disciples asked him: "Sir, I agree with all you say, but how exactly does one conquer one's ego?"

"A very good question," replied our philosopher. "I know something about it, because the problem of conquering the ego because of my many achievements is much tougher for me than for any of you. I recommend that each one of you devise your own formula. What I do is to sit *padma asan* and repeat to myself every morning and evening, "I am not so-and-so who stood first in every exam I took. I am not so-and-so who broke all examination records of my university. I am not so-and-so who became President of the University union. I am not so-and-so the most brilliant philosopher of the Orient. I am merely a spark of the divine."

Needless to say, that those of us who spread this story about the formula to conquer the ego came in for some very uncharitable lambaste from this human spark of the divine.

The second reason for our lacking in humour is that we are very touchy about a large number of topics. We must not make jokes about God or religion; we must not make jokes about our elders; we must not make jokes about revered figures of our history except those which have been sanctioned by tradition—like for example those of Akbar and Birbal or about Maharaja Ranjit Singh and Akali Phula Singh. Try and crack a joke about Chattrapati Shivaji within earshot of a Maharashtrian and you'll understand what I mean.

We are equally sensitive about community jokes, which form a rich storehouse of humour of other countries. Although we have lots of proverbs of different castes and sub-communities like *Julahas, Naees,* Jats, Banias, Marwaris and others, we do not think it is right to relate these or jokes based on stereotypes in the presence of members of those sub-groups. Perhaps the largest number of jokes current today are what are known as Sardarji jokes. What is surprising about this genre of joke is that although most of them are made up by Sardarjis themselves, narrated with great gusto by them and arouse guffaws of healthy laughter, heaven help a non-Sardarji who is foolish enough to take the same liberty in the company of Sardarjis. Sardarjis are a unique combination of a people able to laugh at themselves but totally unable to stand other people laughing at them. This phenomenon is in acute contrast to the Jews who have been through somewhat similar experiences of persecution and discrimination in their long history as the Sikhs. Jews not only tell jokes about themselves but heartily participate in jokes other people tell about them.

With so many taboos, what are we left with? Precious little. Turn the pages of any of our magazines. Most of them devote a page or more to what they think is humorous. The most popular form is an item entitled "Answers to your questions" where readers' queries are answered by a hired wit or by the editor himself. When I read them I do not know whether to laugh or cry. The other item usually bears some silly title like "Smile awhile", "Laugh", "Laffs" or "Laughing Matter". Without exception, all the jokes printed under this heading are taken from some international syndicates or lifted from foreign magazines and occasionally rephrased to make them sound Indian. Almost all the strip-cartoons and comics are likewise taken from foreign sources. I have a sizeable collection of books on humour; I have yet to come across one on Indian humour which is not almost entirely plagiarised.

States' Legislatures and Parliaments are a rich source of humour in all countries. This particular brand of humour requires a ready wit so that the retort can be fired back as soon

as a remark is made, not thought of much later—what the
French call the staircase wit—something you think you should
have said going down the stairs after the party is over. We
have some parliamentarians who were quick-witted in their re-
partees but for the life of me I cannot recollect anything really
memorable. Let me narrate some that have stayed in my memory. One of my favourites is from the Haryana Assembly. A
lady member of the Opposition was fiercely attacking the
Chief Minister and his government. The Chief Minister lost his
temper and described the lady member as *charitraheen*—woman
of loose character. The lady was understandably furious and
roundly abused the Chief Minister describing his mother, wife,
sisters and daughters as *charitraheen*. There was an uproar in
the House. The Speaker had the'exchange of abuse expunged
from the record and ordered both of them to apologise to each
other. The Chief Minister made amends and asked the lady to
forgive him and added: "I regard her as my own sister." When
it came to the lady's turn to apologise, she said: "I concede
your sister is not *charitraheen*. But I cannot say anything about
your other family relatives who I don't know."

Mrs Gandhi's late husband, Feroze Gandhi, was known
for his sharp sense of repartee. But the one repartee most often
quoted seems to have been thought out well ahead of the time
of its delivery. The unhappy recipient of Feroze's barbed shaft
was the then Finance Minister T T Krishnamachari. Old TTK,
as he was known to friends had a very acid tongue and had
been known to refer to Feroze Gandhi as Prime Minister
Nehru's lap dog. Feroze's opportunity came when he had to
open the debate on the Mundhra scandal in which TTK's name
was involved. As he came into the House he went up to the
Treasury Benches and addressed the Finance Minister: "TTK, I
believe you have been describing me as a lap dog. You no
doubt regard yourself as a pillar of the State. Today I will do
to you what a lap dog does to a pillar."

These make a very poor collection when you compare
them to the sallies of wit and humour fired by A P Herbert,
Aneuran Bevan and above all Winston Churchill in the British

House of Commons. I will not narrate them as most of you are likely to have heard them before. But let me tell you an abso-lute gem of a retort that I picked up from, of all places, the Parliament of Uruguay. An opposition member was attacking a minister. The minister got up to intervene. The member shouted back, "But I haven't finished yet." This was repeated many times but every time the minister rose to defend himself the opposition man yelled, "Sit down! I haven't finished yet." When at long last the man finished his speech, the minister asked: "Have you finished now?"

"Yes," replied the man taking his seat.

"Then pull the chain," snapped the minister amidst thunderous applause.

Poverty in Indian Life

One sultry summer afternoon in Calcutta I was entertaining an English lady I had known in my college days in England at lunch. She had never been to Calcutta but had seen Louis Malle's documentary and read about Mother Teresa's work among the poor. She had travelled extensively in Africa and Asia, seen Arab refugees encampments in Lebanon and Syria and met "the boat people" in Malaysia. "I've had all the culture shocks sociologists talk about," she said smiling confidently, "I am shock proof."

We were in a large glazed verandah on the first floor of Calcutta's gourmet restaurant, Firpos, overlooking one of Calcutta's busiest streets, Chowringhee. Being a Sunday, there was hardly any traffic. A line of taxis were parked across the road with their sleeping drivers' legs dangling out of their open doors. Beyond the cab rank was a vast esplanade of emerald green grass with massive rain trees with people sprawling in their shade. It looked very calm and peaceful. The chilled lager had made me drowsy and I was finding it hard to keep up with the cheerful chatter of my lady companion.

All at once there was hubbub in the street below. Men were running from different directions towards the rank. I saw a dozen men slapping, punching and kicking a man who was reeling between them like one drunk. I ran down the steps of the restaurant followed by my companion. We pushed our way through the crowd. Two burly Sikhs held a small, dark Bengali clad in a loin cloth by the tuft of his hair. He was whining piteously. "What's the matter?" I asked. "What has the fellow done?"

"He's a thief," answered one of the Sikhs. "The mother-
fucker was trying to remove the hub cap of my taxi when I
woke up." "These fellows won't learn their lesson until we
stick a greased pole up their dirty arses." To emphasise his
point he gave the fellow a violent kick with his bare feet.
"Don't beat him," I pleaded, "hand him over to the police."
    "No ! no ! in the name of Rama, not the police !" whined
the man as he clutched my legs with both his hands. "Let them
beat me to their hearts' content. But let me go. If the police
take me, my wife and children will not know where I am.
They haven't eaten for two days and they'll think I am dead.
Please save me." He set up a loud wail and slapped his belly:
"I am hungry; I've had nothing to eat for many days." Tears
ran down his eyes; blood oozed down his nose and mouth. I offered to pay the price of the hub cap. The taxi drivers refused
the offer with contempt. I pleaded with them to let the fellow
go as he had received enough punishment. The police arrived,
handcuffed the thief and pushed him into their black van. All I
was able to get was the man's name and the locality where his
family lived. And blotches of blood on my white shark-skin
trousers.
    We were able to track down the thief's family. They had
been pushed out from underneath the suburban railway bridge
where they had spent the monsoon season to a sprawl of gun-
nysack awnings along the rail track. Dust and smoke hung in
the air; stench of sewers mixed with the smell of cooking and
the all pervasive smell of faeces and urine. Garbage emptied
by municipal vans lay in mountainous heaps. Pigs, pi-dogs and
naked children rummaged for cartons and leaf-cups to lick
whatever stuck on their insides of food or grease. The woman
was cooking rice-gruel on an open fire (her husband had lied).
I told her of her husband's arrest. She shrugged her shoulders
and said: "If he can't get work, what is he to do? We have to
fill our bellies." She took the ten rupee note offered by my
friend without a word of thanks. "Thank you" is not in the
vocabulary of India's poor.

My English friend who had chatted merrily in the afternoon was strangely silent all evening. Later she confessed that she had not been able to eat her supper and had thrown up in the bathroom.

When it comes to squalor and scenes of poverty and human degradation no city in the world can beat Calcutta. But similar sights can be seen in other cities including the richest Bombay and the capital Delhi. If one only saw the city slums, one would only get what Mahatma Gandhi aptly described as a drain inspector's report of India. But since Independence, many things have changed for the better. India has inched forward at a snail's pace towards improving living conditions of the poor. This may not be evident to the eye and although official statistics are not always reliable, they cannot be fouled on all the claims they make. A fair balance sheet of achievements and failures would run somewhat as follows:

Since Independence India has had no major famine or epidemics. Production of foodgrains went up from a heavy deficit to self-sufficiency, literacy from under 16 per cent to well over 40 per cent. In the same period India's population more than doubled from 318 million to over 800 million; the average span of life which was 32 years has become over 52; the rate of increase showed a miniscule drop. It is the explosive increase in numbers that negatived much of the progress made because the State has been unable to keep pace with it by providing the required number of schools, hospitals, transport facilities, community centres. No industry, either state controlled or privately owned, showed as much buoyancy as was hoped for. Hence we have a situation full of paradoxes. India is amongst the poorest of the poor of the world, the tenth from the bottom of the list of impoverished nations just above countries like Upper Volta, Ethiopia, Mali, Chad, Afghanistan, Nepal, Bhutan, Bangladesh and Burma. It is also the world's seventh largest producer of industrial goods and has next to the United States and the Soviet Union, the third largest pool of scientific and technical manpower. India today produces just about everything it needs from needles to computers, automobiles, tractors, aircraft and steamships; it has put satellites in orbit. It has exploded a nuclear device and has a chain of eight nuclear power plants. Why then does the poverty sit so heavily on India like the old man on the back of Sindbad?

ON PEOPLE, WITH 'MALICE'

"I cannot resist making fun of name-droppers, calling liars liars on their faces. And I love abusing the arrogant.... And since most name droppers, self-praisers and arrogant men go from success to success, become ministers, Governors and win awards they don't deserve, my anger often explodes in print."

Giani Zail Singh

When Giani Zail Singh was sworn in as the seventh Rashtrapati of the Republic on 25 July 1980, I was rash enough to forecast that despite his modest education and inability to speak English he would prove to be the most popular President the country has had so far—outstripping the suave Rajendra Prasad, the scholarly Radhakrishnan and Zakir Hussain, garrulous V V Giri and Neelam Sanjeeva Reddy and the all-too pliable Fakhruddin Ali Ahmad. He started off with a bang.

On Thursday, 8 July 1980, he came to the Central Hall of Parliament to bid farewell to fellow Parliamentarians and announce the termination of his long association with the Congress party. He was a few minutes late and was visibly embarrassed as Prime Mnister Indira Gandhi was addressing the assemblage. She further embarrassed him by her words of welcome: "See, he is blushing like a bride!" So the Giani didto the roots of his glossy-black dyed beard. His farewell speech to fellow politicians was *a tour de force* of sentimental oratory, the like of which is rarely heard these days. He ended with a reference to Mrs Gandhi's quip about his blushing, admitting that he felt like an Indian bride taking leave of her parents, brothers and sisters when every member of the family is in tears. "You have decided to retire me from politics; however mine will be a kind of a *shaahee* (royal) retirement," he concluded.

His first few months as Rashtrapati were roses, roses all the way. Wherever he went, he was welcomed by mammoth crowds. He regaled them with rustic anecdotes, Urdu couplets, Persian and Punjabi poetry, quotations from sacred Sanskrit texts, the *Quran* and the *Granth Sahib*. Here at last was a *people's Rashtrapti*: of the earth, earthy; one who could talk on the same level to the peasant and the artisan; enter into a dialogue with the Pandit, the Maulvi and the *Granthi*. The only class with which he neither tried nor was capable of making an equation was the westernised woggery. They cracked their Sardarji jokes at his expense at their cocktail parties. He often exposed himself to their jibes as he did when criticising the Darwinian theory of our descent from the apes: "How could the Buddha be a progeny of a monkey?" he asked naively. But few wags dared to take him on in public because they knew they could not hope to match him in witty repartee. He ignored their existence.

The one thing that had irked the sophisticated sections of society was his exaggerated deference to the "royal family". He said he would be willing to sweep the floor if Mrs Gandhi so desired and acknowledged the then seeming heir-apparent, Sanjay, as his *rehnuma* (guide). Few people realised that *darbardari* (flattery and court-craft) was deeply ingrained in his psyche as he was born and brought up in the courtly atmosphere of Faridkot Raj where only sycophancy and cunning ensured survival.

Within a few months, things began to go awry. It was his own community which had earlier lauded his elevation as the first Sikh Rashtrapati that began to deride him. The Akalis launched their *dharma yuddha morcha* against the government. The Giani mocked them: "*Akali, akal kay khalee*—Akalis are empty headed". They retaliated by describing him as a *sarkari* Sikh and the Prime Minister's rubber stamp. Akali demonstrations against the 9th Asiad gave Bhajan Lal's Haryana constabulary freedom to harrass all Sikhs coming to Delhi by rail and road. For the first time in the history of independent India, Sikhs came to be discriminated against. It was ironic that this should have started when a Sikh presided over the country. His stock amongst the Sikh community began to decline. Then events overtook him with rapid succession: "Operation Blue-star" was followed by "Operation Woodrose" to comb the Punjab countryside of terrorists.

Gianiji had been kept in the dark about Bluestar but the Sikhs held him responsible for it. High priests of the Takhts summoned him to explain why he should not be declared a *tankhaiya.* In many gurdwaras posters with his pictures were laid out on the floor at the entrance for worshippers to tread on. His TV appearance visiting the Harimandir Sahib after the carnage wearing a rose in his *sherwani* caused a wave of re-sentment. He was virtually written off by his community. Then came the assassination of Mrs Indira Gandhi followed by the massacre of Sikhs in towns and cities of northern India. Being a Sikh, the Giani had to suffer the odium with which Hindus began to regard his community.

Hardly had the country returned to normalcy and the Giani regained his equipoise, then the new Prime Minister, Rajiv Gandhi, began to exhibit boorishness unbecoming of a young man of his lineage towards an elder to whom he initially owed his position. The Giani felt isolated and unwanted. I was pretty certain that he was looking for a suitable opportunity to resign and to go out of the Rashtrapati Bhawan with the same fanfare with which he had entered it. I was wrong. He stepped out of his mansion not with the proverbial bang, but not with a whimper either.

In the last six months, he has given Rajiv Gandhi and his advisers a taste of their own medicine and many sleepless nights. What is more, if they have any illusions of making up for lost sleep after Gianiji has quit Rashtrapati Bhawan, they may be in for a nasty surprise. Unlike his predecessors, who disappeared into pastoral oblivion after their retirement, we will have a retired President living in the Capital and deter-mined to level his score with the Prime Minister. If I am any judge of character, I foresee Gianiji becoming the patron saint of those disenchanted with the regime. Although he did not fulfil my prophecy of being the most popular President of the Republic, he will undoubtedly go down in the pages of history as the most talked about President of the Indian Republic.

What was there in this man of humble origin and little academic learning that helped him overcome one obstacle after another and pedestal himself to triumph, to reach the pinnacle of aspiration and become the head of state? I will let incidents in his life speak for him.

Zail Singh was an active worker of *Praja Mandal* of Faridkot State. The Raja had personally ordered him to be jailed and kept in solitary confinement. When India became independent and Faridkot was merged into PEPSU, the central government was looking for suitable men to run the new state. Sardar Patel summoned Zail Singh. Zail Singh did not have the money to buy a third class return ticket from Faridkot to Delhi and had to ask friends for a loan. In Delhi, he stayed in Gurdwara Sis Ganj. He did not have money to hire a tonga to take him to Sardar Patel's residence at five in the morning. He walked the entire four miles and was late for his appointment. Sardar Patel's daughter brusquely dismissed him. It was the kindly secretary, V Shankar, who let him see the Deputy Prime Minister. Zail Singh was told that he was being made Minister of State in PEPSU. He walked back to the railway station to return to Faridkot. He never looked back. The remarkable thing about this man was that he did not forget his humble origins nor let power go to his head. Success was to him a gift given by the Great Guru, not something owed to him by virtue of his abilities. One of his favourite couplets warns one of the dangers of hubris:

Jin mein ho jaata hai andaz-e-khudaee paida,
Hum nay deykha hai voh butt toot jaatey hain.

Mortals who allow notions of divinity to germinate in them. We have seen those idols shattered and come to grief.

There is not even a suspicion of arrogance or self-esteem in this man. Besides humility, his faith in religion taught him to be honest and truthful. He is one of the breed of politicians now almost extinct who though handling vast sums of money never feathered his own nest nor those of his relatives. He owns no house, flat or tract of land except the little he inherited. Nobody has ever accused him of telling a lie.

As a junior minister, Zail Singh set about assiduously cultivating the support of the lower and discriminated castes. He is a Ramgarhia (carpenter); Punjab has always been dominated by the Jat and Sikh politics constipated with caste consideration. Zail Singh broke the Jat hegemony over the state and successfully mocked Akali pretensions of being *thekeydars* (monopolists) of the Khalsa Panth. He was able to convince the Sikhs that he was a better Sikh than all the Akali leaders put together. His speeches were always full of quotations from the *Gurbani* and episodes from Sikh history. No other politician, either from the Akali party or the Congress, could build this kind of Gursikh image for himself as did the Giani. By the time he made his presence felt in the state, a precedent had been established that the Chief Minister of the Punjab should be a Sikh. There was no better Sikh than Giani Zail Singh to fill the role.

Zail Singh's six-year tenure as Chief Minister was perhaps the most peaceful and prosperous the State has ever seen. They were the years of the Green Revolution. They were also the years without *morchas, bandhs* or strikes.

The Giani was able to rekindle pride in Punjabiyat. From England he acquired the dusty remains of Madan Lal Dhingra who had been hanged for the murder of Curzon-Wylie, and of Udham Singh hanged for the murder of Sir Michael O'Dwyer, Governor of Punjab at the time of Jallianwala Bagh, and he raised martyrs' memorials over them. He sought out the long-forgotten and ailing mother of Bhagat Singh, gave her a handsome grant and had her honoured as Punjab *Mata*—Mother of Punjab. The road connecting Anandpur to Fatehgarh was named Guru Gobind Singh Marg; horses believed to be descendants of the Guru's steed were taken along the marg for the populace to see and marvel at. A new township was named after the Guru's eldest son, Baba Ajit Singh Nagar. Massive *kirtan darbars* were organised all over the State. In his eagerness to wrest the Akali monopoly over the affairs of the Khalsa Panth, he unwittingly set in motion a Sikh revivalism which turned into fundamentalism under Bhindranwale.

Gianiji could not have forseen this development, much less wished it, because his relations with Punjabi Hindus including the somewhat anti-Sikh Mahasha press of Jullunder remained extremely cordial. And if gossip is to be believed, more than cordial with the smaller Muslim community. Giani Zail Singh achieved the incredible: he had no enemies. Besides being the Punjabi paradigm of a *dostaan da dost*—of friends the friendliest — he has the knack of winning over detractors. Even in the hey day of his power as Chief Minister and Home Minister he never tried to settle scores with people who had persecuted or humiliated him. He won them over by granting them favours and making them ashamed of themselves. If there was anything he could do for anyone, he never hesitated to do it. He has an incredibly good memory for names and faces; he has been able to gain friends by simply recognising people he had met briefly.

During the Emergency, while he had put many people in gaol, he went to see them; he sent a wedding gift to Badal's daughter when her father was in prison and went to receive the *barat* at the house of a friend's daughter in Kalka when her father was locked up. If he heard a friend was sick he would find time to visit him in hospital and quietly slip a bundle of currency notes under his pillow. Virtually the only man he was unable to win over was Darbara Singh who succeeded him as Chief Minister of Punjab.

To describe Gianiji as a far-sighted statesman would be an exaggeration; to describe him as a cunning politician would be grossly unfair because the stock-in-trade of a cunning politician is the ability to tell a blatant lie. And the one thing no one can accuse Giani of is falsehood. He is best described as a shrewd judge of men and events. After Mrs Gandhi's murder, there were many claimants to the prime ministership. Oddly enough, one of the seniormost civil servants at the time and later a confidante of the present Prime Minister even suggested to Gianiji that he take over the Prime Ministership himself. Sensing the anti-Sikh climate of the day, it was Gianiji who brushed aside this inane suggestion and decided to offer it to Rajiv Gandhi in the belief that as the descendant of Nehru and Indira Gandhi, he would be best suited to hold the country together.

And currently, when the Opposition tried to put him up for second term and Congress dissidents assured him of a substantial vote from the Congress party, he carefully weighed his prospects before turning it down. He is not a gambler, he plays to win. It was the same when pressure was brought on him to dismiss the Prime Minister or permit his prosecution on charges of corruption. Gianiji had little to lose and he could have made things very hot for Rajiv Gandhi. He refused to succumb to temptation, teaching Rajiv a lesson for his bad behaviour, because he felt that the nation's future was paramount and India was more important than Rajiv Gandhi or Zail Singh.

He has often quoted a couplet to the effect that while he put a rose in the palms of Rajiv Gandhi, Rajiv took a stone to hurt him. There is an equally apt couplet for him to mull over in his days of retirement:

> *Zakhmee hooey jo hont to mahsoos yeh hua*
> *Chooma tha mainey phool ko deevanagee kay sath.*

It was the bruises on my lips that made me comprehend with what thoughtlessness I had kissed the rose.

M Hidayatullah

I first met him at a small dinner party given by the then West German Ambassador. When he introduced himself I did not catch his name. Since he did not tell me what he did for a living I did not know who he was. In the course of conversation he casually told me that he had that morning struck down D H Lawrence's novel *Lady Chatterley's Lover* as obscene. I was impressed by his modesty: he had not proclaimed himself as the Chief Justice of India. I was not so impressed by his literary judgement. And told him so. "It is by no means Lawrence's best work; but compared to what modern novelists like Henry Miller, Saul Bellow, Philip Roth and Norman Mailer write, it is kindergarten stuff." He did not want to bandy words with me and quickly changed the subject to Urdu poetry.

My next meeting with him was in print. I reviewed two volumes of his reminiscences for the papers. His Victorian sense of morality came through clearly. So did his familiarity with the classics of various languages: Latin, Persian, French, Urdu, and English. Thereafter I met him several times in and out of the Rajya Sabha. He had an excellent memory; his conversation was invariably embellished with apt quotations and anecdotes. I do not recall any other senior Indian statesmen, barring C Rajagopalachari, Nehru and Radhakrishnan, who more answer to Plato's concept of a philosopher-king than he.

Though an extremely modest man, Hidayatullah loved to air his knowledge of literature. He was in his element when he bailed me out in a privilege motion moved against me by a bunch of Congress (I) members whose knowledge of English was as poor as their sense of humour. While he mercilessly punctured their self-esteem, he also had a few digs at my "Dog Latin".

Predictably, at his last appearance as Chairman of the Rajya Sabha most speakers spiced their tributes with quotations from the classics: Amir Khusrau, Shakespeare, Longfellow, Thackeray and Iqbal. Instead of simply thanking them for the kind words they had said, Hidayatullah proceeded to admonish them for quoting wrongly. Ghulam Rasool Mattoo had ascribed to Khusrau what partly belonged to Hazrat Nizamuddin. And Pranab Mukherjee had got his Shakespeare wrong. For once, Hidayatullah's memory failed him. Mukherjee, complimenting Hidayatullah on his ready wit, said that he disproved Shakespeare's saying that "When the age is in, the wit is out." Hidayatullah corrected him saying that the actual words were "When the wine is in, the wit is out." He received loud laughter and applause. Back home I checked the quotation. It is from *Much Ado About Nothing*. It reads:

A Good old man Sir; he will be talking, as they say: "When the age is in, the wit is out."

Pranab Mukherjee was right, Hidayatullah wrong. However, though I am not sure whether Hidayatullah drinks much wine, neither wine nor age had dulled his wits—only taken a toll of his memory.

An unspoken tribute was also paid to Hidayatullah by the staff of official reporters who compile our *Hansard*. Few parliamentarians or Press reporters had noticed that this motley group of men in floppy clothes had suddenly become very spruce in their attire. This was one of Hidayatullah's parting gift to these highly qualified but rarely noticed group of stenographers.

With a couplet which I wanted to quote but which had at the time eluded my memory—I am fast catching up with Hidayatullah—I bade farewell to this God's own gentleman:

Raah-e-manzil mein kucch aisey nishaan paon key
chorhey hain,
Key jinhen deykh kar unkee hamesha yaad aati hai.

On the path of destination such footprints has he left
behind when you see them he always comes back to mind.

Balwant Gargi

I don't recall when I first met Gargi, except that it was in the home of a good-looking lass whom he had succeeded in leading astray from the straight and narrow path of matrimony. What had she found in him? He was a short, squat man who punctuated his talk with feminine gestures. He walked with a mincing gait like one afraid of slipping. He was said to be a good playwright. Since he wrote in Punjabi and only rarely were his plays staged, few people knew his real worth. He was certainly an engaging talker and had the knack of surrounding himself with attractive women and persuading quite a few of them that a Dunlopillo mattress was not necessary to make bed an exciting place. I did not read or see any of his plays but did get to read an anthology of profiles. They were the wittiest pieces of prose I had ever read in Punjabi. They were obviously designed to hurt and succeeded in doing so. Thereafter, every time Gargi produced a book, he lost a dozen of his closest friends. He made up the loss by acquiring new admirers. In his younger days he professed communism (we all did), then jettisoned it (so did we) and landed a job to teach Indian drama at Seattle University. He produced an excellent book on the Indian theatre in English. I complimented him on writing 300 pages on a subject that did not exist. He arrived back from Seattle with a lovely blonde American wife, Jeannie. All of Balwant's friends fell in love with the Gargis.

It was a misalliance. Balwant's diet was literary *sarson ka saag;* Jeannie's was American apple pie. Gargi wanted appreciation of what he wrote and produced; Jeannie never bothered to learn Punjabi and was therefore unable to become a part of her husband's *claque*. Gargi was gregarious, open-hearted in his hospitality, with not much in his kitty to be open-hearted about. Jeannie cherished the privacy of her home and could not stomach people dropping in at all hours. She also had an enormous appetite for food which embarrassed Balwant for the simple reason that his friends might think he did not give her enough to eat at home.

It was Balwant who took the irrevocable step to break the marriage by committing adultery. He gives an emotionally charged account of his lustful encounter with one of his girl students, in a garage from where he could see his wife and children through the window. The affair was entirely physical. "While making love to Raji, I always came out with the wildest truths—the sins I had committed. How I had slept with a seventeen-year-old girl when I was twenty-three. Once her mother caught us and lost her temper. When I broke down, she soothed me, 'Son, you must know my daughter is to marry soon. She is innocent. I cannot allow it... It's a sin.' She caressed me and held my head in her lap with a purity and affection that I had not known. At night, she seduced me, kissing me like a mother and then suddenly changing her passion into naked lust, whispering 'my son, my son!' all the time. After that she would allow me to take her daughter. I began to sleep with both of them."

Raji laughed, "If I were your mother, I would also have seduced you!"

The affair with Raji, whose breasts he says had opium on them, came to a sticky end. By then Jeannie had launched on a liaison of her own. Balwant's machismo was deeply wounded. The injured tone he adopts over Jeannie's behaviour is hard to swallow.

Balwant Gargi is like a cactus flower. He hurts anyone he touches. In his autobiography, *The Naked Triangle* , he barely conceals the identity of the people he writes about. Some are mentioned by their real names. There is the writer, film producer, Rajinder Singh Bedi, recounting his affair with a nineteen-year-old girl who bared her bosom to him as a sort of introductory "how do you do?" It makes nice erotica. But one does not need, much imagination to know how the lady in the episode, Mrs Bedi, her children and grandchildren, will react to this disclosure.

Balwant Gargi's book is largely set in Chandigarh. The Punjab University's academic circles are up in arms against him for having portrayed them with their shirts up, pants and *salwars* down. Balwant Gargi will have to find new friends in Delhi. I will be one of them—till he writes about me.

The Man Who has Seen God

I would like to introduce the latest addition to my small circle of friends. He is unlike anyone I have befriended so far and at times I feel that I treat him more as good copy than as a friend. We have very little in common: his ambition is to make lots of money; mine to become a famous author. He has achieved what he set out to do: I am not likely to earn fame. He has hardly any formal education and has picked up a little Urdu and English; I have exaggerated respect for men of learning. He believes in God; and God has been good to him. I don't believe that anything is to be gained from God or prayer. Nevertheless I look forward to his visits. I shall divulge his identity when I have finished telling you his true life story.

I first set eyes on him on the Diwali of 1986. He came to greet me but as he had made no appointment I refused to see him. He rang up from a neighbouring house to tell me that all he wanted was to wish me well. I apologised and asked him to come over. He was upset with me and refused to sit down. "I wanted so much to talk to you but don't want to any more— *mera mood kharaab kar ditta.*" I apologised again and asked him to tell me why he wanted to see me. "Not this time," he replied. "I wanted to tell you that I have seen God face to face."

"You mean you have really seen Him?" I asked in a voice loaded with disbelief. "How? Where?"

"As closely as I am seeing you now. But I am not going to tell you about it today: *mera mood kharaab kar ditta,*" he repeated.

Last Diwali he surfaced again. This time after having fixed a time for his visit. And this time I held him captive till he told me of his seeing God.

"**In** August 1947 I came out of Pakistan with my widowed mother and two younger brothers. We belonged to a half-Hindu, half-Sikh family. I being the eldest was brought up as a Sikh; my brothers remained Hindus. All we had was a hundred rupee note and a gold bangle my mother wore on her hand," he began. "We were sent to Saharanpur refugee camp. I was only 15-years-old but the responsibility of looking after the family rested squarely on my shoulders. I got one of my brothers a job of rinsing dirty utensils in a *halwai's* shop at Rs. 7 per month and the other as a cycle-rickshaw puller. I persuaded my mother to let me sell her gold bangle and trade on the money I got for it. She threw the bangle at me saying she knew I had had my eyes on it but since she had kept it for the girl I would marry, I could do whatever I liked with it."

"Where does God come in to all this?" I asked impatiently. "Patience!" he counselled. "I am coming to it. With the Rs. 700 I got for the bangle, I began to trade in whatever anyone suggested. Having failed in trading with dry fruit, I bought sacks of black-pepper in Calcutta to sell in Delhi."

"God made you buy black-pepper?" I asked sarcastically. "In a way, yes," he replied ignoring my sarcasm. "At Patna station while I was making enquiries about prices of pepper I missed my train. I felt I was ruined. I cried for help. I got a taxi to the next station, Danapur. The train had left Danapur two hours earlier. I was frantic. I begged the station master to send a message to the next station to off-load my sacks of pepper. He refused to help and threatened to have me arrested for travelling without a ticket. I never bought tickets—just eluded ticket collectors or bribed them. I told him that if he did not have my goods off-loaded, I would jump in front of the next train that passed. He bluntly told me to go and kill myself anywhere I liked except at his station. Then I recited *Sukhmani* (Guru Arjan's hymn of peace). I pleaded with God to give me back my bags of pepper. I took a bus to the next station. I ran into the train standing at a signal. It had been there for two hours. Nobody knew why. I did. It was *Sukhmani Sahib* that did it. I sold the pepper at a handsome profit in Delhi and put the thousands of rupees I had earned in my mother's lap. She thought I had robbed a bank. I have never looked back since then."

"Where did God come in?"

He looked dismayed. "Who stopped that train at the signal when there were no other trains for it to let pass and there were two rail tracks? If that does not convince you about the existence of God, I don't know how else I can."

"It could be a coincidence. I need stronger proof than His concern for your black pepper. When did you see Him next?"

"I will tell you at our next meeting. And if that does not convince you, nothing will."

It was *Bakr eid*. This 14-year-old boy saw the village butcher leading a young heifer down the lane. "O Fakira, where are you taking this beautiful cow?"

"To the slaughterhouse. Today is *Bakr eid*. She is to be sacrificed."

"How much have you paid for it?"

"Seventy rupees."

"I'll give you Rs. 100 for it," said the boy who didn't have a paisa in his pocket.

Fakira hesitated. If Muslim villagers got to know he'd sold a sacrificial cow, he'd be in trouble. But the extra Rs. 30 settled the issue. The boy borrowed the money from a neighbour and took the cow to a *pinjrapole*. Fakira slaughtered an older animal and thought all was over. Secrets don't remain secrets in villages for very long. Fakira and the boy were hauled up before an all-Muslim *Panchayat*. The *lambardar* sternly questioned the boy about his misdeed. The boy admitted guilt. "I know nothing about *Bakr eid* or sacrifice. I saw that it was a beautiful young animal and my heart was overcome with compassion. I borrowed money on interest to save it. You can punish me."

The *lambardar* was moved by the boy's honest admission and let him off with a warning. A few days later when he had gone to a *mandi*, he was stricken with fever and laid himself down on a *charpoy* shivering with high fever. In his delirium he dreamt of the cow he had saved. "You have no fever now," the cow told him. "You will never have fever again. Get up and go home." When the boy woke, the fever had left him.

"That was the last time I ever had fever," he concluded with evident pride. "I was then 14, today I am 65. Isn't that clear proof that there is God?"

"No", I replied. "I am almost ten years older than you and I don't remember having had fever. I know thousands of people in their 80s who have never been ill."

His face showed distress. Nevertheless, he continued his narrative. "You may call it a coincidence or whatever you like but I firmly believe that it was the cow I saved which made me take up milk business. I started in a small way buying milk unfit for human consumption and turning it into glue. Then expanded it to a dairy. Today I have a fleet of milk-tankers plying across the length and breadth of this land. I send good, fresh chilled milk to our *jawans* wherever they may be. I personally took a tanker right into East Pakistan past Pakistani troops to our own while the war of Bangladesh liberation was at its height. Who could have protected me except God?"

I did not answer. I don't think that only those who believe in God rise from rags to riches. This man has succeeded by dint of hard work, integrity and liberal doses of good luck. He has known stark poverty; today he runs a vast business as a supplier of milk, producer of country liquor and owner of real estate; he lives in a marbled mansion and owns a fleet of imported automobiles. He has printed a brochure on himself; it is full of quotations from English and Urdu poets. Amongst them, there is one of Allama Iqbal which he believes applies to him:

> *Yaqeen Mahkam, amal paiham, mohabat fatah-e-Alam*
> *Jihaad-e-Zindgani mein hain yeh mardon kee Sham-*
> *sheeren*

In life's crusade, a man's weapons are three:
>   Conviction that his cause is just,
>   courage to strive till eternity, compassion that em-
braces all humanity.

I concede that this man's faith in God and prayer has sustained him. The moral, if any, that can be drawn from his life story is capsuled in the adage: *himmate-mardaan madad-e-Khuda* — God helps those who help themselves.

The subject of this true story is Nanak Singh.

If he could do it, why can't you?

K L Gauba

The initials K L stand for two names, Kanahya Lal and Khalid Latif. Both belonged to the same man. No one knew which really applied to him. Now no one will ever know because last week when he died, he took both with him.

Half-a-century ago, if the name of K L Gauba had been in any general knowledge examination paper, almost every candidate would have got the answer correct: eldest son of the banker-millionaire and first Hindu minister of Punjab, Lala Harkishan Lal Gauba; barrister, author, politician; a man who took his religion and his women as it suited him; much censured and much reviled for whatever he did. But a living example of *badnaam agar hongey to kya, naam na hoga.* The world didn't give a damn for K L Gauba; K L Gauba didn't give a damn for the world. He left it, unsung and unhonoured as he would have liked and as he deserved.

K L Gauba made his debut in Indian society as the author of *Uncle Sham,* a reply to Katherine Mayo's *Mother India.* As Mayo had maligned India, Gauba maligned Mayo's motherland, the United States of America. *Uncle Sham* was a scissors-and-paste job consisting largely of reports of incest, juvenile prostitution, dope and drink and all that was seamy in American life. He followed it up with another best-seller on the lives of Indian princes entitled *His Highness.* The book began with a memorable quote which ran somewhat as follows: "Some people begin their morning with a cup of tea, some with the morning paper; His Highness prefers a virgin." It was a scandalous account of sex orgies performed by our Maharajas.

What made Kanahya Lal Gauba the odd man out in every society is not very hard to guess. His father was the most distinguished and respected Punjabi of his times. K.L., as he was popularly known, flouted social norms of the times, by going through a much publicised conversion to Islam almost entirely to hurt his father—as Mahatma Gandhi's son had done to him. He was careful to retain his initial identity and never used his new name Khalid Latif in full. As a convert, he won the hearts of Punjabi Muslims and cashed in on his popularity by winning an election to the Punjab Assembly from a purely Muslim constituency which included Lahore's notorious red light district, Hira Mandi, where he had been a familiar figure even before his conversion. Although he wrote a book on the life of the Prophet Mohammed, it was common knowledge that his conversion was *nam ke vastey* and *kam ke vastey*.

I first met K L Gauba some time in 1948 in Lahore. He was then married to a Muslim lady (our cartoonist Anwar Ahmed's sister) and lived in considerable style in a spacious bungalow along the canal bank. I devilled for him in a number of cases. Then he wrote a very scurrilous book on Chief Justice Sir Douglas Young, accusing him of womanising and taking bribes. It was odd that K.L. who had renounced Hinduism only to spite his Hindu father went out of his way to malign Young who had jailed his father. He was hauled up for gross contempt of court and was sent to gaol. He, however, succeeded in blackening the face of Douglas Young who was given a very cool farewell by the Lahore bar and died in obscurity in South Africa.

On the partition of the country, Khalid Latif Gauba did not stay on in Muslim Pakistan but migrated to India with other Hindus and Sikhs. A few months later I ran into him in Simla. He had acquired a very lovely, young, burqa-clad Begum from Hyderabad. After some time the Hyderabadi Begum vanished and was replaced by another lady and later yet another. K.L. settled down in Bombay but his practice never picked up. He moved from big to smaller apartments and then to a lodging house. He tried to add to his meagre income by writing articles and books. He churned out another scissors-and-paste job listing atrocities committed against Indian Muslims which, though entirely unauthenticated, provided plenty of propaganda fodder to Pakistan. K.L. gradually sank into poverty and spent his last years living on the charity of his step-brother, M L Gauba and his generous-hearted Sindhi wife, Gopi.

In his later days K.L. could be seen in his sola topee and tattered clothes, shuffling along Flora Fountain towards the Asiatic Society where he spent all his days reading magazines and sleeping in armchairs. The last time I saw him, he was sitting on the pavement outside a Parsee fire-temple munching parched gram out of a paper cup. It was a pathetic sight: the story of from the log cabin to the White House in reverse; from a palatial Punjab mansion to the pavement of Pherozeshah Mehta Road. Fifty years ago, K L Gauba's cortege would have been followed by half the city of Lahore; last week he did not have a dozen to mourn his departure.

POLITICS

"*I* have said a lot of things on a lot of subjects, particularly Punjab, and have been constantly misunderstood .... Let me add, and finally put on record: I never have, nor do, nor ever will compromise with anyone who in any way insults the Constitution of this country. I never have, nor do, nor ever will have any truce with anyone who fouls the Indian air by flying foreign flags, whether they be made here or made outside. I never have, nor do, nor will ever compromise with anyone who talks about dismembering this country. Let that go on record once for ever."

(Khushwant Singh in his farewell speech in Parliament; 18 March, 1986.)

My Years in Parliament

One afternoon in April 1980 when I was editor of *New Delhi,* a fortnightly journal of the Ananda Bazar Group, I got a call from Giani Zail Singh who was then Home Minister in Mrs Indira Gandhi's cabinet. "Congratulations! Your name has been recommended for nomination to the Rajya Sabha," he said. And added as a legpull, "I trust you have no objection to accepting it. I have yet to get the President's consent."

I had been expecting the call for some days. Two days earlier Mrs Indira Gandhi had wanted me elected from Maharashtra. I missed the chance because my name was not on Maharashtra's electoral rolls. This time I had been assured of the nomination by Sanjay Gandhi. He never broke his word.

I had no illusions of being either a distinguished writer or an editor. There were many writers and poets more distinguished than I. And although I had earned a certain amount of notoriety as editor of *The Illustrated Weekly of India,* there were journalists enjoying greater public esteem. However, I was as happy as a child given a whoppingly expensive birthday present. I rang up my wife. She rang up my son and daughter. I shouted out the news to my office colleagues and shook hands with all of them. I told everyone I met in the corridors of the PTI building from managers, clerks, liftmen and *chaprasis.* I drove to my aged, 90-year-old mother and woke her up from her siesta to tell her. "Your father would have been very happy to hear this," she said with tears of joy flowing down her cheeks. My father had been member of the Upper House half-a-century earlier.

By the evening when the names of new members were announced on All India Radio, my telephone began to ring incessantly and congratulatory telegrams began to pour in. I knew I would have no peace for the next few days. Early next morning I got out of Delhi and drove away to my summer villa in Kasauli.

The swearing-in ceremony came more than a month later. The only thing that marked me out as different from other new MPs was that while they took their oaths in the name of God, I, being an agnostic, made an affirmation. To my great delight I found myself seated next to my college days' heart-throb, Nargis Dutt.

I had planned not to open my mouth in the first session but to watch the proceedings, familiarise myself with the way the House conducted itself and get to know other members. My self-imposed vow of silence was rudely shattered within the first week. As I arrived in the House one morning, I found a note from R K Dhawan awaiting me saying that Mrs Gandhi wanted to see me urgently. I hurried to her office. Dhawan handed me a cyclostyled copy of the speech made by Bhupesh Gupta the afternoon earlier and a small book of rules with relevant passages marked in ink. Bhupesh had described me as Mrs Gandhi's sycophant. Mrs Gandhi wanted me to rebut the charge.

Instead of making my debut with a speech on a matter of national importance, I had to defend Mrs Gandhi nominating someone undeserving as a Member of the Rajya Sabha. My problem was how to avoid beating my own trumpet and yet effectively put across that I was neither wholly undistinguished and undeserving nor simply a *chamcha* of the Gandhi family.

I did the best I could. I quoted people like L K Advani for my having pleaded for the release of the leaders held in captivity during the Emergency and having been even-handed in my praise and blame of political leaders irrespective of their political bias. I said that it was unfair of Bhupesh Gupta to have maligned me when I was not present in the House but if he withdrew the offending remark, I would be happy to shake hands with him and call it quits. Bhupesh replied: "I am a Communist. We never withdraw our words." I lost my temper and let loose a string of Punjabi epithets reflecting on the morals of his female relatives. There was an uproar of protests from Communist MPs. My volley of abuse was struck off the record. No matter, I had said what I wanted and felt lighter. It was not a very auspicious beginning of my career as a parliamentarian.

It did not take me very long to size up my fellow MPs. Gupta had a great reputation as a parliamentarian. But since I had suffered the sting of his forked tongue, I never got to like him nor ever spoke to him. He was a sick man and died soon after.

I was impressed by Piloo Modi; he was a good orator and a ready wit. Unfortunately, he could not resist acting the clown and keeping a running commentary going through the proceedings. He had many clashes with the over-loyal and loud J K Jain. Piloo scored over Jain every time. Piloo's sudden death deprived the house of a lot of laughter.

Amongst the Opposition members there were a number of excellent speakers, notably L K Advani, Jaswant Singh, Hukum Narain Dev Yadav, Ladli Mohan Nigam and Dinesh Goswami. Amongst newcomers there is Jayalalitha. Besides being a classic beauty, she is a hard-working girl and a gifted speaker. Only she does not take the Rajya Sabha seriously and is often absent. Another equally impressive woman speaker is Margaret Alva. Somehow, no sooner than she switched over from the Opposition to the treasury benches, much of the fire went out of her. The same happened to Satyapal Malik when he quit the Lok Dal. I was not particularly impressed with any of the Congress party backbenchers save Chaudhary Sultan Singh, Rafiq Zakaria, Saroj Khaparde and later G L Bansal. They had and have a number of lady members but most of them made their presence felt by barracking Opposition speakers. Amarjeet Kaur, who has the making of a good parliamentarian continues to read prepared texts. Manners of some members left much to be desired. The pachydermatous Kalpnath Rai, who was later elevated to a ministerial post was often ticked off by the chairman for unseemly behaviour. His friend Sita Ram Kesri (picked up, put down and picked up again) could often be crude beyond words. We also had a large number of irrepressible windbags. There was Rameshwar Prasad Singh who was perpetually raising *viyavastha kay prashna* (points of order), getting into hot arguments with the very gentle and tolerant Hidayatullah and staging walk-outs. His place has been taken by a much abler Suresh Kalmadi who knows his facts and often takes on the ruling party single-handed. He is loud, aggressive but also impressive and is about the only member that the present chairman, Venkatraman, cannot subdue.

There was something ill-omened about my presence as one after another people allotted seats next to mine were "called to their heavenly abodes". First, it was the beautiful Nargis Dutt. Her place was taken by the poet, Bhagwati Charan Verma. He had been there long before me but treated the House as a pleasant place for a peaceful snooze. He used to arrive at the end of the noisy Question and Zero Hour, exchange *namaskars* with me and then doze off. Once I asked him the name of a member who was speaking. With a beatific smile on his face, Vermaji replied: *"Naam vaam to main kisee ka nahin janta* (I don't know anyone's name or anything)." After a few months, he too died. During my last session, my neighbour was the 90-year-old ornithologist, Salim Ali. May Allah transfer some of my years to him!

Before the advent of Rajiv Gandhi, the Rajya Sabha was indeed the House of Elders. The average age of members was well over 50. Half a century of striving in sedentary jobs essential to bring them into the realm of possibles for the Rajya Sabha had played havoc with their digestive systems. A fair proportion of them were diabetic or dyspeptic and suffered from constipation, piles and other diseases of ageing, notably flatulence. Besides natural infirmities that come with age, we Indians are singularly insensitive about others' feelings. Belching loudly is almost an accepted form of expressing gratification. Breaking wind in public, though frowned upon, is condoned. I had to put up with at least three shameless farters given seats not far from mine. One was in the row behind mine and sat next to H L Kapur. He was a rotund, cherubic member from an eastern region and believed in expressing himself from his rear end. This could be most disconcerting to anyone who was speaking. Once he broke wind so loudly that even the ever-suffering Kapur turned to me and asked. "Does this amount to contempt of the House?" I thought to myself that one day before I retired, I would ask Chairman Venkataraman for a ruling on the permitted decibels allowed for this form of expression. Also to request him to install a stinko-meter which records the pungency of malodorous vapours a member is allowed to emit per session. It was my misfortune that for two years the seat once occupied by the lovely Nargis Dutt was occupied by a member who believed in the Christian principle of keeping his right and left hand neighbours guessing the source of his benevolence: he believed in *gupta daan* of the most malodorous intensity while pretending to be deeply absorbed in the debate.

Nominated members are Harijans of the House of Elders, treated more as decorative trimmings and expected to maintain a golden silence. When they want to speak, they have to await their turn till representatives of all the political parties have had their say. This is usually late in the evening when the House is almost empty and the press gallery left with only correspondents of the two major news agencies. Being frustrated at this state of affairs, I joined a group of 17 consisting of representatives of Congress(S), the National Conference, Socialist and Republican Party and a couple of Independents. We chose S W Dhabe as our leader and Ghulam Rasool Mattoo as deputy leader. The chairman agreed to consider us as a party and allot us precedence and time according to our strength. At the time, Akali members resigned from both Houses and affairs of Punjab started coming to the boil. Willynilly, I became the spokesman of the independent but antigovernment point of view on the Punjab. Although I spoke on many other topics, particularly those concerned with foreign affairs (notably relations with Pakistan on which I usually defended Pakistan), information, broadcasting and the media, education, railways and cultural problems, it was on the Punjab, Sikhs and Akalis that I was listened to with a certain amount of attention as an expert. I soon found myself in the ranks of the Opposition. Thereafter, the Congress party had its own guns lined against me.

The tragic succession of events brought out whatever I had in the way of oratory within me. I was as outspoken in condemning Bhindranwale as comrade Harkishen Singh Surjeet. When the government broke its word, given many times, that it had no intention of ordering the invasion of the Golden Temple by the army, I not only returned my Padma Bhushan but also mounted single-handed the most blistering attack on Mrs Gandhi on what I denounced as "a grave error of judgement". I had the entire House, including the Opposition, against me; Mrs Gandhi did me the honour of referring to my speech as being "against national interests". I became India's villain number one. That did not deter me. I continued to press for the immediate release of Akali leaders and re-opening a dialogue with them. I pleaded for compassionate treatment of Sikh soldiers who deserted their regiments following Operation Bluestar. I was dubbed as a Sikh communalist by the entire media of the country.

A few months later came Mrs Gandhi's assassination. I sought special permission from the Chairman to pay her tribute. I did so with all the eloquence at my command because despite all my differences, I loved and respected her. My tribute was more sincere and therefore better worded than any paid to her in the House. This is what I said: I thank you for giving me this opportunity of paying tribute to our departed leader Indira Gandhi. I speak of her in four capacities. First, as one who for a brief period had the privilege of her friendship and to whom I owe my presence in this august assembly today. Secondly, as a critic of her policies, particularly in so far as they concerned the Punjab and earned her displeasure for doing so. Thirdly, as a Sikh and a member of the same community to which her assassins belonged and bearing the stigma that many of my countrymen have imprinted on us. Finally, and above all, as an Indian who feels passionately that the most befitting tribute we can pay this great woman is to strive to achieve her unfulfilled dream of creating a united, strong, prosperous and happy India.

Mrs Gandhi's place in history is assured. No one person in the history of the world, neither dead nor living, neither man nor woman, held the destinies of so many people for so long a time in her hands as did Indira Gandhi. No monarch ruled over so vast a territory inhabited by so numerous a people as diverse in race, creed, language and ways of living as did Indira Gandhi. She did not inherit an empire nor was sat upon a throne by a set of courtiers. She was put on the seat of authority by the free will of her own people. She wore no crown save the crown of thorns that rulers often have to wear. She bore the awesome burden of office with conscientious responsibility, fortitude and cheerfulness. I recall how in the 1979 election campaign, she toured the country by plane, jeep, bullock cart and on foot, non-stop and without rest or sleep for 36 hours or more and arrived at a social function looking as fresh, smiling and as radiantly beautiful as she always did. I know of no other woman who combined in her appearance regal dignity with feminine charm as she did and answered Hillaire Belloc's description of a really beautiful woman:

> Her face was like the king's command
> When all the swords are drawn.

She took the hazards of life with unparalleled courage, and ultimately paid the price for it with her own life. As the bard said: "She and comparisons are odious." Before her the great figures of history, the Ceasars of Rome and the Tsars of Russia, the Bonapartes of France and the Kaisers of Germany, the monarchs of England, the Presidents and Prime Ministers of our times pale into littleness. "She was not of this age but for all time." We will not see the likes of her in our lifetimes. About her we can say with conviction: She will forever be honoured, forever mourned.

Mrs Gandhi did not subscribe to any dogmas. Her one political commitment was to keep the country united. That persuasion and belief ripened into faith and that faith became a passionate intuition.

While paying my personal tribute to Mrs Indira Gandhi, I cannot overlook mentioning the fact that her killers were men entrusted to watch over her safety. They betrayed their sacred trust because they were blinded by fanatic hate after what had happened in Amritsar in the first week of June.

I have no hesitation in condemning this dastardly act in the strongest of terms. I have, on several occasions, described Operation Bluestar as an error of judgement and I am convinced that but for that one error of judgement, we would not have had to pay so heavy a price as the loss of a Prime Minister we loved and respected and the loss of thousands of innocent lives that followed. Rulers have many hard decisions to take and Mrs Gandhi must have weighed all the consequences before she made that fateful decision. However, I have not the slightest doubt in my mind that nothing would have hurt her more than to see that for a crime committed by two or more individuals, their entire community would be stigmatised. I fervently hope that our new rulers will honour the memory of our leader by seeing that the Sikhs are once again rehabilitated as trusted and loyal citizens of their motherland.

And finally, since the nation has chosen Mrs Gandhi's son to lead the country, let me assure him that as long as he treads the right path we will lend him our unstinted support in his endeavour to lead the country to prosperity. Let this be our prayer: "Today he puts forth the tender leaves of hope, tomorrow may he blossom and may the fruits of honour come thick upon him."

However, hardly a word of it was reproduced in the press, All-India Radio or Doordarshan because in between I had also lashed out in angry condemnation of the deliberate and planned massacre of thousands of innocent Sikhs in towns and cities of northern India. This holocaust hardly stirred the emotions of either the Congress or the Opposition MPs. Once again I felt isolated and alone.

Despite my deep-seated reservation against the policies of the ruling party in dealing with Punjab's problems, when Rajiv Gandhi signed the accord with Sant Longowal, I applauded it as the birth of a new dawn. Twice I had occasion to speak on the resurgence of terrorism—the transistor bombs in Delhi and the chain of killings following Tohra's abduction of authority by handing over the Golden Temple complex to the Damdami Taksal, and gangsters of the United Akali Dal. Besides condemning them as common criminals, I recommended forcible entry into the Golden Temple to oust illegal squatters; peaceful if possible, by force if necessary. I roundly condemned the hoisting of Khalistani flags as acts of treason and warned the authorities that the Punjab was ready for another blood-letting but sooner the surgical operation was performed, the less bloody it would be; the longer it was delayed, the greater would be the danger of the cancer spreading. This is for the record of those who glibly describe me as a Sikh communalist.

In the six years I was member of the House I reckon I made an average of two major speeches and at least half-a-dozen other interventions during the Question Hour, or as Special Mentions in every session. Whatever satisfaction that gave me, I became more and more aware of the irrelevance of Parliament in directing the country's affairs. Primarily, it is the fault of the members themselves because they do not take Parliament seriously enough. Almost every day the hall empties after the Question and the Zero Hour. In the afternoon there are seldom more than two-dozen members present. Ministers pay scant attention to what Members are saying and are usually busy whispering to their cronies or reading their files. The press is equally guilty of indifference. No. sooner than Members file out of the House, they disappear from the press gallery leaving only the PTI and UNI representatives to record whatever they can or wish. Without exception, most reporting of Parliamentary debates which appear in our national newspapers under the caption "From Our Parliamentary Correspondent" are tinctured re-hashes of versions put out by the wire-services. I know this from experience as an editor and a Parliamentarian. It is not surprising that there is no follow-up of suggestions made by the Members.

Once when I was feeling particularly frustrated with Parliament, I vent my feelings in the column I write for *The Hindustan Times*. I was emboldened by one article written by Auberon Waugh in *The Spectator* in which he had many nasty things to say about British MPs: useless, arrogant, illiterate were some of the expressions he had used in describing them as dogsbodies.

I concealed my real feelings by prefacing each paragraph with the sentence "Dare I use the following words for our own MPs?" And liberally quoted Waugh. Very promptly Satpal Mittal, Congress MP from Punjab, had a large number of his partymen and women sign a Motion of Privilege against me and presented it to M Hidayatullah demanding that I be hauled up for contempt of the House. Hidayatullah gave his ruling a few days later. He first read out what I had written; then the construction put on my words by Satpal & Co., then proceeded to dismiss their understanding of my words in his usual witty and erudite manner.

Instead of hauling me up, he poked fun at them for lacking in a sense of humour. He said every thing short of calling them a pack of assess. In his farewell speech to the House he referred to this privilege motion against me as the most enjoyable and memorable event in the six years of his chairmanship.

Despite the growing feeling of disenchantment with the relevance of Parliament to national affairs, I was anxious to get a second term either by nomination or being elected from the Punjab. If nothing else, being an MP makes you member of the elitist of clubs in India. Once having tasted the privileges and perks that go with it, I was loath to lose them. I made half-hearted attempts to get back into the Rajya Sabha on the plea that my voice still mattered more with educated Punjabis than that of any other individual. I must have over-estimated my importance. Neither the President nor the Prime Minister shared my self-esteem and did not think I deserved a second term. They may be right. What difference does it make whether or not an MP opens his mouth? The caravan marches on.

Khalistan

S ikhs who form under two per cent of the population of India are nevertheless a formidable minority. Unlike the other minorities like the Muslims and the Christians who are scattered in different parts of the country, almost 85 per cent of Sikh population is concentrated in the Punjab on India's sensitive border with Pakistan. They are the most prosperous agricultural community of India, form at least a tenth of India's defence forces and have more representation in civilian services than warranted by their numbers. They are also more conscious of their rights and being somewhat aggressive by nature, when roused can become a major problem to the administration. A section of them have started a movement demanding an independent sovereign state of their own, Khalistan. Although so far the movement has very limited support, it has enormous potential for mischief and has got the Indian government very worried.

Ever since the initially pacifist Sikh community founded by Guru Nanak (1469-1539) was baptised by the last of its ten Gurus, Gobind Singh (1677-1708) into the militant fraternity called the *Khalsa* (pure) in 1699 AD, every congregational prayer in Sikh temples (Gurdwaras) has ended with a chant *Raj Kareyga Khalsa* — the Khalsa will rule. In actual fact the Sikhs ruled the Punjab for barely 50 years till 1849 when their Kingdom was annexed by the British and made a province of India. Since then the resolve to become rulers was regarded by the Sikhs themselves as no more than a ritual chanting of a pious but improbable hope.

The partition of India in 1947 found the Sikhs equally divided with almost half their population in Pakistan. They were driven out of Pakistan with considerable violence and in their turn drove out Muslims in East Punjab with bloody slaughter. Then for the first time in their history the Sikhs found themselves in a majority in certain districts of Indian Punjab. Taking advantage of the principle of demarcation of State boundaries on the basis of language they pressed for a unilingual Punjabi speaking State. After much agitation, a Punjabi *Suba* (Punjabi speaking State) was conceded in 1966 in which they formed 55 per cent of the population with the Hindus, who were also Punjabi speaking, reduced to a minority of 45 per cent. Ever since, Indian Punjab has, except for a short period of six months, been ruled by a Sikh Chief Minister.

Sikh's grievances against the government are basically propaganda material for political parties. Before partition they were a community of landlords; after partition they were reduced to small-holders who had to till their own lands. They enjoyed several privileges during British rule: they formed almost a quarter of the British Indian army and were well represented in the British colonial police; their abolition of separate electorates put them on par with other religious communities. Sikh politicians found many grievances against the government which they could air to gain political leverage: Punjabi speaking sub-districts in neighbouring Haryana, Himachal and Rajasthan have not been incorporated into the Punjab; Punjab has to share its capital, Chandigarh, and its High Court with Haryana; Sikh squatters in the Nepal Terai (Uttar Pradesh) have been served with notices of ejection after they had cleared the malarial swamps and made them productive; the Punjab has not been given the control of hydro-electric complexes like Bhakra-Nangal which lie in its territory and substantive portions of the river waters which run through it have been allocated to other States; the Punjab has hardly any heavy industry and much of its income invested elsewhere. And so on. Along with these grievances, which have, some substance, they have added others, mainly against the government's interference in the religious affairs of the Sikhs by manipulating elections to governing bodies of their innumerable Gurdwaras.

Thousands of Sikh Gurdwaras scattered all over India are governed by an apex body, the Shiromani Gurdwara Prabandhak Committee (SGPC) located in the Sikh's holy city, Amritsar. Ever since its inception in 1925, it has been controlled by one or the other factions of the Akali party. The SGPC wields enormous patronage. The incomes from the Gurdwaras is over Rs 6 crores per year. Apart from appointing priests, hymn singers and caretakers to these Gurdwaras, there are dozens of colleges and hundreds of schools and orphanages run by it. The president of the SGPC enjoys a unique religio-political status. The present incumbent is Gurcharan Singh Tohra. His chief rival is Jagdev Singh Talwandi, leader of a splinter Akali group. In addition, there are another six sub-groups of Akalis. The jostling for power requires every group to outdo the other in championing Sikhs' grievances. Waiting in the wings is the Congress party which also has a sizeable following among the Sikhs. But having to keep up the pretence of being secular it has not been able to openly enter the fray over control of religious institutions.

The demand for a sovereign Sikh state was first raised in 1971 by Dr Jagjit Singh Chauhan, one time Minister of an Akali government of the Punjab. No one in India took much notice of it and the best Chauhan could do was to gather a few supporters among Sikh emigrants living in Canada, the United States and England. He also got some encouragement from the Pakistan government. He was received both by the late Mr Bhutto and General Zia-ul-Haq. Pakistan radio, which beams a regular service consisting of chanting of Sikh hymns to India has always highlighted this demand.

The movement slowly gained adherents among some Sikh intellectuals. At a meeting of the Akali party in 1973 in Anandpur, where Guru Gobind had first baptised the Khalsa, a resolution demanding a self-determined status for the Sikhs was passed. The sentiment was taken a step further when the

SGPC presided over by Tohra declared the Sikhs to be a nation apart from the Hindus. Last year, the Sikh Educational Conference, a body known for its conservatism allowed Ganga Singh Dhillon, a prosperous businessman living in Washington D.C. to introduce a resolution to the effect that the Sikhs should apply to the United Nations for recognition as a separate nation and be granted "associated status". Although the organisers of the Conference later rescinded the resolution, the mischief had been done. For the first time the government took serious note of this new development in Sikh politics. Both Chauhan and Dhillon have since been refused entry into India.

Meanwhile, yet another extremist faction rose under the leadership of an almost unknown and semi-literate head of a religious group located in village Bhindranwale near Amritsar. This was 37-year-old "Saint" Jarnail Singh who had been conducting parties of hymn singers to different Sikh villages and persuading Sikhs who had been straying from the spartan traditions prescribed for the Khalsa (to wear their hair unshorn, not to smoke, etc.) to be rebaptised. Bhindranwale's followers clashed with followers of a Sikh subsect called the Nirankaris who rever a living guru as a reincarnation of the founder of the faith, Guru Nanak. This is unpardonable heresy for orthodox Sikhs. There were several bloody encounters between Bhindranwale's armed men and the Nirankaris with killings on either side. On April 24, 1980 the Nirankari guru, Baba Gurbachan Singh was slain in Delhi. His assassins are still untraced. The murder was followed by slaying of other Nirankari leaders and wild spree killings of innocent Hindus by Sikh extremists including Lala Jagat Narain, an aged proprietor of a chain of Hindi, Punjabi and Urdu papers which had vociferously opposed Khalistan. By fortuitous circumstances Bhindranwale came to be associated with the demand for Khalistan and the leader of Sikh crusaders against Hindu domination. He was arrested on September 20, 1981 but only at a place and time of his own choosing. He was later released for lack of evidence connected with the slayings. An Indian Airlines plane was hijacked by his followers demanding his release and recognition of Khalistan. Jarnail Singh and Bhindranwale have emerged as the most powerful force in the Sikh community.

Khalistan has no support among Indian Sikhs living outside the Punjab. It has gained some adherents in the central districts of the Punjab and amongst young hot-heads of the Sikh Students Federation. It continues to draw most of its sustenance from Sikh emigrants in the United States, Canada and England who have hardly any stake in its establishment. And it continues to be exploited by both its supporters and its opponents to extract concessions from the government.

There is a strong element of emotional insecurity behind all the demands of exclusiveness that have from time to time been voiced by Sikh leaders. The vast majority of Sikhs are converts from Hinduism and their relationship with the Hindu community continues to be very close. Till recently, many Hindu families of North-West Punjab and Sindh brought up one of their sons as a Khalsa Sikh, gave their daughters in marriage to them and more often than not preferred to worship in Sikh gurdwaras rather than Hindus temples. The border line between Sikhism and Hinduism was always very blurred: a Khalsa Sikh who cut off his long hair and beard became, for all practical purposes, a Hindu living in Sikhism. Professor Lorimer, a well-known philologist, once lecturing on the religious communities of Northern India was asked: We've heard about Hindus and Muslims, but who exactly are Sikhs that you have been speaking about?" The learned Professor replied: "It is awfully hard to define a Sikh; he is a kind of vicious Hindu."

Since independent India opted for secularism and abolished privileges based on religious affiliations which the British had given to the Sikhs, an ever-increasing number of young Sikhs have been giving up the external forms of the Khalsa and relapsing back into the Hindu fold. It has been surmised by some scholars of Sikhism that if the pace at which young Sikhs are abandoning their Khalsa traditions continues, it will not be long before Sikhs become a subsect of Hindus. This fear has haunted the orthodox leadership which tries to harp on differences and whip up resentment against discrimination practised on Sikhs by the Hindus. One of the commonest is that Hindus look down upon the Sikhs as a naive, stupid people. The Sikhs, they allege, because they have long hair bound under heavy turbans feel the heat excessively and loose their wits at noon time. All one has to say to a Sikh is *bara bajey* (its twelve o'clock) and see his intemperate reaction to the insult. A whole *genre* of Sardarji (the title by which Sikhs are addressed) jokes are current. Though many are manufactured by Sikhs themselves, heaven help a non-Sikh who takes the liberty of cracking one in their company. The latest on Khalistan is about a dialogue between a Hindu and a Sikh. Asked the Hindu: "Why are you Sikhs demanding Khalistan? Don't you realise how dangerous this demand can be for the unity of India?

"Not at all!" replied the Sikh. "Khalistan will protect your north-western frontier from Muslim invaders."

"How?" demanded the Hindu.

"By providing a duffer state."

A TRAVELLER'S DIARY

"*I am a muftkhora— a free liver. I have been round the globe dozens of times and visited almost every country in the world but rarely, if ever, paid for my travel or hospitality. But with the years I have also become an araamkhor—luxury loving. And that is not always available to me. Every time I set out of my home for the Indira Gandhi International Airport, I ask myself; 'Is this journey necessary?' I resolve never to accept a foreign invitation again. At my age, I share Samuel Johnson's sentiment: 'Worth seeing? Yes, but not going to see'.*"

Australia : Lone Land of Magnificent Distances

On the afternoon of 24 March 1977, Morarji Desai was sworn in as Prime Minister of India. The next day I was on my way out of the country. My friends said: "You are running away because Mrs Gandhi and Sanjay are out and Morarji-bhai will put you in gaol."

I am sorry that Indira is out. But I am also glad that it is Morarji who is in and nobody else. Although I don't like his self-righteous sermonising, I know he is a good, honest and able man. And I don't care if he rams *neera* down other people's throats, I hope he won't ram it down mine. If I want to drink *lattha* and kill myself, I will drink *lattha* and kill myself. However, I am on my way to Australia.

The first thing Danny Lewis asks me as we are airborne is: 'Would you like a drink?" Morarjibhai is of the opinion that journalists can't afford to buy drinks and when they get them free they do not tell the truth about those who give it to them. It is true Air-India is offering me the drink free, but it is not true that I cannot tell the truth about Air-India. It is much the best of the world's air services that I have flown. Their staff is the most courteous and their food delectable. And they murder the English language as any patriotic Indian would like to murder the language of a race that ruled us for 200 years. At one time linguicide was performed by our pretty air-hostesses; now it is performed with greater efficiency by the captains of our air fleet in the few seconds they use the internal communication system.

I spend the first hour listening to music over the plane's stereo system. I switch on to Zubin Mehta conducting *Bach* and *Beethoven*. But I am already nostalgic about the country I am said to be fleeing and switch on to Hindi film songs. How many can tell whether *Raina beeti jaaye* and *Jaaiyey aap kahan jayenge* is sung by Lata or Asha? I can. And how many have heard Vani Jairam sing the soul-uplifting *Bol re papihara*? I have heard it a hundred times and a hundred times has my soul been uplifted. And how many can tell the voices of Kishore Kumar, Mohammed Rafi, Mahendra Kapoor and Yesudas from the voice of P Sushila? I can. I am 100 per cent lowbrow Hindustani. Mukesh keeps reassuring me that though my shoes are Japani and my jacket Englishstani, my head is wrapped in a Finlays turban and my heart is very, very Hindustani.

Five hours after my flight from my native land, we descend on a very brightly-lit Singapore. I find myself in the transit lounge with rows of duty-free shops run by Indians and Chinese. Indians steal the show in more ways than one. They put out all their stock of toys: tail-wagging, yapping puppy dogs; chimps bashing away cymbals; miniature aeroplanes with blinking lights going in circles. It is the Indians, not the Chinese, who solicit custom. They do it in Tamil, Arabic, English and ungrammatical Hindi: "*Kya mangta*". I buy a bottle of eau-de-cologne from one store and go into the next. "How much you pay for that?" asks the shopman. I tell him. "I give you five dollars cheaper." I am dismayed. Bargaining for standard products at an airport shop! I discover only the Indians do it—not the Chinese. Fellow Indians, if you happen to be in the transit lounge of Singapore airport, avoid your countrymen like the plague. The Chinese are more honest.

I reboard the Emperor Akbar. Four-and-a-half hours later I wake up in Perth. Two Australians fumigate the plane with insecticide. One can never be sure of disease-carrying Orientals, can one? Once sterilised, the Australians are not bothered with what else you are carrying. I step out into a pitch-black, wind-blown darkness where the heavens are studded with stars

I have never seen in the Northern Hemisphere. I spot the Southern Cross, the emblem of Australia. From the 22nd floor of my hotel window I get a view of Perth. The grey light of the dawn unfolds neon-lit, wide, empty avenues, and colonial bungalows amidst handsome skyscrapers, expanses of lawns and beyond them the blank nothingness of the Swan river.

Perth has a population of some 700,000 souls. Of these, about 3,000 are Indians or Pakistanis, mostly in the civil services or in the professions such as teaching or medicine. There are said to be over 30,000 Anglo-Indians in the region who have completely obliterated the oriental part of their heritage and become "dinkum" Aussies (good Australians).

I spend the morning window-shopping with Krishen Malik of Air-India. All the major stores, arcades, etc., are located within a radius of a quarter mile. The rest of Perth is just pavements without pedestrians and wide roads with too many cars. The vegetation is familiar—hibiscus, palm, banyan, cacti—but every one of them bigger and healthier than in India. In the Governor's residence there is a hibiscus tree over 50 feet high and in the park alongside, a massive yucca tree with more than a dozen candelabra-like clusters of flowers at different points. The birds, except for the common mynah, are alien to me. Parakeets are a peacock blue, bright and slate grey crows wear white waistcoats. Other birds I cannot recognise at all.

I return footsore to the hotel lobby and espy a figure in a sari. It is Raj Sahni (nee Chawla), once a journalist, now a businesswoman. She exports garments and handicrafts to Australia.

Handstitched clothing, textiles (mainly from Bombay Dyeing) and steel are all that the Australians buy from us in exchange for the massive quantities of wool and wheat we buy from them. A country with a population of 13 million sells us food and winter clothing. Disgraceful !

By Saturday afternoon, the little evidence of life there is in the streets is gone. Perth looks like a wilderness of cement and glass and long stretches of asphalt roads lined with eucalyptus swaying to the breeze. Perth is the third windiest city of the world. I turn in to watch television. There are only two channels, both very clear and colourful, both devoted to sport—soccer, rugger, motor-racing. Physical fitness is an obsession with the Australians. They have a high incidence of skin cancer caused by exposure of their bare bodies to the sun.

In the evening, Shaikh Maqbool Ahmed, an Amritsar-born Pakistani, now an Australian citizen, comes along with his wife and sister-in-law. As a young man he acted as Mr Jinnah's personal bodyguard. He was soured with the dictatorship of Ayub and Yahya and decided to emigrate. He's done well for himself. A lovely bungalow at City Beach, three cars, a Pakistani servant, a son studying in Hong Kong, two daughters in school and a collection of rare Persian manuscripts including a copy of the *Ain-i-Akbari*. More valuable than all those, a heart of gold which knows no distinction between Pakistani and Indian, Muslim, Hindu or Sikh.

I leave for my dinner date with local journalists. It is in a motel known for its gourmet food. I run into a wedding reception. Most of the guests are in high spirits. The newly-married couple are on view kissing and pawing each other. They can hardly wait to get into bed. Their friends tell them how to go about it in the bawdiest language. We get down to the dinner. As usual, I count up the cost of the meal and compare it to what the same fare would cost in India. My order of oysters (much smaller than ours), dhufish—a local favourite which tastes like a poor relative of our pomfret—and apple strudel comes to 18 dollars. Australian wine adds another 12 dollars to the bill making it 30 dollars per head. This is Australia's middle class fare.

Next morning, Krishen Malik drives me over to City Beach to Shaikh Maqbool's villa for breakfast. The atmosphere is very Indo-Pakistani. The men eat, the *begamat* cook and serve. And there is the dulcet voice of Farida Khanum singing *Jab sey huey hum kalam, Allah! Allah!*

We drive back through King's Park overlooking Perth

and the Swan river. It is a magnificent sight of blue water and green hills. There is also a massive trunk of a 334-year-old eucalyptus, 230 feet high. I didn't know eucalyptus could grow to such dimensions and live so long. Australia has over 300 varieties of eucalypti—they call them gum trees.

Farewell to Perth and on to Melbourne. Two airway companies operate the route, one owned by the State, the other by a private company. I take Ansette, the private line. Healthy effects of competition are apparent. Buttons of carnations for the lady passengers; continuous service of tea, coffee, cookies, beer and spirits—a massive five-course lunch with wines thrown in free of charge. Every single seat in the aircraft is occupied.

Australia is a big country. It takes a jet five hours to traverse it from one end to the other. We take off from Perth at noon and land at Melbourne three-and-a-half hours later. The sun has beaten us by another two hours and it is 5.30 p.m. The sky is overcast and squally. "We need the rain," Les Zellner of Air-India informs me. "Look how dry it has become," he adds, waving to a stretch of dried grass. Zellner is a Romanian who opted for Australia 20 years ago and has never looked back. And of Australia's cities, Melbourne, the second largest after Sydney, remains his favourite. But he resents its sudden growth (3 million), its changing landscape of sky-scrapers and the evils that beset large cities—dope, prostitution, young thugs (Larrikins) and bad manners. It is not surprising that he has booked me in the old-fashioned Hotel Windsor rather than the flashy Southern Cross. My room faces the stately multi-colummed House of Legislature and a two-spired cathedral.

An hour after my arrival, there is a reception hosted by the very colourful Captain Peter Jansen. He looks a somewhat smaller version of our Kabir Bedi. Although he shows no great interest in women, he is a fast man, being one of Australia's ace car-racers. That afternoon he was racing in Sydney. He took a helicopter to fly back to Melbourne for the party. His apartment sprawls over the entire roof of the hotel. Every room is cluttered with paintings, prints and photographs taken by him. He has a wine loft and 14 beds in odd corners at different elevations. He has a 20-year-old blonde lass and an 18-year-old youth as his girl-boy Fridads. He makes a short speech of welcome (in a very British la-di-da accent), presents me with an autographed picture of himself with Fateh Singh Gaekwad of Baroda and retires to his study to enjoy his Scotch in peace.

The guests are largely Indian. Melbourne has nearly a hundred Indian doctors and some ьtudents in its three universities. The "foreigners" include Mellhuish who was once Australian Consul-General in Bombay. Among the many guests are the Sklowskys whom I had befriended 40 years ago on a skiing holiday in the French Alps. Geisha was Polish Jewish; Celia (nee Weigall) as Nordic as any Aryan maiden after Hitler's heart. They fell in love, married and settled in Melbourne. They have aged gracefully. He sports a rabbinic beard; she has greyed as handsomely as Vijaya Lakshmi Pandit. We step out of the party to talk about our children and grandchildren.

I turn in to catch up with some reading on Australia.

Australia has been aptly described by one of its leading writers, Henry Lawson, as "... the lone land of magnificent distances and bright heat; the land of reliance and never give-in, and help your mate." And so it is: vast stretches of desert growing grisly, stunted, bushes and shadeless eucalypti where only lizards survive; it has some oases round water-holes where thirsty kangaroos, wallabys and Galah parrots come to quench their thirst. Here the miserable Indian pi-dog has run wild and as a Dingo, hunts in packs like wolves; camels let loose by Baluchi camel drivers who came to lay rail-road tracks have also run wild; and so have their buffaloes which have acquired the size and ferocity of bison. No wonder even human beings have become bigger, stronger and suspicious of their neighbours. The fierce competition of the earlier days has left its scars. An unfriendly Aussie can be meaner than anyone else—so mean, goes a saying, that "he would not let even his dog drink from a mirage."

In a country which puts a premium on ruggedness, the man who robs, kills and gives away is the paradigm of virtue. The great hero of the Australian bush is Ned Kelly, a cattle thief who was a kind of Robin Hood and William Tell rolled into one. He murdered three policemen and was hanged in 1880. He proved to be somewhat of a prophet. When the judge, Sir Redmund Burry, passed the sentence of death on him, Kelly responded, "When I go to the great beyond, I will see you there." Kelly was hanged on 12 November; Sir Redmund died 11 days later.

Australians set great store by physical prowess. Next to the heartless thug, they admire the record-breaker in the world of sport. In the 1840s there was a baker, William King, who walked 192 miles non-stop in 48 hours. Hence the adoration of fast bowlers who make double hat tricks or the Bradmans who hit five centuries.

It is an Aussian illusion that, despite adulation of men of violence and physical endurance, he is ease-loving, lazy, phlegmatic and difficult to provoke. "The Lord made Australia at His leisure, and the cornstalk is the chosen people." The cornstalk is a slov -to-move day-dreamer. But once roused he can be terrible.

Much has been written about the Australian's language. There is now a dictionary devoted to its new vocabulary.

'Tis the everyday Australian
Has a language of his own,
Has a language or a slanguage
Which can simply stand alone,

And a "dickin pitch to kid us"
Is a synonym for "life,"
And to "nark it" means to stop it,
And to "nit it" means to fly!

And a bosom friend's a "cobber"
And a horse a "prad" or "moke",
While a casual acquaintance
Is a "joker" or a "bloke",

And his ladylove's his "donah",
Or his "clinh" or his "tart",
Or his "little bit o' muslin",
As it used to be his "bart".

Most Australian place names reflect the nostalgia of the early emigrants for the mother country, England. Just about every English town, street and square is represented: King's Cross, Hyde Park, Picadilly, Leicester Square, Brighton, Camberwell—you name it, Australia has it. There are a few which encapsule experiences of the early comers: near Sydney there are Pinchgut (where convicts were hanged) and Ultimo from the use of the word in a document; Dripping Valley from food given to convicts or when the ration was only onions "Fossicks Dinner". Some are highly original, e.g., Katamite does not derive from the pansy who plays the female role in a homosexual act but from a drunk who was for ever asking his wife: "Kate, am I tight?" Miepoll comes from a magistrate whose *takia kalam* was "my poll says". Advale from Mrs Ada Stevens who lost her veil crossing a creek, Tinaroo from the discovery of a tin mine "Tia hurroo". Then there are Jackeroo and Jilleroo, Australian counterparts of a cowboy and cowlass. The more attractively mouthfilling are aboriginal names, some listed in verse:

I like the native names, as Parramata,
And Illawarra, and Wooloomooloo,
Nandowara, Woogarora, Bulkamatta,
Tomah, Toongabbie, Mittagong, Meroo;
Buckobble, Cumleroy and Coolangatta,
The Warrangumby, Bargo, Burradoo;
Cookbundoon, Carrabaiga, Wingecarribee.
The Wollondilly, Yurumbon, Bungarribee.

The most famous of Australian vocabulary are the pejoratives used for the Englishman. At one time the old settlers were "currency", the new arrival "sovereign". How the sovereign became a "pome" is not known. One theory says it is an acronym of Prisoners of Mother England. Nor do we know why the word bastard came to be attached to it. But last time the English cricket team played a test match against Australia in Sydney, many Aussie lasses expressed their contempt in bikinis—across their bras was printed POME and on their brief backsides BASTARD—and at times right across the T-shirt: F . . . YOU!

It is the 28th day of March and though the beginning of autumn in the Southern Hemisphere, the weather is very much like spring in England—cool, cloudy, squally. I have a breakfast date with the Sklowskys. I take a cab to Camberwell.

In Australia, you sit with the driver and discuss world affairs. I give him a 'silver' rupee as a tip. We breakfast on bacon and eggs. Geisha drives off to his office. Celia shows me her recent paintings. I hope she will present me with one: she gives me photographs. (That's what being married to a Jew does to you!) However, she drives me to Alexandra Park, a botanical garden with a rich collection of cacti, oak, cedar and auricana (monkey puzzle).

I pack up and join Zellner and Bhupinder Singh for lunch at a very ye olde restaurant in downtown Melbourne. Fortified with lobster and white wine, I face a gruelling cross-examination over my support for Sanjay Gandhi from Chakrapani of Australian Broadcasting. I sound even more enthusiastic for whatever Sanjay did than ever before.

So to my last assignment in the city. I face a packed hall at the Indian Studies Centre of Melbourne University now eight years old under the stewardship of a somewhat asthmatic Dr S N Ray (Indian Studies in Australian universities are dominated by Bengalis) and a very gentle Dr Desao. The questions are all about the Congress debacle, Indira Gandhi and Sanjay. The encounter is followed by a sherry party in the very British academic tradition. Amongst the guests is the lovely Mrs Bruce Grant whose husband was the Australian High Commissioner in India till the fall of Premier Whitlam. The Grants were close friends of Mrs Gandhi. She rewards my loyalty to the Gandhis by an unexpected but wholly welcome hug and two kisses on my beard. What a wonderful finish to my sojourn in Melbourne!

Scintillating Sydney and *Guru Ka Langar* with the 300-strong Sikh community of Coff's Harbour are among the high spots of the second half of the sojourn.

Sydney is Australia's largest city—its real commercial, political, social and cultural capital. Sydney is to Australia what New York is to America, Bombay and Calcutta to India. Canberra is like Washington and New Delhi a babu city with lots of greenery basking in a small-town atmosphere.

Sydney scintillates with life. In some parts, like King's Cross, there is traffic all the 24 hours of the night and day: brothels, strip-tease joints, blue cinemas, junkies and street-walkers. What makes a city a city is the fragrance of stale beer, cigar smoke and perfume; a little bit of sin is like a drop of Angostura in a tot of gin. Sydney has a big dollop of sin in its cocktail. I had asked to be allowed four days in Sydney.

My hosts are Captain Mohan Singh Kohli, the man who put nine Indians atop the Everest, and his wife, Pushpa. From the airport I go to his garden house in the suburbs. The guests include our Consul General, Virendra Pal Singh, Hemant Gupte and I.C. Khanna of our Tourist Office and John Foxlittle, PRO of Air-India (that really is his name). There is also Sridhar Rao, head of the Tea Board, and his very Telugu film-star-looking wife Saraswati, grand-daughter of ex-President V V Giri. If all Giris grandchildren look like Saraswati, I am glad the Giris gave India 16 sons and daughters.

I try and gather statistics of the Indian community in Australia. It is estimated that there are about 20,000 Indians and over 1,00,000 Anglo-Indians who no longer acknowledge their Oriental ancestry. Gujaratis are the most numerous, followed by Punjabis (mainly Sikhs), Tamilians, Mangaloreans and Goans. All of them are doing well. A few names are mentioned as outstanding: Balwant Singh Saini, Head of the Department of Agriculture, Brisbane University, Professor Raj of the Department of History, Queensland University, Gurcharan Singh Siddhu of the CSIR and Dr Hariharan, son-in-law of the late Sir Alladi Krishnaswami Aiyar.

However, the professions do not give the same sense of belonging as does shopkeeping and more than shopkeeping, working on the soil. That distinction goes only to the Sikh farmers who have taken root in Australian soil. Their success forms a sub-chapter of the Indians' success story. And they are the ones who make light of all they have earned by toil and sweat.

This Sardarji story (variations of which you might have heard elsewhere) is narrated to me. Two new emigrants, Santa Singh and Banta Singh (popular names for characters in Sardarji jokes), arrived in Australia. A few days later Santa Singh was seen driving a Mercedes Benz. "*Oi, Santeya!* How did you come by this fancy motor?" enquired Banta. Replied Santa: "There was this golden-haired *mutiar* who picks me up at a traffic-light. She drives me into the jungle and parks the car. She strips herself and says, "Take whatever you want to take." So I take her car. Wasn't that something?" Banta is not impressed. "Why did you leave her clothes? We could have sold them and had a good meal."

As may be expected, where there are Indians, there is a proliferation of Indian Associations. There is the India League of Australia, the Indo-Australian Society, several Sikh, Bangla, Gujarati and Goan Associations. None of them gets on with the others.

My window looks down upon the massive Sydney Bridge and the petal-shaped Opera House, the pride of Australia. It is an ugly building which has become the Mecca of Australian ballet and classical music. The Australians are a remarkable combination of talents—the world's best cricketers, tennis players, swimmers and now hockey players as well. They have also produced some of the world's best singers, ballet dancers and writers. Opera singer Melba was Australian. So are Joan Sutherland and ballet director Sir Robert Helpman. Morris West (*Devil's Advocate, The Shoes of the Fisherman*), Patrick White, Nobel Prize-winner for literature in 1973 (*Happy Valley, The Tree of Man, Riders in the Chariot, The Living and the Dead, Voss, The Aunt's Story*), Alan Moore-Head (*The White Nile, The Blue Nile, No Room in The Ark*), the brothers Colin and Graham McCinnes, Judith Wright and a host of others rated tops in the English world of letters are Australian. Nolan and Drysdale, painters of international repute, are Australian. I muse over all this as I watch the sun come up over Sydney Harbour.

The morning is wasted in a television studio telecasting the woman's hour. I am sandwiched between two lovelies from Air-India, Sidhwa and Turner. They demonstrate the art of wearing the sari, the excellence of Indian tea. In between the wrapping and un-wrapping of saris, I explain the Janata-CFD victory and the downfall of Indira and Sanjay Gandhi. I don't know how the Australian *Shrimatis* take this cocktail of garments, politics and *chai*. However, the next hour I am put through a gruelling cross-examination by Caroline Jones over the radio network. By the time I emerge from the studio there are a sheaf of messages from listeners, many of whom I had known 40 years ago, asking me to ring back. Among the callers is Peggy Holroyd, wife of Derek, who was BBC representative in Delhi 20 years ago and is now settled in Perth. It would appear that Australians keep their transistors going while they work.

My notion of a holiday abroad is to stroll about the streets, look at the shop windows and ogle at pretty girls. They leave me little time for this indulgence. I manage to give the slip to my escorts and walk across Sydney Bridge, through Hyde Park (a small, squarish plot of green) into the main shopping centre. I pick up the statuesque Leila Siddhu—Norwegian-born blonde wife of a Sikh engineer—and with her help buy bras and panties for a variety of Indian ladies.

Then comes the ordeal. I am scheduled to deliver a lunch-hour talk to the students of Sydney University. I am mentally prepared to speak to a small group of Indians and their Australian girlfriends (or vice versa) in a small classroom. What confronts me is a vast sunlit quadrangle with a thousand boys and girls swilling beer, munching sandwiches, gossiping or cuddling. It requires market-place oratory which vendors of herbal medicines and Christian missionaries practised half-a-century ago. I yell over the microphone. I fight a losing battle against beer and smoking. By the time I finish, I am a nervous wreck.

A few hours later I am subjected to a reverse experience at the New South Wales University. I am scheduled to speak on the Sikhs. I prepare myself for mass oratory. I find myself at one end of a table alongside Professor Mukerjee with a dozen very scholarly-looking academics, including Marie Munster who has written a thesis on the Sikh community in Australia. The experience is more unnerving than the lunch-hour nightmare. I ramble on and on interrupted only by a kookaburra which alights on the window sill and mocks my academic pretensions with its jackassish laughter.

From the quantities of liquor I put down in the faculty canteen, Mohan Singh Kohli guesses my need for compensation for what he has put me through. He drives me down to King's Cross and says, "I know you like an after-dinner stroll."

So we saunter round the lovely thistle-bloom fountain, past sex shops, underclad ladies with cigarettes hanging from their lips and their hands on their hips. Past blue cinema houses and striptease joints.

Then we dive into one of them to see "how Aussies do it". The lady stripping herself looks more Oriental than Australian. Of the audience of about a dozen men, at least ten are

Chinese or Malays. The lady on the stage takes a painfully long time to denude herself and then only a miserable second or two to show what she has. The second and the third do much the same. I feel cheated of the money that Kohli has spent on me. The final *coup de grace* is delivered by a youngster sitting in the front seat. He turns round and greets me with a very knowing *Sat Sri Akal*. It is time to go to bed.

As the sun rises, a Fokker Friendship plane takes off from Sydney and heads northwards. It flies along the Pacific coast over a succession of cities interspersed by green hills, rivers and lakes. An hour-and-a-half later it lands at Coff's Harbour. A warm, damp air floods into the plane. You are in tropical Australia where grow banana, avocado and pineapple. At Coff's Harbour, a bearded, beturbaned Sikh is a familiar sight; so is his Sardarni in her *shalwar-kameez* wheeling a trolley in the super-market. In the region live about 150 families of Sardar farmers. Their coming to the region and their prosperity make a heart-warming fairy-tale.

Some time in the 1880s one Inder Singh, a Jat from village Malpur Arkan in district Jullundur, looking for a living happened to find his way to the Pacific coast where white settlers were trying to grow cane and bananas. Inder Singh worked as a labourer. He saw that wages were plentiful, land even more so. He returned to his village and spread the word. He came back with a few friends and relatives. They worked as labourers and as soon as they had saved up enough, they bought land which would yield harvest to their tillage. Most of these Sikh farmers or their parents migrated to Australia between 1880 and 1890. In 1901 the Australian Government introduced the visa system based on the White Australia policy; Italians, Greeks, Turks, etc., were welcome. Indians, Chinese and Blacks were not.

The welcome is in Indian style: marigold garlands and clasping of both hands synchronised with a *Sat Sri Akal*. Then we drive in a cavalcade through Coff's Harbour and into the open country along the Pacific Highway which joins Sydney to Brisbane. We have the banana-covered hills on our left and the Pacific on our right. Tall tapering eucalypti, massive banyan and pine. Motels and gas stations are all very American looking. And suddenly atop a hill on the right is a snow-white square building with a small onion-shaped dome. Beside it is a flag-pole drapped in yellow with the Khalsa emblem of a quoit and crossed swords fluttering in the ocean breeze. A signboard announces. Guru Nanak Sikh Temple, Woolgoolga.

There is a line of swarthy, bronzed men armed with garlands. Some sport turbans and beards, others are "mechanised". More *Sat Sri Akals* before we enter the clean, spacious temple to make obeisance to the *Granth Sahib* and a copy of its translation in English which shares the pedestal with the holy book. Teja Singh Garewal who performs the functions of a priest chants an appropriate hymn from the *Granth*, says a few words of welcome and we are off.

As is well known, where there are two Indians there are two factions: where there are two Sikhs, there are three factions. The miniscule Sikh community of Woolgoolga (300) has two temples and is split into sub-factions too numerous to count. A visitor must not offend any one; if he has breakfast with one, he must have lunch with the other and a small Scotch accepted from one must be compensated for by a double from his rival. The results can be devastating for the stomach and the liver.

Kulbir Singh Atwal takes over. He came nine years ago as a son-in-law. Now he owns his own plantation called "Golden Glow", a lovely bungalow and three cars. He first takes me to visit his mother-in-law. Beneath the shade of a banyan tree, a grey-bearded patriach puts down three cans before he finally wipes the froth off his whiskers.

Our conversation is in rustic Malwa Punjabi and Australian English. It takes me some time to catch on that nime is name, kine cane, try tray, bison basin and snikes snakes. No wonder they call the Australian language Strine (Australian)!

We report for lunch in the home of Tejpal (Paul) Atwal in Sandy Beach. The ladies in *shalwar-kameez* are baking *chapatis*—the men, including the aged patriarch, resume swilling beer. I go out to spot a kookaburra: it looks somewhat like a cross between our roller (neelkanth) and a white-breasted kingfisher. Its call is reminiscent of the laugh of a villian in Hindi films—hence the popular name Laughing Jackass. The lunch is an enormous spread of *pulao, chapatis,* chickens, *matar paneer* followed by pineapple cake. The patriarch washes each morsel down with a healthy swig of beer and while I top my lunch up with black coffee, I see him open another couple of cans for internal irrigation. There's a Punjabi peasant for you! Beer is the next best thing to *lassi*.

At 5 p.m. we re-assemble in the Gurdwara. Once more there is recitation from the *Granth* and singing of hymns. We are about 150 people in the tiny chapel atop a green hill. There is a clap of thunder and lightning and rain—the avocado, pine and cypress blow in the gale. A loneliness envelopes me. Then a sense of pride in these manly men and their handsome women who, 10,000 miles away from the land that gave them birth, keep the flag of their faith flying. They want me to make a speech; I can barely wish them to be of good cheer (*charhdi kala*) and may the Guru's hand always rest on their shoulders.

We adjourn to the *Guru Ka Langar* in the refectory besides the temple. The women are busy in the kitchen. On the refectory table in the main hall are dozens of tumblers; in the corner a barrel holding 58 gallons of beer. For me they have a bottle of Scotch and a dozen bottles of soda. It is not long before our voices rise and we begin to shout at each other. I tell them some bawdy jokes in Punjabi, they explode with laughter. They sing bawdy songs. I double up with a bellyache of laughter. They recite a doggerel in my honour alluding to me as the *Jathedar* of the weekly *akhbar*. Within one hour the barrel of beer is empty—it is more than a gallon to each man. I plead for dinner, threaten to walk out, sulk. They give me dinner. What would the great Guru think of such a *Langar*!

It is time to say farewell. I turn to one of the ladies who

has been busy in the kitchen to thank her. I ask her how she likes being thousands of miles away from her village. She replies in Australian-Punjabi: *"Bhai itthey libbing* (living) *bada good ya."* Bless her soul!

There always comes the last day when you ruminate over what you could have seen and done—and didn't. I have neither seen a kangaroo nor a wallaby, neither a koala bear nor the duck-billed platypus. I haven't "done" an opera or a ballet. All I saw was an exhibition of Chinese treasures. Not a picture likely to be banned in India; nor a blue film. Not even the Lady Jane beach (remarkable choice of name after Lady Chatterly) where everyone goes naked. Captain Kohli compensates me by driving me to Bondi beach which is near Sydney airport. But after what I was expecting, the girls appear obscenely overdressed in their bikinis. "If you stayed a little longer I could have driven you to Lady Jane," says the mountaineer. I can't stay any longer because Air-India had trouble in finding me a seat on their flight to Bombay. Mercifully, a party cancelled its bookings at the last minute and so I am on.

The economy class is again packed with Greeks, Turks and others on their way to Europe. Many take Air-India to go on to England or the United States. If only Bombay airport had more to offer than its morgue of duty-free stores and a shorter halt for onward-going passengers, Air-India could run a daily Jumbo service between Australia and New York and mint a fortune in foreign exchange for India.

Captain Dhillon invites me to join him in the cockpit as we begin our descent over Perth. I recognise some of the landmarks: the Swan river, the bridge, the parks and hotels. In the transit lounge I find myself in the arms of Peggy Holroyd and her husband Derek. They are English by birth but their heart is in India. Every time Peggy talks of Delhi and her many Indian friends her lovely eyes are clouded. "I am homesick for India," she says as the flight is called. "Give every one my love," she adds, giving me a sample of what she is sending to 600 million Indians. I am also homesick for India. So farewell Australia.

Pakistan: Sweet and Sour

I return to the country where I was born, brought up and sustained for the first half of my life as a stranger. If its people had turned hostile towards me I would not bother to go back to it: what is a country if not its people! However, despite the three bloody wars we fought with them and despite the fact that our leaders spit abuse at each other and the air is thick with rumours of a fourth war, I go to Pakistan as a Hindu goes to Varanasi, a Muslim to Mecca. It is my *teerathsthaan* where I perform my *Haj* and my *Umra*. This is where my roots are. I have nourished them with tears of nostalgia and sheltered them from venomous winds of hate with my bare hands.

I am not alone in my resolve never to let hate overcome my love for my neighbour. What if years ago we divided our patrimony and parted company? There are millions of others who though they do not share my senile sentimentality for the land of their birth are tortured alternately by love and hatred towards it. There is my 90-year-old mother who demands: "Has some *hakeem* ordered you to go to Pakistan? These Pakistanis are a *bari zaalim qaum* (very cruel people); they'll kill you. When you get to Lahore, give my love to Asghari, Akhtari, Jameela, Rabbia, Nusrat, Yasmeen. Sister Allaha Rakhi has been dead for some years but if you meet any of her children tell them their *massi* (aunt) sends them her love. How I miss my village Mitha Tiwana! I wish I could see it once before I go. But must you go to Pakistan? They are very *zaalim*..." And so on.

The start is auspicious. The police officer at Palam frisks me with his bare hands and then goes over my body with his metal detector. He pays special attention to my turban—I could be concealing a revolver in its folds—and to my side where I could be carrying a *kirpan*. The detector passes over my head and sides in silence. But as it is run down my frontage it lets out a loud bleep of complaint. The officer tries again. And again the tell-tale bleep. What could I possibly conceal in my trouser front? Prem Bhatia, Editor of *The Tribune* who is in the queue behind, offers an explanation: *"fauladi hai!* What he's got there is made of steel?" Everyone around bursts out in laughter. The culprit is my zip fastener.

After clearing security at the airport we line up along the PIA jet on the tarmac. It is a bitterly cold winter evening but we have to await our turn for a second body search. Two fierce-looking, hook-nosed Pakistani commandos in awami suits re-examine our hand bags and give us another frisking before they let us in the aircraft. Pakistanis are more vigorously re-searched and re-frisked than us Indians. They are not afraid of us but of their own countrymen owing allegiance to Bhutto's *Al Zulfiqar*.

I judge airways' companies by the looks of their stewardesses and their clientele by its manners. I am glad to note that Indian Airlines girls look better than their Pakistani *hawaii* sisters but the manners of Pakistani passengers are as deplorable as those of Indians. Where the Indian girls score is with their smiles. In Pakistan a girl who smiles is still regarded as wanton. (It is the same with their television announcers: waxen, frozen-faced with no animation in their voices). Where Indian passengers score black marks for ill-behaviour is in the liberties they try to take with air hostesses. Recently a fellow MP was reportedly unable to resist the temptation of letting his hands stray on the shapely figure of a lass taking something out of an overhead locker. Such behaviour in Pakistani aircraft could entail risk of the errant hand being lopped off and its owner's backside being subjected to a few well-deserved lashes. Consequently, ill-mannered Pakistani passengers content themselves by being rude to stewardesses.

Lahore is just a half-hour hop away from Delhi. Everything has the same feel as Delhi—climate, birds, trees. Only their humans look much healthier, bigger and better-dressed. There are signs of poverty but none of starvation. Pakistanis are more forthcoming in their exhibitions of friendship. A handshake is regarded as too cold, it has to be a bear-hug. It takes all your wiles to avoid strangers pumping teas, coffees and cokes into your system.

Rawalpindi is another half-hour hop from Lahore. And Islamabad a half-hour drive from the airport. It is a sprawling, half-born city at the foot of the Murree hills and much cooler than Lahore. This time of the year chill winds blow over a frosty landscape of leafless trees and uncompleted multi-storeyed buildings. Everything except the strapping Pathans is in miniature: tiny shops with little worth buying; dimly lit during the grey mornings and closed by 5.30 p.m. because of shortage of electric power.

Prohibition is as much of a farce in the Islamic Republic of Pakistan as it was in Morarji Desai's India. A drinking man can find liquor in the mirages of the Sahara desert. In Pakistan it does not run like the river Ravi in spate, but it does trickle in tumbler fulls in most well-to-do Pakistani homes. You may have whisky served in metal tumblers or in a tea-pot and have to sip it from a China cup. It costs more than twice as much as in India but also goes down twice as well because it tastes of sin.

Religion lays its heavy hand on the social life of the country. At Lahore, morning *azaans* blare forth in succession from dozens of mosques lasting a full 25 minutes followed by recitation from the Quran till the roar of traffic overcomes the incantations from the holy book.

Our seminar on as secular a subject as relations between nations of South-east Asia began with the recitation of a *tilawat* and every Pakistani speaker including the ex-Foreign Minister, Agha Shahi, started their orations with *Bismillah-hir-Rehman-e-Rahim*. One night I watched a debate on Pak television between the Minister of Information and Broadcasting and three divines on the role of media in spreading the message of Islam. A Maulvi Sahib who looked like a twin brother of the Shahi Imam of the Jama Masjid of Delhi was upset that not enough was being done to emphasise the "two-nation theory".

The other man, the principal of a Peshawar college, was unhappy that not enough emphasis was laid on the beauty of Islam. The third, a grim looking lady in dark glasses with her head covered, was disturbed at the exposure of the limbs of girls at play. The minister *sahib* was on the defensive throughout. The next evening I happened to be sitting on his right at an official dinner hosted by him for the visiting Indian delegation. He read out a very formal speech of welcome. I had to respond. I had a little liquor inside and was emboldened to refer to his interview the evening before and offered him an appropriate *sher* (verse) for his next confrontation with orthodoxy:

> *Mulla, gar asar hai dua mein*
> *To masjid hila ke dikha!*
> *Gar naheen to do ghoont pee*
> *Aur masjid ko hilta dekh*

> Mulla, if your prayer has power
> Let me see you shake the mosque!
> If not, take a couple of pegs of liquor
> And see how the mosque shakes on its own

There was a roar of applause in which the minister joined. Then he whispered in my ear: "If these fellows had their way, they would make our girls' hockey teams play in burqas."

The difference between Indian and Pakistani college girls is that in India you look at their assemblages to see if there are any pretty faces among them; in Pakistan it is the other way round: you look to see if there is any who is not pretty. Hence, despite a very tight schedule of interviews and visitors, when Mrs Phailbus, principal of Kinnaird College for Women, asked me to come to speak to her girls, I readily agreed to do so. My friend M A Rahman warned me: "You know it is now a government college and very conservative. Be careful about what you say. Or the parents would want to know why the principal invited a man like you."

I told them exactly what I had in mind: that I had agreed to come because as Sadia Dehlavi had said of me that if I was a woman I'd be always pregnant because of my inability to say no. The girls roared with laughter. I told them that I wished their principal (she is as attractive as her girls) had a similar inability to say no, the consequences might have been more fruitful. Another burst of laughter with the principal joining in. I told them never to take anything for granted—neither God nor scriptures nor social norms but think for themselves and reject whatever did not stand the test of logic and reason. They took it in their stride. I told them to learn to make their own mistakes and not let important decisions like who they should marry and what careers they should adopt to their parents. They cheered wildly. Then I told them about the difference between them and Indian college girls. They yelled triumphantly as if they had won an Indo-Pak war. Far from being upset with me for what I had said, Mrs Philbus thanked me profusely for saying things which would make her girls think and talk about for many days. "You get away with murder," said Rahman ruefully on our wayback home.

For me Pakistan is Manzur Qadir, the greatest human being I have known. He was the ablest, the most truthful and the humblest of men, I have ever met. He has been dead for many years but I feel his presence around me whenever I have to make a decision. I visit his grave every time I am in Lahore the same way as devotees do *ziarat* at the tombs of Khwaja Mueenuddidn Chishti at Ajmer or at Hazrat Nizamuddin Auliya's in Delhi. The only difference is that although Manzur was also somewhat of a Sufi he was denounced as a *mulhid* (Unbeliever) by the *thekeydars* of the faith. He wrote some poetry in praise of God but was much more spirited when he recited his highly pornographic compositions.

Miani is Lahore's biggest graveyard. It has thousands of graves scattered amidst dusty mounds, *mazars* and jujube trees.

Manzur's wife, Asghari, and her sister, Husnara, were with me
when we drove into the maze of narrow lanes. It took us quite
some time to locate our destination. Word had gone round of
my intended pilgrimage. A cluster of men with Munshi Saleem
(Manzur's assistant) were present with flowers and a Press
photographer. Manzur's grave was covered with fresh rose
petals and joss sticks sending up fragrant smoke. I was very
disappointed. I wanted a few quiet moments with my friend
and to recite the *fateha*; they made it into a kind of a Press
conference. I decided to get away as fast as I could.

It was a grey, misty morning. And there was a long way to go.
I had to cross three rivers: Ravi, Chenab and the Jhelum before
I would get to my destination, village Hadali, over 300 kilome-
ters away. I was loaned a new Japanese station-wagon with
retired Colonel Gul Hayat Awan to act as my escort. Driver
Ameen Khan, a Pathan from Bannu, placed his hands on the
steering-wheel and intoned loudly, "*Bismillah!*" Every journey
in Pakistan begins with the name of God. And quite often with
Noah's prayer before he set out on his famous Ark: "Go safely
and return safely."

Over the years Lahore has become more and more unrec-
ognisable. New buildings come up to smother the old. Dual
highways with overbridges have been laid to cope with its
exploding population and the chaotic traffic of cycles, rick-
shaws, scooters, tongas, donkey and camel carts and buses
which bulge on either side as if doubly pregnant. On the way
out of the city I could barely recognise landmarks I had once
known well: Chauburjee, D.A.V. College (since Islamised),
Gol Bagh, the law courts and Government College. We passed
the Badshahi mosque and Ranjit Singh's *samadhi* to cross the
Ravi. Jehangir's mausoleum was lost in the morning mist.

Sheikhupura I remembered well. Other towns we passed
through had become faint echoes of the past: Choor Kana,
Pindi Bhattian, Chiniot, Rabwah (headquarters of the Qadiani
Muslims), Sargodha. The contrast with our Punjab was telling:
bumpy roads, not many tractors and vast tracts of uncultivated

land. I did not see a single seed, fertiliser or insecticide depot; only one cold storage plant and one silo. The *chaikhanas en route* had none of the basketful of eggs that have become the main features of Haryana-Punjab *dhabas*.

We arrived at our destination two hours behind time. I was born there 70 years ago and had not been back since the family migrated to Sargodha and then to Delhi 60 years ago. All I remembered of Hadali was a tiny hamlet with less than 300 families—mostly Muslims of Baloch extraction divided into clans, Waddhals, Mastials and Awans. Tall, rugged, handsome men with Romanesque features proud of their horsemanship, falconry (the nobs sported hawks on their hands) and martial tradition. The tiny railway station had a marble plaque stating that 437 men of the village (which meant every able-bodied adult) had fought in World War I and seven had laid down their lives—the highest proportion of fighting men of any village in India. Their women, I recalled, were equally tall, slender-waisted, well-rounded and carried three pitchers of water on their heads and one under each arm as they glided by with downcast eyes.

Hadali was then lost among sand dunes stretching as far as one could see up to the Salt Range of Khewra. The only vegetation were some date palms. There were a couple of saline ponds (*tobhas*) which we shared with our buffaloes and which were our chief sources of drinking water as wells were deep and often dry. Sand dunes were our playground. We boys went out together in the evenings to defecate. We watched dung beetles roll our excreta into balls and push them into their subterranean larders. We played on the sands through dusk under starlight and moonlight till impatient voices summoned us home.

No Hindus or Sikhs remained in Hadali after partition. My ancestral home was taken over by Muslim refugee families from Rohtak. My generation of villagers slept in dusty graveyards. How would their sons receive me? Would anyone of them remember the names of my forefathers?

As we pulled up near the side-road beside the signpost in Urdu reading "Hadali", our car was surrounded by elders of the village. They introduced themselves: Malik Khuda Baksh Tiwana, Malik Habib Nawaz Tiwana and names I failed to memorise. They shook me by both my hands, embraced me and smothered me with gold tasselled garlands inscribed with words of welcome. Rockets exploded and burst into coloured showers. I was put back in the car to be driven through the village lanes. Men stood in the doorways shouting *"Khush Aamdeed,"* women flung flower petals from roof-tops. The house I was born in was specially decorated for the occasion. It was a hero's welcome given to a man who had done nothing heroic besides wanting to see what his native village looked like after six decades.

Nothing remained of the sand dunes or the *tobhas*. A canal had turned the desert into greenery and village ponds into swamps covered with hyacinth. The population of Hadali had more than trebled. The one building that they preserved and left unoccupied was the *dharamsal* where Sikhs and Hindus had worshipped.

In the government school compound the entire male population of Hadali was assembled round a flagmast flying the Pakistani flag. After recitation of *tilawat* from the Quran, addresses of welcome were read out by a succession of notables, all beginning with *Bismillah-e-Rahman-e-Rahim*—and in execrable Urdu which has become the language of oratory. I replied in my village dialect. All I could say to the entirely Muslim audience was that to me coming to Hadali was my *Umra* and my *Haj*. Overcome by emotion, I broke down, and made an ass of myself. They loved me all the more as I had given a demonstration of my affection for the village which was once mine and was now theirs. I still regard it as my *vatan* (homeland).

There is something elemental about one's place of birth. It is said that when Prophet Mohammed after eleven years of exile in Medina returned in triumph to Mecca, he quickly did the rounds of the *Kaaba*, and asked to be left alone. He spent the night crying by the grave of his first wife, Khadijah. If they had left me alone, I would have spent the night wandering about the lanes of Hadali in the moonlight.

Southern Safari

It must have been the massive inferiority complex from which we Northerners suffer *vis-a-vis* the "Madrasis" that brought it on me. As the plane began its descent towards Meenambakkam airport, my ears began to lose their power of hearing—the roar of the engine faded in the distance; announcements to fasten seat-belts followed by no smoking, fold tables and keep chairs upright were barely audible. Nothing unusual in poorly pressurised aircraft. The cold and sore throat which I had carried with me from Goa made it worse. I apologised to the gentlemen who had come to receive me, "I've gone deaf". They assured me it would pass in a few minutes. It did not. For the two days and nights I was in Madras I had to have every question put to me repeated louder; while orating at the IIT and later to the Inter-Faith group at Hotel Connemara, I could not hear my own voice. I am sure I must have been shouting like most deaf people. Neither wax dissolvents, nor trying to blow air out of the ear helped. What did help was getting the flight out of Madras to Bangalore; the further north you go from Tamil Nadu, the less the inferiority complex and the psychosomatic illnesses that follow. Moral: Punjabis unsure of matching their wits against Madrasis should stay away from Tamil Nadu.

I was expecting to see a bit of rain in Madras. There was not a drop. It was hot, humid, and still. Gulmohars were in flower just as they are in Delhi before the monsoon sets in. Like Delhi in mid-summer, electric power went off without prior warning and taps went dry. No great problem for me, as I was staying in an old mansion with high ceilings and thick walls. When my mouth was full of toothpaste and not a trickle of water came out of the tap, I rinsed my mouth with Campa Cola. There was plenty of that about as my hostess Surjit Kaur's son (Sunny) ran the fizz plant. Fluoride toothpaste and Cola make pleasant mouthwash. Washing my face and getting shampoo out of my beard was a problem I could not solve on my own.

Other surprises awaited me. Lunch at the Madras club, the oldest and swankiest in town, was a non-starter. My hostess assured me it had the best chef in town and I could invite any friends I liked. Rajmohan Gandhi was one; dimpled and ever-smiling Geeta (Padmanabhan), a doctor, was the other. She warned me not to go barefoot to the club (she had seen me always shoeless in the hotel at Goa). We drove in to the stately club portico and walked through its spacious Victorian lounge into the dining room. A black-coated and necktied waiter scanned me from turban to toe and announced. "Not allowed, Sir. You have to wear socks and shoes. Also must have collar in your shirt. Club rules." I was the only defaulter in the party. "I told you so", reprimanded Geeta. "I am not barefooted," I protested, "I have sandals". They were not good enough. We were turned back. In this very club when Rajaji (Rajmohan's grandfather) and prohibition ruled, I had been surreptitiously served Scotch in metal tumblers.

"Very conservative city, Madras", remarked Rajmohan Gandhi. "They don't like changing." Too true. Somehow I could not reconcile austere caste-marks and white shirt-lungi-wearing addicts of the spiritual columns on the back page of *The Hindu* who form the backbone of the city allowing clubs to get away with nonsensical rules about socks and shoes.

"When there is a place like this why should anyone live anywhere else?" I asked myself as I stepped out of the Airbus into the cool, fresh air of Bangalore. Why must we suffer the stifling heat and the dust-storms of the northern plains when we have this place where rain-soaked breezes blow throughout the summer months? Why shiver in the biting cold when you can enjoy a warm sun throughout the winter? Here we have our own garden of Eden where you awaken to the piping notes of the whistling thrush and open your window to a casement of dew-washed trees in flower: pink cassias, African tulips, Begonias—all in full glory amid weird-shaped arucarias. All day long koels and barbets call from dense green foliage and the evenings are fragrant with jasmine and maulsari.

There are many reasons why we cannot all be living in Bangalore. For one, it is already bursting at the seams with its three million inhabitants and cannot take another 680 millions. In any case we can't abandon the rest of *Bharatvarsha* just to be able to live more comfortably in Karnataka, can we? There is a stronger reason why people like me must put aside any notion of migrating to Bangalore for some time to come. Gundu Rao regards journalists as vermin, like snakes and scorpions fit only to be trod upon. He may have learnt this from the experience of his predecessor. Devaraj Urs tried to win journalists over by granting them land at throw away prices to build houses of their own. They sold their allotments at profit. Today Bangalore has a journalists' colony with no journalists.

Compared to homes of northern Indians of the same class, South Indian homes appear very bare. The climate is not conducive to having carpets; apart from the elderly who may have grandfather armchairs to doze and day-dream in, others sit and eat on the floor—so there is a minimum of furniture. Pictures, if any, will be colour prints of gods, goddesses or calendars. Almirahs are for storing things; nails in the walls or just a string across the room on which shirts and lungies can be hung are their wardrobes. This is likely to be the style of living of a family with an income of Rs. 3,000 per month. The only things of ostentation are the gold and diamonds that the ladies wear in their ears and noses. And their ornate silk sarees. The south Indian woman's pride is her kitchen in which she spends more time than women of the north. They are rightly proud of their cooking which is most sensible being easy to digest and extraordinarily tickling to the palate. Any Indian who is doing a sedentary job would be best advised to shun the greasy northern Indian diet and switch over to *uthapam, vada, idli* and *dosa* with delicate chutney. A new dish which I can recommend is *thayir saadam*, a delicious rice-n-curd preparation spiced with ginger, garlic and caraway seeds.

In the few hours I spent in the city, I could not find out the origin of its odd-sounding name. It has become quite a favourite with makers of crossword puzzles; a city full of prohibitions (Banllgalore), a city of a noisy tale (Bang lore), a place in South India which tells a Bengali story (Banga lore), and so on. The only explanation given by a local was that the name is derived from Banglooria, meaning parched gram and was so adopted when Kempe Gowda occupied it and found nothing to eat except this cereal. *Hobson Jobson*, otherwise very knowledgeable on such matters, has nothing to say on the subject. And Balfour's *Cyclopaedia of India* (1983) has a brief entry to the effect: "The climate is almost European, but at the most exposed parts is unfavourable to young children.... Bangalore Pettah or civil town was taken by storm by the British on 21st March, 1791. See silk, tea." One could add a lot of items to the list of things to be seen in Bangalore: aircraft, telephones, watches, electronic equipment, mangosteen, avocado pears, petite lasses with slender waists, knee-length hair and eyes as dark as the pools of Heshbon.

Calcutta

There was a time when I thought that there were no people on the earth more civilised than the Bengalis and no women easier on the eye than theirs. I even thought that if we had to choose a capital for Culturistan, it would have to be Calcutta. Those were the days of Gurudev Tagore, Rathi Babu, Nandalal Bose, Jamini Roy, New Theatre with Uday Shankar coming up on the horizon. As the years passed, my enthusiasm for everything Bengali began to wane. This was entirely due to repeated exposures to Calcutta. I saw it decline from a grand metropolis to an unkempt, unwashed city with more people than was good for its health. Soon it became, as Kipling had described it, a "packed and pestilential town" with death hanging over it like dirty smog. I began to dislike it and avoided going there. In the last two years my dislike for Calcutta has turned to dread; I am frightened of the city and its denizens. Every time I walk down the corridor of Grand Hotel and come face to face with the solid wall of humanity flowing down Chowringhee, I stop in my tracks and want to run back to my room. I have to muster up all my courage to plunge into the smelly human stream, suffer jostling and buffeting, then stumble over uneven, broken pavements, avoid slimy ooze that is always there, dodge oncoming, overloaded buses and cabs which bear on me from all sides. I have developed all the phobias associated with filth and squalor, most of all claustrophobia—fear of crowds. No crowd in the world is more hostile than that of Calcutta. If a car brushes a pedestrian, a mob will collect, rock it till it turns over and set it on fire. I still believe that Bengalis have more going for them than any other Indians and their women have the longest, loveliest hair and the largest, loveliest eyes. But I cannot understand why they have Calcutta. And if they can't do without it, why don't they do something about it like, for instance, blow it up.

I now go to Calcutta only when I have to. I had to once, to cover the 77th plenary session of the AICC for *The Telegraph*. I also have as insatiable an appetite for gossip as our politicians have of catering to it. The foregathering of the Congress clan promised quite a feast of scandal. I also hoped to pick up a whisper or two about the next general election and see for myself how Rajiv Gandhi was shaping as a politician. The five days I spent there proved to be quite rewarding: they confirmed my loathing for the city, provided me with lots of juicy tales of Congressmen's peccadilloes, a wide range of views on the impending elections, and many opportunities of seeing Rajiv Gandhi in action.

The bandobast which seemed at first sight to be very *puccka* really turned out to be very *kuchcha*. The sessions were held in the Netaji Stadium designed to hold Table Tennis matches. No one had bothered to check its acoustics. The echo made the speeches inaudible; you could hear them better outside than inside the stadium. As a result, no one paid any attention to what was being said and indulged in the national pastime of small chat. Apart from the general hubbub of thousands of people talking, there was not a moment when at least a couple of hundred people were not coming or going from somewhere to nowhere. Quite understandably, Mrs Gandhi was in a bad temper throughout the five days and kept reprimanding people for lack of discipline (the worst culprits were press photographers) and repeatedly admonishing the audience: "Why don't you listen?" Equally understandably, the audience paid no attention to her command. They could not hear clearly, they had heard the same kind of thing said a few weeks ago in

Bombay and in every other speech Mrs Gandhi had delivered since then. So what was she so fussed about! However, two things she said stayed in my mind. We should not plant eucalyptus trees which, though quick-growing, do harm to the soil. And advising Congress leaders to set an example of simple, unostentatious living. Most of the *netas* were lodged in Calcutta's two most expensive hotels, Grand and Park.

Discipline? There was none. Shoving, pushing, gate-crashing and smashing window panes. Scuffles between Seva Dal volunteers and visitors were a daily affair. The only person who seemed to keep his cool and occasionally get the crowd under control was Rajiv Gandhi. I was pleasantly surprised to see his stage presence and impressed by the way he spoke. Although he once boobed over his facts and figures, what he had to say, he said with dignity and clarity. He was mercifully free of the wind-baggery that afflicts his partymen.

The last afternoon was nightmarish. From noon onwards, an unending procession of slogan shouting Congressmen wended their way towards the Maidan to hear Mrs Gandhi. Till 4 p.m. there was no let up and I had only an hour left to get to the airport. If it had not been for the ingenuity of our driver I would not have made it on time. I was told that not since the visit of Khruschev had a larger assemblage been seen in Calcutta. Then it was a left-oriented crowd come to greet a Communist leader. This time it was of a people expressing their resentment against Communist rule.

It was a jolly crowd on the aircraft taking us back home to Delhi. And never before had I seen so many important personages on one plane. There were at least twelve ministers of the central government, some chief ministers and over two dozen Members of Parliament. "If this plane goes down, I won't even get an obituary notice", I announced cheerfully "That is why I decided to fly it myself", replied Captain Chaddha, the seniormost of the Indian Airlines pilots. "Don't worry", assured Shankaranand, "I am accident-proof. Nothing happens to anyone when I am present." So we relaxed. I told H K L Bhagat, Makwana, and Salve the latest Punjabi jokes and indulged in some *sheroshairi* with lady MPs and the airhostesses. I must have roused some envy amongst the mighty. Chaudhary Bansi Lal presented me with a glossy picture of a bridal couple, a grey-bearded, turbaned bridegroom with a very young and comely bride. "This is you", he said pointing to the aged groom. "And this is..." I can't tell you who the Chaudhary Sahib had mated me with, except that I was more than willing, A cheerful end to a momentous session!

I always return to Delhi as a man returns to his mistress when he has had his fill of whoring in other cities. What a welcome my beloved city gives me! It is a hot, sticky night. As soon as I am in my apartment, I peel off my clothes, go into the bathroom and turn on the tap. A muddy ooze oozes down into the bucket followed by a trickle of muddy water. Then a fart. No water. I give up.

I go to my study, pick up the phone and dial the caretaker. Two girls are on the line yapping away about their Daddyji and Uncleji. I put down the receiver to try again. They are still on the line now discussing their Mummyji and Auntieji. I make an obscene reference to their parents. "Some dirty fellow on the line", says one, "buzz you later".

I dial my number. Engaged. I dial again. Engaged. I dial "complaints". She tells me to dial "assistance". I dial "assistance". She tells me "number out of order, dial complaints". I dial "complaints". The telephone is dead.

I go to my bedroom to let the air-conditioner cool my naked flesh and raw temper. It welcomes me with a distinct lowering of tone. Its drone lulls me to slumber. It resents my indifference and goes off in a sulk. The bedroom becomes like the Black Hole of Calcutta.

Power cut. No light. No fan. I spend most of the night sitting in a chair in the lawn slapping mosquitoes and counting the stars. A pale old moon wanders into the sky. The morning star glitters. I go indoors and throw open the windows. A cool breeze, fragrant with Madhumalati, drives away the dank fuzz of yesterday's dead air. Through the dark foliage of the mulberry tree appears the grey dawn. A magpie robin begins to warble; its dulcet notes awaken the koel which screams to announce the birth of another day.

Flying-foxes wing their soundless way to their perches on massive Arjun trees. The old lady who lives above comes slish-sloshing along the road, looks round to see if anyone is looking, quickly plucks a few hibiscus flowers from my hedge, tucks them in her dupatta and slish-sloshes towards the temple. Her old man follows. He also stops by my hedge, looks around to see if anyone is listening, presses his paunch and breaks wind. He walks on with lighter step and a "who did that" look of innocence on his wrinkled face. A light goes up in the opposite block. A woman draws her curtains, ties her untidy hair into a bun and stretches her longing arms towards me. Crows begin cawing to each other. Sparrows start quarrelling in the hedges. From the neighbouring mosque, the muezzins' voice rises to the heaven, proclaiming the glory of Allah. Temple bells peal to awaken the gods from their slumbers. A milkman cycles round the block clanging his milk cans. Another man also on a cycle follows him calling in a heavy voice: Paperwallah—Ishtaitman, Taim of India, Aikspraise, Hindustan Trime, Paperwallah! I hear the shush of papers being pushed under my door.

NATURE

"*There is much in India that remains unwritten because its leading scribes wear blinkers which restrict their vision to political tittle-tattle. There is the world of nature, an inexhaustible reservior of things beautiful ... Much remains unexplored and unexploited.*"

The Month of May

May is the month of the laburnum. Although *gulmohars* continue to blaze their fierce scarlets, oranges and yellows, you can see they are losing some of their fire and passing Nature's baton as it were, to the laburnums.

The laburnum (*Cassia fistula*) or *amaltas* has become a great favourite of Delhiwalas as the *gulmohar* for the simple reason that both are quick growing and colourful. Of the two, the laburnum makes the more spectacular entry. It first sheds its leaves; by the second fortnight of April only the long, brown-black tubular (hence 'fistula') fruit can be seen hanging from its bare branches. Then suddenly blossoms appear in clusters like bunches of golden grapes. The beauty of the Indian laburnum defies description. No poet or writer has ventured to put it to paper. Only painters have been able to do it justice. Alas! its glory has a very short lease—less than a fortnight—after which its leaves take over. The seed of the laburnum when crushed makes a powerful purgative and its bark, which is aromatic like cinnamon, is also used for tanning.

An equally beautiful flowering tree which is in bloom this time of the year and outlives the laburnum by several weeks is the pink cassia (*Cassia javanica*). It is a thorny tree with slender branches adorned with pink and white blossoms like bracelets on the arms of a beautiful woman.

May is also the month of searing heat with the glass seldom falling below 40°, often touching 42° and even 45° in the shade. As one wag remarked. 'India has only two seasons: hot and hotter. With the heat comes the *loo*, the hot wind from the deserts of Rajasthan. Our *loo*, like the equally warm *khamsin* (sirocco) and the chilly *mistral* takes its toll of life. On the hottest days its torrid embrace beguiles the unwary and lulls them to eternal sleep.

Kipling has many memorable descriptions of the heat dust and sandstorms that visit northern India during May and June. In his story *False Dawn*, he writes: 'I had felt that the air was growing hotter and hotter, but nobody seemed to notice it until the moon went out and a burning hot wind began lashing the orange trees with a sound like the noise of the sea. Before we knew where we were the duststorm was on us and everything was a roaring, whirling darkness.' Kipling depicts in another poem the lassitude and weariness that come with the endless days of heat and dust:

No hope, no change! The clouds have shut us in.
And through the cloud the sullen Sun strikes down
Full on the bosom of the tortured town,
Till night falls heavy as remembered sin
That will not suffer sleep or thought of ease,
And hour on hour, the dry-eyed Moon in spite,
Glares through the haze and mocks with watery light
The torment of the uncomplaining trees. Far off, the thunder
bellows her despair
To echoing earth, thrice parched. The lightnings fly
In vain. No help the heaped-up clouds afford,
But wearier weight of burdened, burning air,
What truce with Dawn? Look, from the aching sky
Day stalks a tyrant with a flaming sword!

The days, hard enough to bear, get longer and longer. On the first of the month the sun rises at 5.40 a.m. and sets at 6.56 p.m. giving us more than thirteen and a quarter hours of hell. By the end of the month the sun rises 16 minutes earlier (5.24 a.m.) and sets 17 minutes later (7.13 p.m.) adding more than half an hour of unwelcome daylight. However, dry heat is easier to bear than the moist, sticky, warm stillness that pervades our coastal towns and cities. Even though perspiration is profuse, it is healthier than the body ooze that surfaces on the skin in humid climates. There is of course the nuisance of prickly heat (*pitt*) which erupts round the neck, but I hold to the theory my grandmother used to expound—that prickly heat is a sign of good health. For those who find it too oppressive, there are air coolers which convert hot winds into fragrant breezes by blowing them through dampened screens of *khas* fibre. These smell of the earth after the first drops of rain.

May is also the month of duststorms, cloudbursts and hailstorms. They come with little warning. There is of course a preliminary lull, but after days of windless calm you hardly notice it. Only pariah kites wheeling in the grey sky portend that something is on the way. Then suddenly it sweeps across with gale fury, blowing dust into your eyes and nostrils. It is usually followed by a cloudburst. The gale and rain take their toll of trees. I have seen ancient banyans which had stood for years like gigantic sentinels on either side of Parliament Street, torn up from their roots and ignominiously flung across the tarmac road. One May afternoon a weather beaten *neem* on Kasturba Gandhi Marg, under whose shade half-a-dozen cars sheltered from the blazing sun, came crashing down and broke a Fiat car into two. A 50-year-old mulberry (the only leafy tree outside my apartment, to whose shade I staked my claim every summer by parking my car under it in the early hours of the morning) was mauled by one of these storms. One afternoon as I left for the swimming pool, a fierce wind came up. I had barely gone a hundred yards when three branches of the mulberry were torn from the trunk and fell down on the exact spot where my car had rested. If my frail new Maruti had been there it would have been mashed to a pulp. If I had been in it, I would not be writing this. That afternoon I drove through lashing rain along Moti Lal Nehru Marg, up Shankar Road to the Ridge past Buddha Jayanti Park. The entire route was littered with branches of *jamuns, neems* and *mahuas*. Since fragile eucalyptus trees have no branches worth speaking of, many had been brought down to earth in one piece. It was hazardous driving along these avenues and for safety I drove in the middle of the road.

Despite the intense heat during May and June, you can also have, besides duststorms and cloudbursts, an occasional hailstorm which brings the temperature down for a few hours. Usually the hailstones are very small, almost like gravel but sometimes they are of the size of pigeons eggs. Hailstones of the size of cricket balls have been known to kill cattle and humans. A hailstorm in Moradabad in 1888 is said to have killed over 246 people in a few minutes.

Deciduous trees like *neems, banyans, peepuls* and *mahuas* continue to shed their leaves and don new vestments. *Semuls* have by now yielded all they have to give to humans. In May you will see families of poor gathering *semul* cotton in sacks to sell to the makers of pillows and quilts.

Petals shed by flowering trees lie about their boles. Laburnums spread golden carpets about their feet; *maulsaris* weave them in beige, *papris (Pongamia glabra)* in pink and white looking very much like a spread of tiny hailstones.

What is true of the flora is true of the fauna. In the feathered world, May is the month of birdsong, courtship and fulfillment. Kites and vultures which began courting in the winter sit hunchbacked watching over their nests high up in the branches of the ailanthus or *semul* trees. The screams of koels become louder and more strident. Crows grow more suspicious of koels' intentions and can be seen chasing them away as soon as they come anywhere near their nests.

If you listen attentively to the koel's calls, you will notice a clear pattern. It is amongst the earlier callers. As soon as the eastern sky turns grey, male koels lay claim to their airspace by a series of staccato *Urook, Urook, Urook,* repeated over half-a-dozen times. In human language this could be interpreted as a warning to other males: Keep off and that means you! The rest of the day the call is a monotonous *Koo-oo, Koo-oo.* While courting, it is the female pursued by her suitor who emits sharp cries of *Kik, Kik!* as she courses through the foliage. One rarely sees koels in the act of mating. Once the female is ready to lay her eggs, her paramour takes the lead in luring crows away from their nests. The female koel then quickly deposits her egg amongst the clutch of crows' eggs and signals to her partner that her mission has been successful by triumphant cries, *Kuil, Kuil, Kuil!*

This cuckolding of crows requires a lot of cunning and a fine sense of timing. Koels have first to locate a crow's nest which has some eggs already laid, otherwise the crows would become suspicious. The eggs must resemble those of crows and must hatch earlier. While the crow's eggs take over a fortnight to incubate, koel chicks are ready to emerge a couple of days earlier. They also have the capacity to edge crow chicks out of the nest and hog all the food their foster parents bring. By late August and early September you can often see koel chicks being fed by crows and hear them cawing like their foster parents.

Pied mynahs rebuild their homes. For many years I have seen a pair remake theirs in the same cleft of the *siris* which stands at one end of the tennis court. And while playing I catch the honeyed notes of golden orioles from *sheesham* trees, the trumpet calls of peacocks from a neighbouring park and *papeehas* calling, in the distance.

I generally see more of nature at dawn on my way to the Club, in the hour I play tennis and on my way back home, than I do during the rest of the day which I spend closeted in my study. I did not realise for years, being too absorbed in the game, that the source of the fragrance that pervaded the courts was the *siris*. By the middle of May its pale yellow powder-puff blossoms fall and mingle with the dust to look like bedraggled fluffs of wool. It was the same with the *gulmohar* under which chairs are laid out for people awaiting their turn to play. I had taken its presence for granted and rarely did my gaze rest on it till one summer the elements compelled me to open my eyes and take notice of its flamboyant beauty.

For three days and nights dust had hung in the air like a pestilent cloud. Not a leaf stirred, not a bird sang. The once green lawn in front of the apartment had turned a sere yellow: flowers had withered in their beds. I said to myself: 'Only cacti thrive in this cactus land!' When the days were at their hottest, the fan stopped churning hot air, leaving me to sweat it out and nurse the prickly heat that had erupted round my neck. In the evening when I stood under the shower to wash the day's dust and sweat off my body, the turn of the tap only produced a few apologetic coughs but not a drop of water. One night, the air-conditioner died on me, converting my cool bedroom into the Black Hole of Calcutta. Why do I have to live in this God-forsaken land? I asked myself.

The next afternoon a duststorm swept across the city with demonic fury. An ancient banyan on Parliament Street which I had regarded as the emblem of eternity was pulled out by its roots and hurled across the road, bringing traffic to a halt for several hours. It limbs had to be hacked off before the stream of traffic could resume its flow. The storm raged for almost an hour until twilight. Sounds of thunder and flashes of lightning pierced the dust-laden air. Then came the rain. It lasted only 15 minutes but in that short burst it filled the gutters to overflowing, flooded the roads, knocked out the electric supply and slew most of Delhi's telephones stone dead. 'Why do I suffer these humiliations? I swore. Why don't I live somewhere else where things are better managed?

Early next morning I set out for my game of tennis. Every leaf of every tree had been washed clean. The soft fragrance of *siris* floated in the air. Golden orioles called. The *gulmohar* trees along the tennis court were ablaze with scarlet and yellow. A magpie robin (*shama*) alighted on the topmost branch of one and burst into song:

> *Amon deshti kothao khojay*
> *Paabey no ko toomee,*
> *Shokol desher rani shejey,*
> *Amaar jonmo bhoomee.*

Search where you may, you will not find a land as beautiful as this, she is the queen, this land of my birth.

How could I have ever thought of living elsewhere?

FICTION

"*My earliest foray into the world of fiction was bragging, when I came home for vacations from England, of my exploits with English girls.*"

Karma

S ir Mohan Lal looked at himself in the mirror of a first
class waiting room at the railway station. The mirror was
obviously made in India. The red oxide at its back had come
off at several places and long lines of translucent glass cut
across its surface. Sir Mohan smiled at the mirror with an air
of pity and patronage.

'You are so very much like everything else in this country, inefficient, dirty, indifferent,' he murmured.

The mirror smiled back at Sir Mohan.

'You are a bit of all right, old chap,' it said. 'Distinguished, efficient—even handsome. That neatly-trimmed moustache—the suit from Saville Row with the carnation in the
buttonhole—the aroma of eau de cologne, talcum powder and
scented soap all about you! Yes, old fellow, you are a bit of all
right.'

Sir Mohan threw out his chest, smoothed his Balliol tie
for the umpteenth time and waved a goodbye to the mirror.

He glanced at his watch. There was still time for a quick one.

'Koi Hai!'

A bearer in white livery appeared through a wire gauze
door.

'Ek Chota,' ordered Sir Mohan, and sank into a large
cane chair to drink and ruminate.

Outside the waiting room, Sir Mohan Lal's luggage lay
piled along the wall. On a small grey steel trunk Lachmi, Lady
Mohan Lal, sat chewing a betel leaf and fanning herself with a
newspaper. She was short and fat and in her middle forties.

She wore a dirty white sari with a red border. On one side of her nose glistened a diamond nose-ring, and she had several gold bangles on her arms. She had been talking to the bearer until Sir Mohan had summoned him inside. As soon as he had gone, she hailed a passing railway coolie.

'Where does the *zenana* stop?'

'Right at the end of the platform.'

The coolie flattened his turban to make a cushion, hoisted the steel trunk on his head, and moved down the platform. Lady Lal picked up her brass tiffin carrier and ambled along behind him. On the way she stopped by a hawker's stall to replenish her silver betel leaf case, and then joined the coolie. She sat down on her steel trunk (which the coolie had put down) and started talking to him.

"Are the trains very crowded on these lines?"

'These days all trains are crowded, but you'll find room in the *zenana*.'

'Then I might as well get over the bother of eating.'

Lady Lal opened the brass carrier and took out a bundle of cramped *chapatties* and some mango pickle. While she ate, the coolie sat opposite her on his haunches, drawing lines in the gravel with his finger.

'Are you travelling alone, sister?'

'No, I am with my master, brother. He is in the waiting room. He travels first class. He is a *vizier* and a barrister, and meets so many officers and Englishmen in the trains—and I am only a native woman. I can't understand English and don't know their ways, so I keep to my *zenana* inter-class.'

Lachmi chatted away merrily. She was fond of a little gossip and had no one to talk to at home. Her husband never had any time to spare for her. She lived in the upper storey of the house and he on the ground floor. He did not like her poor illiterate relatives hanging about his bungalow, so they never came. He came up to her once in a while at night and stayed for a few minutes. He just ordered her about in anglicised Hindustani, and she obeyed passively. These nocturnal visits had, however, borne no fruit.

The signal came down and the clanging of the bell announced the approaching train. Lady Lal hurriedly finished off her meal. She got up, still licking the stone of the pickled mango. She emitted a long, loud belch as she went to the public tap to rinse her mouth and wash her hands. After washing she dried her mouth and hands with the loose end of her sari, and walked back to her steel trunk, belching and thanking the gods for the favour of a filling meal.

The train steamed in. Lachmi found herself facing an almost empty inter-class *zenana* compartment next to the guard's van, at the tail end of the train. The rest of the train was packed. She heaved her squat, bulky frame through the door and found a seat by the window. She produced a two-anna bit from a knot in her sari and dismissed the coolie. She then opened her betel case and made herself two betel leaves charged with a red and white paste, minced betelnuts and cardamoms. These she thrust into her mouth till her cheeks bulged on both sides. Then she rested her chin on her hands and sat gazing idly at the jostling crowd on the platform.

The arrival of the train did not disturb Sir Mohan Lal's *sang-froid*. He continued to sip his Scotch and ordered the bearer to tell him when he had moved the luggage to a first class compartment. Excitement, bustle, and hurry were exhibitions of bad breeding, and Sir Mohan was eminently well-bred. He wanted everything 'tickety-boo' and orderly. In his five years abroad, Sir Mohan had acquired the manners and attitudes of the upper classes. He rarely spoke Hindustani. When he did, it was like an Englishman's—only the very necessary words and properly anglicised. But he fancied his English, finished and refined at no less a place than the University of Oxford. He was fond of conversation, and like a cultured Englishman he could talk on almost any subject—books, politics, people. How frequently had he heard English people say that he spoke like an Englishman!

Sir Mohan wondered if he would be travelling alone. It was a Cantonment and some English officers might be on the train. His heart warmed at the prospect of an impressive conversation. He never showed any sign of eagerness to talk to the English as most Indians did. Nor was he loud, aggressive and opinionated like them. He went about his business with an expressionless matter-of-factness. He would retire to his corner by the window and get out a copy of *The Times*. He would fold it in a way in which the name of the paper was visible to others while he did the crossword puzzle. *The Times* always attracted attention. Someone would like to borrow it when he put it aside with a gesture signifying 'I've finished with it.' Perhaps someone would recognize his Balliol tie which he always wore while travelling. That would open a vista leading to a fairy-land of Oxford colleges, masters, dons, tutors, boat-races and rugger matches. If both *The Times* and the tie failed, Sir Mohan would '*Koi Hai*' his bearer to get the Scotch out. Whisky never failed with Englishmen. Then followed Sir Mohan's handsome gold cigarette case filled with English cigarettes. English cigarettes in India? How on earth did he get them? Sure he didn't mind? And Sir Mohan's understanding smile—of course he didn't. But could he use the Englishman as a medium to commune with his dear old England? Those five years of grey bags and gowns, of sports blazers and mixed doubles, of dinners at the Inns of Court and nights with Picca-dilly prostitutes. Five years of a crowded glorious life. Worth far more than the forty-five in India with his dirty, vulgar countrymen, with sordid details of the road to success, of noc-turnal visits to the upper storey and all-too-brief sexual acts with obese old Lachmi, smelling of sweat and raw onions.

Sir Mohan's thoughts were disturbed by the bearer an-nouncing the installation of the Sahib's luggage in a first class coupe next to the engine. Sir Mohan walked to his coupe with a studied gait. He was dismayed. The compartment was empty. With a sigh he sat down in a corner and opened the copy of *The Times* he had read several times before.

Sir Mohan looked out of the window down the crowded platform. His face lit up as he saw two English soldiers trudg-ing along, looking in all the compartments for room. They had their haversacks slung behind their backs and walked unsteadily. Sir Mohan decided to welcome them, even though they were entitled to travel only second class. He would speak to the guard.

One of the soldiers came up to the last compartment and stuck his face through the window. He surveyed the compartment and noticed the unoccupied berth.

'Ere, Bill,' he shouted, 'one ere.'

His companion came up, also looked in, and looked at Sir Mohan.

'Get the nigger out,' he muttered to his companion.

They opened the door, and turned to the half-smiling, half-protesting Sir Mohan.

'Reserved!' yelled Bill.

'*Janta*—Reserved. Army—*Fauj*,' exclaimed Jim, pointing to his khaki shirt.

'*Ek Dum jao*—get out!"

'I say, I say, surely,' protested Sir Mohan in his Oxford accent. The soldiers paused. It almost sounded like English, but they knew better than to trust their inebriated ears. The engine whistled and the guard waved his green flag.

They picked up Sir Mohan's suitcase and flung it on to the platform. Then followed his thermos flask, briefcase, bedding and *The Times*. Sir Mohan was livid with rage.

'Preposterous, preposterous,' he shouted, hoarse with anger.

'I'll have you arrested—guard, guard!'

Bill and Jim paused again. It did sound like English, but it was too much of the King's for them.

'Keep yer ruddy mouth shut!' And Jim struck Sir Mohan flat on the face.

The engine gave another short whistle and the train began to move. The soldiers caught Sir Mohan by the arms and flung him out of the train. He reeled backwards, tripped on his bedding, and landed on the suitcase.

'Toodle-oo!'

Sir Mohan's feet were glued to the earth and he lost his speech. He stared at the lighted windows of the train going past him in quickening tempo. The tail-end of the train appeared with a red light and the guard standing in the open doorway with the flags in his hands.

In the inter-class *zenana* compartment was Lachmi, fair and fat, on whose nose the diamond nose-ring glistened against the station lights. Her mouth was bloated with betel saliva which she had been storing up to spit as soon as the train had cleared the station. As the train sped past the lighted part of the platform, Lady Lal spat and sent a jet of red dribble flying across like a dart.

The Riot

T he town lay etherized under the fresh spring twilight. The shops were closed and house-doors barred from the inside. Street lamps dimly lit the deserted roads. Only a few policemen walked about with steel helmets on their heads and rifles slung behind their backs. The sound of their hobnailed boots was all that broke the stillness of the town.

The twilight sank into darkness. A crescent moon lit the quiet streets. A soft breeze blew bits of newspaper from the pavements on to the road and back again. It was cool and smelled of the freshness of spring. Some dogs emerged from a dark lane and gathered round a lamp-post. A couple of policemen strolled past them smiling. One of them mumbled something vulgar. The other pretended to pick up a stone and hurl it at the dogs. The dogs ran down the street in the opposite direction and resumed their courtship at a safer distance. Rani was a pariah bitch whose litter populated the lanes and by-lanes of the town. She was a thin, scraggy specimen, typical of the pariahs of the town. Her white coat was mangy, showing patches of raw flesh. Her dried-up udders hung loosely from her ribs. Her tail was always tucked between her hind legs as she slunk about in fear and abject servility.

Rani would have died of starvation with her first litter of eight had it not been for the generosity of the Hindu shopkeeper, Ram Jawaya, in the corner of whose courtyard she had unloaded her womb. The shopkeeper's family fed her and played with her pups till they were old enough to run about the streets and steal food for themselves. The shopkeeper's generosity had put Rani in the habit of sponging. Every year when spring came she would find an excuse to loiter around the stall of Ramzan, the Muslim greengrocer. Beneath the wooden platform on which groceries were displayed lived the big, burly Moti. Early autumn, she presented the shopkeeper's household with half-a-dozen or more of Moti's offspring. Moti was a cross between a Newfoundland and a Spaniel. His shaggy coat and sullen look was Ramzan's pride. Ramzan had lopped off Moti's tail and ears. He fed him till Moti grew big and strong and became the master of the town's canine population. Rani had many rivals. But year after year, with the advent of spring, Rani's fancy lightly turned to thoughts of Moti and she sauntered across to Ramzan's stall.

This time spring had come but the town was paralysed with fear of communal riots and curfews. In the daytime people hung about the street corners in groups of tens and twenties, talking in whispers. No shops opened and long before curfew hours the streets were deserted, with only pariah dogs and policemen about.

Tonight even Moti was missing. In fact, ever since the curfew, Ramzan had kept him indoors tied to a cot. He was far more useful guarding Ramzan's house than loitering about the streets. Rani came to Ramzan's stall and sniffed around. Moti could not have been there for some days. She was disappointed. But spring came only once a year—and hardly ever did it come at a time when one could have the city to oneself with no curious children looking on—and no scandalised parents hurling stones at her. So Rani gave up Moti and ambled down the road toward Ram Jawaya's house. A train of suitors followed her.

Rani faced her many suitors in front of Ram Jawaya's doorstep. They snarled and snapped and fought with each other. Rani stood impassively, waiting for the decision. In a few minutes a lanky black dog, one of Rani's own progeny, won the honours. The others slunk away.

In Ramzan's house, Moti sat pensively eyeing his master from underneath his charpoy. For some days the spring air had made him restive. He heard the snarling in the street and smelled Rani in the air. But Ramzan would not let him go. He tugged at the rope, then gave it up and began to whine. Ramzan's heavy hand struck him. A little later he began to whine again. Ramzan had had several sleepless nights watching and was heavy with sleep. He began to snore. Moti whined louder and then sent up a pitiful howl to his unfaithful mistress. He tugged and strained at the leash and began to bark. Ramzan got up angrily from his charpoy to beat him. Moti made a dash toward the door dragging the lightened string cot behind him. He nosed open the door and rushed out. The charpoy stuck in the doorway and the rope tightened round his neck. He made a savage wrench, the rope gave way, and he leapt across the road. Ramzan ran back to his room, slipped a knife under his shirt, and went after Moti.

Outside Ram Jawaya's house, the illicit liaison of Rani and the black pariah was being consummated. Suddenly the burly form of Moti came into view. With an angry growl Moti leapt at Rani's lover. Other dogs joined the melee, tearing and snapping wildly.

Ram Jawaya had also spent several sleepless nights keeping watch and yelling back war cries to the Muslims. At last fatigue and sleep overcame his newly-acquired martial spirit. He slept soundly with a heap of stones under his charpoy and an imposing array of soda water bottles filled with acid close at hand. The noise outside woke him. The shopkeeper picked up a big stone and opened the door. With a loud oath he sent the missile flying at the dogs. Suddenly a human being emerged from the corner and the stone caught him squarely in the solar plexus.

The stone did not cause much damage to Ramzan but the suddenness of the assault took him aback. He yelled 'Murder!' and produced his knife from under his shirt. The shopkeeper and the grocer eyed each other for a brief moment and then ran back to their houses shouting. The petrified town came to life. There was more shouting. The drum at the Sikh temple beat a loud tattoo—the air was rent with war cries.

Men emerged from their houses making hasty inquiries. A Muslim or a Hindu, it was said, had been attacked. Someone had been kidnapped and was being butchered. A party of goondas were going to attack, but the dogs had started barking. They had actually assaulted a woman and killed her children. There must be resistance. There was. Groups of five joined others of ten. Tens joined twenties till a few hundred, armed with knives, spears, hatchets, and kerosene oil cans proceeded to Ram Jawaya's house. They were met with a fusilade of stones, soda water bottles, and acid. They hit back blindly. Tins of kerosene oil were emptied indiscriminately and lighted. Flames shot up in the sky enveloping Ram Jawaya's home and the entire neighbourhood, Hindu, Muslim and Sikh alike.

The police rushed to the scene and opened fire. Fire engines clanged their way in and sent jets of water flying into the sky. But fires had been started in other parts of the town and there were not enough fire engines to go round.

All night and all the next day the fires burnt and houses fell and people were killed. Ram Jawaya's home was burnt and he barely escaped with his life. For several days smoke rose from the ruins. What had once been a busy town was a heap of charred masonry.

Some months later when peace was restored, Ram Jawaya came to inspect the site of his old home. It was all in shambles with the bricks lying in a mountainous pile. In the corner of what had once been his courtyard there was a little clearing. There lay Rani with her litter nuzzling into her dried udders. Beside her stood Moti guarding his bastard brood.

RELIGION

My Sentiments regarding places of worship are summed up in a beautiful little couplet by a Punjabi Sufi poet:

Masjid ddhaa dey, Mandar ddhaa dey
Ddhaa dey jo kuchh ddhenda
Ik kisey da dil na ddhavein
Rabb dilaan vicch rehndaa

Break down the mosque, break down the temple
Break down whatever there is besides;
But never break a human heart
That is where God Himself resides.

The Magic Words

All religions have a few words believed to have powerful protective and curative potential. It is difficult to unravel the mystery behind them. In Hinduism we have the mystic syllable *Om* or *Aum*. It is chanted in its elongated form and believed to have the entire range of sounds in it. Intoned by itself or in combination with one of the names of God, Hari, as *Hari Om*, it does produce a soothing effect on jangled nerves and brings peace of mind. The Sikh equivalent *Ek-Onkar* (there is one God) is derived from it, but does not enjoy the same popularity among Sikhs as does *Aum* among Hindus.

The Muslims do not have any single word to match *Aum*, but they do have some which, like *Allah-o-Akbar*, are repeated while telling the beads of a rosary. They also recite select passages of the *Quran* which are believed to be more powerful than others. The most frequently quoted is of course the opening lines of the holy book, *Al-Fatihah:*

All Praise Be to Allah
Lord of all the worlds,
Most beneficent, ever merciful,
King of the Day of judgement,
You alone we worship, and to You alone we turn for help.
Guide us (O Lord) to the path that is straight,
The path of those you have blessed,
Not of those who have earned Your anger, nor those who have gone astray.

—Ahmed Ali

Next to *Fatihah,* the second most popular verse is the *Ayat-ul-Qursi,* the throne verse:

God: There is no god but He, the living, sustaining, ever self-subsisting.
Neither does somnolence affect Him nor sleep.
To Him belongs all that is in the Heavens and the earth;
and who can intercede with Him except by His leave?
Known to Him is all that is present before men and what is hidden.
(in time past and time future)
and to even a little of His knowledge can they
grasp except what He will.
His set extends over heavens and the earth and He tires not protecting them:
He alone is all high and supreme.
There is no compulsion in matter of faith.
Distinct is the way of guidance now from error.
He who turns away from the forces of evil
and believes in God, will surely hold fast
to a handle that is strong and unbreakable,
for God hears all and knows every thing.

— Ahmed Ali

The *Ayat-ul-Qursi* is embossed on medallions and worn by Muslim ladies attached to their necklaces. It is also the most popularly quoted verse on Muslim graves. The third in popularity are lines from *Surah Yaseen.* This Surah is also a favourite citation on mausoleums. On the entrance gate of the Taj Mahal, it is reproduced in full.

Amongst Hindus, the *mantra* regarded as the most powerful is the *Gayatri* from the Yajur Veda. To me it appeared as an invocation to the sun and I could not decipher any hidden meaning in it. I turned to my one-time Hindi teacher (I studied Hindi only for two years before I turned to Urdu) for an explanation. Dr Dashrath Ojha, who retired as a professor of Hindi and Sanskrit of Delhi University some years ago, was kind enough to illumine my mind. I share his explanation. First the *Mantra*:

OM
*Bhur bhuvah swah
tat savitur varenyam
bhargo devasya dhimahi
dhiyo yo nah prachodayat*

Literally, the *mantra* means:
"Let us meditate on God, His glorious attributes, who is the basis of everything in this universe as its creator, who is fit to be worshipped as omnipresent, omnipotent, omniscient and self-existent conscious being, who removes all ignorance and impurities from the mind and purifies and sharpens our intellect... May God enlighten our intellects."

Dr Ojha advises that, in order to comprehend the full meaning of the *mantra*, the reciter must pause at the end of each line and let the meaning sink in.

After the incantation *Aum* is *Bhur bhuva swah*, meaning on earth (*bhur*), in the sky (*bhuva*) and in the heavens above the sun (*swah*). *Tat* stands for God, *savitur* God as the creator and the power that sustains creation; *varenyam* indicates that God is transcendent; *bhargo* that He is the light that dispels darkness and purifies impurities; *devasya*—He is the light behind all lights and the bestower of happiness; *dhimahi* is the exhortation to meditate on Him, *dhiyo yo* stands for intellect, *nah* for ours and *prachodayat* is the prayer that God may direct our energies towards good deeds, thoughts and conduct.

According to Dr Ojha, the purpose of reciting the *Gayatri Mantra* is as follows:

"As this *mantra* invokes an integrated form of endless and beginningless God, all limitations which are normally found in the worship of a personal God or Goddess is totally absent in its goal. As such it helps to clean our mind of its impurities in totality as and when it expands in tune with the meaning of its repetition. Thus, gradually, this *mantra* helps us to possess an enlightened intellect. This enables us to know more and more about God in meditation and the mysteries of nature through intellect when it is directed towards objects. This also makes us maintain constant awareness of the very basis of our existence. As this *mantra* directs the imagination of the mind to a limitless state, it strikes at the very root of our basic desires and instincts, not necessarily of this present life, but also many past lives."

There is something inherent in all religious systems which makes them intolerant towards others. This phenomenon is particularly noticeable when a section of believers break away from the main body to recognise sub-prophets of their own with their separate scriptures, places of worship and social organisations. No religious system is known to have escaped the cancer of intolerance.

Hinduism, which makes lofty claims of being the most tolerant of religions (the caste-system notwithstanding) was unable to contain itself either against Jainism or Buddhism, which broke away from it. When Hindusim came back into its own, it wreaked terrible vengeance against Jains and Buddhists and virtually wiped them out as separate communities.

Judaism was unable to accept the emergence of Christ and denounced Him as a heretic. Christians never forgave the Jews for what they did to their Messiah and continue to persecute them to this day. Then Christianity splintered into many churches—Catholic, Greek Orthodox, Protestant and dozens of others. Catholics and Protestants have waged wars against each other and perpetrated massacres of each others' populations. When Islam rose out of paganism, Judaism and Christianity, Muslims suffered the same fate. They repaid the Jews and the Christians in the same way.

Smaller religious communities like the Sikhs did not escape this malaise either. While they were able to make adjustments with the numerically more powerful Hindus and

Muslims, they could not tolerate sub-communities which broke away from the Sikh mainstream.

Two groups, the Namdharis and the Nirankaris, which recognised gurus of their own, were ostracised. Neither of them are allowed inside Gurdwaras and no amritdhari may have matrimonial relationship with them. Bhindranwale turned the wiping out of Nirankaris into an article of faith. Their sacred books, *Avtar Bani* and *Yugpurush*, were condemned as derogatory of the Sikh gurus (I was unable to locate anything offensive in them) and Baba Gurbachan Singh was murdered.

From the outside, Islam gives the impression of being a unified, monolithic religious group. It is nothing of the sort. It broke into two, immediately after the death of Prophet Mohammed. The larger section accepted the succession of the first three Caliphs—Abu Bakr, Omar and *Othman*. A smaller group regarded them as usurpers and recognised only Ali, the Prophet's son-in-law, as the true successor. Ever since, the Islamic world has been split into the Shias and Sunnis. Their hostility continues to this day. While the Sunnis have not had many breakaway groups and only follow different schools of jurisprudence, the Shias have virtually dozens of sub-groups with their own mosques, rituals and graveyards.

Muslim intolerance towards breakaway groups has been noticeably fierce towards the Bahais and the Quadianis. Hundreds of Bahais were executed in Iran for no crime except being Bahais during the reign of Ayatollah Khomeini. Pakistanis did not lag behind in their fervour in persecuting Quadianis. This group, which branched out in 1889 under the leadership of Mirza Ghulam Ahmed of Quadian (now in Indian Punjab) has done more to spread the message of Islam in Africa and Europe than any other set of Muslim missionaries. It has also produced some very distinguished men like Chaudhary Zaffarrullah Khan, judge of the Supreme Court and later Foreign Minister of Pakistan, and Professor Abdus Salam, the only Pakistani winner of the Nobel Prize. But they have, nevertheless, been the target of Muslim fundamentalism. Their township Rabwah, along the Jhelum, witnessed a lot of violence before the country's highest judiciary declared Ahmediyas to be non-Muslims. They are not allowed to call for prayers from the minarets of their mosques and not even allowed to describe themselves as Muslims. They have declared themselves a minority.

The only point of contention is that the Ulema maintains that Islam recognises Mohammed as the last of the Prophets (*Khatmun Nabi*) and anyone who accepts a successor is a heretic. The Ahmediyas strenuously deny that they ever question Mohammed's singular Prophethood and look upon their Mirza Sahib and his successors simply as guides. This is not good enough for the Pakistani Ulema.

The fact that the Aga Khan is regarded as a living God by his Ismaili followers and that there are innumerable Muslim sects based on worship of *peers* is considered besides the point. Logic has never been the strong point of any established religion. Nor has there been room for accommodation of a different point of view in the minds of religious bigots.

Mrs Indira Gandhi ordered the Indian army into the Golden Temple. Her Sikh bodyguards avenged the insult by killing her. Sikhs killed Mrs Gandhi, so Hindus avenged her murder by killing thousands of Sikhs. Mrs Gandhi's murderers were hanged so Khalistani terrorists took revenge by hanging a few innocent Hindus. The spirit of revenge is deeply ingrained in the human psyche. It is not an animal instinct because animals do not kill to take revenge, only in self-defence or for food.

All religious systems have tried in their own ways to exorcise the spirit of revenge from the human mind. Some have achieved notable successes in this direction by adopting penal codes which forbid people settling their scores themselves and making punishment for crime the business of the state.

This significant step was taken in the transition from the Old to the New Testament. Judaism sanctioned "an eye for an eye, a tooth for a tooth". In the sermon on the Mount which forms the most important part of the New Testament, Jesus is quoted as preaching: "Ye have heard that it hath been said, an eye for an eye, a tooth for a a tooth. But I say unto you, that ye resist not evil; but whosoever shall smite thee on the right cheek, turn to him the other also. And if any man shall sue thee at the law, and take away the coat, let him have the cloak also." (Matthew 5:39-40)

One must be fair to Judaism. Although it sanctioned retaliation in equal measure, it did not justify a person taking the law into his own hands. It was not for the individual whose eye had been pierced or tooth knocked out to execute revenge but to lodge a complaint and submit to a court's judgement whether or not the man who did him harm was to be punished in the same manner or compensated by a sum of money. "Love thy neighbour as thyself" was also an integral part of the Judaic faith.

Islam, which took a great deal from Judaism and Christianity, made a similar compromise between crime and punishment. It accepted the principle of eye for an eye, but allowed compensation in place of similar punishment as legitimate and elevated forgiveness to the pedestal of supreme virtue.

Badla or revenge has never been sanctioned by any of the religious systems of Hinduism, Jainism, Buddhism or Sikhism. Jainism made *ahimsa (non-violence) parmo dharma*—the supreme religion—and even forbade killing of animals for food. Likewise, the Buddha preached non-violence in face of violence. Sikhism of the first nine Gurus as compiled in the *Granth Sahib* also preaches the moral superiority of turning the other cheek over retaliation. Amongst the most quoted lines is from the Muslim divine Baba Fareed:

Jo tain maara mukkian
Tina na maaren ghum
Apanery ghar jai kay
Payr tina dey chum

> Those who hit you with their fists
> Do not turn and hit them back;
> Seek them out in their homes
> And kiss their feet.

Guru Gobind Singh, the last of the Gurus, turned the Sikhs into a militant fraternity and exhorted *Dharmayudha*—the battle of righteousness—in face of unwarranted aggression. But he did not justify a person taking the law into his own hands. And sanctioned the use of force by a people only after all other means had been tried and had failed; it was only then that they were to draw the sword. In a memorable passage he wrote:

"I came into the world charged with the duty to uphold the right in every place, to destroy sin and evil. Holy men, know it well in your hearts that the only reason I took birth was to see that righteousness may flourish: that the good may live and tyrants be torn out by their roots."

There are other aspects of the spirit of the revenge that need to be considered. There may be some justification for wanting to avenge the wrong done to you by paying the wrongdoer in the same coin. To wit:

> Tit for Tat;
> Remember that;
> You killed my dog,
> I'll kill your cat.

You may not rest in peace till you have maimed or murdered the man who raped your child. Such levelling of scores has its own logic. But when vengeance is sought to be extended to people of the wrongdoer's caste or community, its implications can be horrifying. This unfortunately has become a regular pattern of our lives. When one man desecrates a place of worship we not only desecrate his people's places of worship, but also seek to avenge ourselves against his clan or community. The sickening incidents of communal riots bear testimony to this extended spirit of revenge. And often we extend the domain of vengeance against the entire society by organising bunds and gheraos, derailing trains, burning buses and causing damage to public property.

It would be naive to expect that religious sermons will curb the desire to seek revenge. Forgiveness is a very rare commodity. There are not many in the world who, like Jesus Christ on the cross, would say of his tormentors: "Lord, forgive them for they know not what they do." However hard it may be to forgive the wrongdoer, it is the only antidote to *badla*.

Israel Zangwill has a lovely short story about how a place can acquire sanctity and people who have blind faith at times benefit from it. It is about a remote village in eastern Poland where lived a poor Jewish wood-cutter with his young wife. Near their home lived a middle-aged woman with her son who had been born paralytic. She had spent whatever she had having him treated, but it had been of no avail.

Came Christmas and the village and the surrounding country was under a layer of snow. The wood-cutter had made a little money selling firewood and was looking forward to eating a square meal after a long while. Early on the morning of Christmas Day, the wood-cutter's wife went out into the woods to pick holly and mistletoe to decorate her home.

After she had gathered what she wanted, she came by a pond frozen with ice. It occurred to her that she had not had a bath for many days and her husband, though Jewish, might wish to celebrate the occasion in other ways. She took off her clothes, smashed the ice and jumped into the icy water. No sooner had she done so than she heard human voices approaching. She got out of the pool, gathered her clothes and ran naked into the woods towards her home.

The human voices belonged to two farmers who happened to be out with their guns to see if they could get a wild

hare or some other game for their Christmas dinner. They saw
the figure of a young girl come out of the icy pool and disappear in the snows. They came back to the village and spread
the story that they had seen the Virgin Mary. Soon the entire
village was out to see the pond. All the signs of someone having bathed in it were there. Surely, if the Virgin had come
there, the water must be blest.

The middle-aged widow heard of the story. She picked up
her paralysed son in her arms and hurried to the pond. With
full faith that a miracle would happen, she ducked her son in
the chilly water. The shock did to the boy what medicines and
therapy had failed to do. He was cured of his paralysis.

The story of the miracle cure spread like wildfire. The
trickle of pilgrims became a regular stream. The Jewish wood-
cutter and his wife made good business. They filled small
phials with water from the pond and sold it at high prices for
its medicinal properties. The site was examined by a representative of the Pope who confirmed that the Holy Virgin had
indeed visited the place and many people had been cured of
their ailments by drinking the water. A huge cathedral was
built in the village and it soon became a place of pilgrimage.
The one to benefit the most was the poor Jewish wood-cutter
who, through the sale of his land and millions of bottles full of
"sacred" water, became a millionaire.

Zangwill's story is, of course, apocryphal. But it does
contain an element of truth in so far as people who have blind
faith in miracles are known to have miraculous recoveries. I
am not sure of the origin of Lourdes in France, but eveyone
who goes there will see innumerable crutches abandoned by
those who could not walk as evidence of their having been
healed. Millions go to Lourdes for treatment. Perhaps a handful, already on the verge of being healed, get healed. But they
perpetuate the legend that such miracles are possible.

Belief in miracles exists in every religious system. The
outstanding example is the Hindu's belief in the purifying
qualities of the waters of the Ganga and various "sacred" tanks
such as those at Kurukshetra and Pushkar near Ajmer. The

"holy dip" is a uniquely Hindu-Sikh phenomenon. Stellar constellations determine the more auspicious days like the *Kumbhs* when the ritual bath is said to be more beneficial. Some even wipe out all sins committed in the past.

Guru Nanak proclaimed: "I have no miracle save the name of the Lord." Despite that, many miracles have become attached to his name and the places he visited. A fresh water spring, not far from Rawalpindi, has an overhanging rock with the imprint of a human palm dug into it. The faithful believe it is the palm of Guru Nanak as he stretched out his hand to stop a boulder loosened by an envious Muslim *peer* on him. The Gurdwara that has come up on the site is known as "Panja Sahib". There is an annual pilgrimage of Sikhs from all over the world to this Gurdwara.

There is another place in the hills where there is a tree growing *reetha,* which is normally very bitter. The fruit of this particular tree is very sweet because the guru sat under its shade. It is no use telling devout Sikhs that there is in fact, a botanical species of *reetha* which bears sweet fruit.

As with the Hindus, so with the Sikhs, waters of temple tanks are endowed with sanctity. Bathing in "the pool of nectar" from which Amritsar derives its name is *de rigeur* for all pilgrims. In addition, water from a sacred spot such as Har Ki Pauri in Hardwar as well as behind the central shrine of the Golden Temple is drunk with reverence and collected in bottles to take home for relatives. The same reverence is accorded to the spring water of Gurdwara Bangla Sahib in New Delhi. Here the infant Guru Harikishen lived for a while before he succumbed to small pox.

It can hardly be maintained that belief in miracles is an integral part of religion. Many devoutly religious people scoff at them as spurious accretions to beguile the superstitious and the stupid. Indeed, a case could be made out to ban propagation of miracles for the harm they do to gullible people. Many years ago there was a film made called *Nanak Naam Jahaz Hai* (the name of Nanak is a ship, to take you across the waters of life). The theme was of a young man who lost his sight in an accident. When all medical treatment failed, he undertook a pilgrimage to the major Gurdwaras. Ultimately, at the Harmandir in Amritsar, a divine light came out of the Temple and restored his vision. Millions of Sikhs and Hindus saw this film many times. The film producer made his millions. And spread a message of crass superstition. Miracles are the biggest money-spinners of institutionalised religion.

Life of Guru Nanak

O n the night of the full moon in the month of *Vaisakh* in
Samvat version—Mehervan's *Janam Sakhi*—on the life
of Guru Nanak, 'Tripta, the wife of Mehta Kalian Das Bedi of
Talwandi Rae Bhoe, was in labour. Three-quarters of the night
had passed. The morning star shone bright in the eastern sky; it
was the hour of early dawn when she was delivered of her
second child, a son.'

Nanak's birth was thus on 15 April 1469. However, in
order to continue an old tradition, the event is celebrated on
the full moon night in the month of November. As to the place
of his birth, it is thought that the name Nanak was given to the
child because he was born in the house of his maternal grandparents or *nankey* which was either in Kahna Kacha or Chale-
wal, two villages in the district of Lahore.

Nanak was a precocious child, smiling and sitting up in
early infancy. When he was only five years old, people noticed
that he did not play with other boys but spoke words of wisdom well beyond his years. The people's reactions were inter-
esting. Whosoever heard him, Hindu or Muslim, was certain
that God spoke through the little boy—and this belief grew
stronger as Nanak grew older.

At the age of seven Nanak was taken to a pandit to be
taught. Nanak apparently turned the tables on his teacher and
his discourse with his teacher is the subject of a beautiful
hymn in *Sri Raga*.

The only real learning (says Nanak) is the worship of
God; the rest is of no avail and wisdom devoid of the knowledge

of the creator is but the noose of ignorance about one's neck. He that repeats the name of the Lord in this world, will reap his reward in the world to come.

Do you know (says Nanak) how and why men come into this world and why they depart? Why some become rich and others poor? Why some hold court while others go begging door to door—and even of the beggars why some receive alms while others do not? Take it from me, O pandit, that those who have enjoyed power and ease in this life and not given praise to the Lord will surely be punished—just as the *dhobi* (washerman) beats dirty clothes on slabs of stones, so will they be beaten; just as an oilman grinds oilseeds to extract oil will they be ground; just as the miller crushes grain between his millstones will they be crushed. On the other hand, those that are poor and those that have to beg for their living, who spend their lives in prayer will receive their honour and reward in the divine court of justice.

He that has fear of God (says Nanak) is free from all fears. But monarch or commoner, he that fears not God will be reduced to dust and be reborn to suffer the pangs of hell. That which is gained by falsehood becomes unclean. The only truth is God. Our only love should be for God who is immortal; why love those that will perish—son, wife, power, wealth, youth— all are subject to decay and death. [Mehervan: *Janam Sakhi*]

A year later Nanak was sent to the village mosque to learn Arabic and other subjects. Here, too, Nanak astounded his teacher:

The mullah wrote down the Arabic alphabet from *alif* to *yea*. Nanak at once mastered the writing and the pronunciation of the letters, and within a few days had learnt arithmetic, accounting and everything else the mullah could teach. The mullah marvelled, 'Great God! Other children have been struggling for ten years and cannot tell one letter from another, and this child has by Thy grace learnt all within a matter of days.' [Mehervan: *Janam Sakhi*]

Nanak was a moody child and often refused to speak to anyone for days on end. He wandered about the woods absorbed in observing the phenomenon of nature: the advent of spring with its bees and butterflies; the searing heat of summer that burned up all vegetation followed by the monsoon which miraculously restored life and turned the countryside green; the ways of the birds and beasts of the jungle. All this mystery baffled young Nanak's mind and he began to ponder over the character of the Creator, Preserver and Destroyer—and to question the efficacy of rituals, both Hindu and Muslim.

When he was only nine Nanak demanded of the Brahmin priest who had come to invest him with the sacred thread, the *janeau:* 'Do the Brahmins and Kshatriyas lose their faith if they lose their sacred thread? Is their faith maintained by their thread or by their deeds?

Nanak was the despair of his parents. He refused to do any kind of work. If he was sent to graze cattle, he let them stray into people's fields; if he was given money to do trade, he would give it away to the poor and the hungry. He was saved from the wrath of his father by his mother and sister— and by the village-folk who bore witness to the many miracles they had seen emanate from Nanak.

At the age of sixteen Nanak was married to Sulakhni, daughter of Mul Chand Chona of Batala. They had two sons, Sri Chand and Lakhmi Das, and perhaps a daughter or daughters who died in infancy. Family life did not divert Nanak's attention for too long. His moods would suddenly descend upon him and he would remain silent for many days and then become argumentative on subjects such as God, man, death, rituals and moral values. And he remained as indifferent to making a living as he had been before he became a husband and father.

One evening in July (says Mehervan's *Janam Sakhi*), the skies over Talwandi were darkened by black monsoon clouds and it began to pour. At night the sky was rent with flashes of lightning and there was a fearful crash of thunder. Nanak began to sing hymns in praise of the Lord. His mother came to him and said, 'Son, it is time you had some sleep.' Just then the cuckoo called 'peeoh, peeoh', and Nanak replied, 'Mother, when my rival is awake, how can I sleep?'

It became evident to the people that it would not be long before Nanak took the hermit's path in search of truth and, once when a group of holy men happened to pass through Talwandi on their way to a pilgrimage, Nanak's mother expressed her apprehensions.

'I know,' she said, 'that one of these days you too will be leaving me to go on a pilgrimage. I do not complain but would like to know what is gained by going to holy places.

'Nothing,' replied Nanak categorically. 'It is in our own body that we have to build our temples, free our minds from the snares of *maya,* renounce evil deeds and give praise to our Maker. This is as good as going to bathe in the sixty-eight holy places of pilgrimage.

"Then tell these holy men that they pursue the path of error,' said Nanak's mother. Tell them that God can be found in their own houses.'

'Let each one find his own path,' replied Nanak. 'Why should I worry my head about their methods?'

The beauty of the woodland in spring cast its usual spell. But, for Nanak, the beauty was now tinged with anguish for he needed to know the truth of the reality that did not change with the seasons. A beautiful hymn in *Raga Basant* sums up the feeling:

It was springtime. The trees were in new leaf; many wild shrubs were in flower. The woods around Talwandi were a beauteous sight. Young men of his village came to him and said, 'Nanak, it is spring. Come with us and let us behold the wonders of nature.'

'The month of *Chaitra,*' said Nanak, 'is the most beautiful of the twelve months of the year because all is green and every living thing seems to blossom into fullness. But my heart does not rejoice at the sight of the blossoming of nature until it is blessed with the name of the Lord. We must first subdue our ego, sing praises of the Lord and then our hearts too will be fragrant.'

'We do not understand what you say,' they protested, 'we want to tell you that in the woods the trees are so green that we cannot find words to describe them; there are varieties of flowers whose beauty is beyond the speech of man; there are fruits whose lusciousness is beyond praise; and beneath them the shade is cool and fragrant. You should see these things with your own eyes.'

'The Lord's grace,' says Nanak,' gave the trees their new foliage. His decrees covered them with blossoms of great beauty and filled their fruits with sweet nectarine. When they have their foliage the Lord makes their shade cool and fragrant. I have such foliage in my own heart with similar flowers, fruit and cool shade, and people seek shelter under it.'

'The great God has given us eyes to see, ears to hear and a mouth to speak and eat the corn that grows. Why has he given us these things?'

'He has given you eyes not merely to gape at the woods but to behold His creation and marvel at it; ears to hear godly counsel; the tongue to speak the truth. Thereafter, whatever you receive is your true wealth and sustenance.'

The young men did not understand all that Nanak said. They tried once more to persuade him to come out with them. 'Spring comes but once a year and nature dons its garb of green but once. Then comes the fall. Trees lose their foliage and the woods are barren of beauty. If you want to see nature at its best, see it in the month of *Chaitra*.

'Months and seasons ever come and go and come again,' replied Nanak. 'Trees and bushes attain foliage at one season, lose it at another and once again become green when the season turns. The lesson for you is to see that those who do good acts reap the fruit of good action and those who do evil, wither and die; those who take the name of the Lord ever have spring in their hearts. The grape only receives its juice during the monsoon but the good man receives his reward at all times of the year and all times of the day and night. Human birth is the springtime of the cycle of birth, death and rebirth; it is the time for you to plant the seed of good action and reap its fruit in life thereafter; in this do not tarry.'

As Nanak grew even more detached from the ties of living, he took no notice of his wife or children, of his goods or of the people about him. His life became one of prayer, almsgiving, ablution and the seeking after knowledge; *nam, dan, isnan* and *gyan*. Lust, anger and pride fell away as Nanak's heart was filled with truth and blessed contentment. Nanak lived in this state 'like one drunk' for some years till his sister, Nanaki, now married, took the situation in hand. She persuaded her husband, Jai Ram, to invite her brother over to Sultanpur, where they lived, and get him employment with his master, Nawab Daulat Khan Lodhi.

Nanak went to Sultanpur accompanied by a family servant, a Muslim named Mardana, who was to become his closest companion. Mardana, the *Janam Sakhi* tells us, came from the brewer caste, and was a gifted musician. Mardana played the *rabab* and also sang hymns.

Nawab Daulat Khan Lodhi was impressed with the integrity of his new storekeeper and accountant. Nanak would not accept bribes from agents and refused to follow the corrupt practices of his predecessors. The people in Sultanpur could not stop praising Nanak.

In Sultanpur Nanak organised his daily life in an ideal manner. Every evening he and Mardana would sing hymns before retiring to bed. Nanak would wake up while it was still dark, and, after a dip in the river close by, sing hymns with the coterie of his followers. After this, at the appointed hour, Nanak would go to the court of the Nawab and apply himself to his work.

Though he won the approbation of his employer and those he dealt with, Nanak was unhappy.

'This has been suddenly put around my neck like a noose,' he said. He began to say to himself that if he had to serve anyone, wouldn't it be wiser to serve his own Master who is within him instead of the person without? It is all very well to seek knowledge and wisdom but one cannot escape the noose of *maya* without sowing seeds of good actions. One cannot earn wages without service and it is the love of the wage which stands in the way of renunciation. Why not then serve the great Master who is the Lord of all? Nanak postponed his decision with the thought: 'I, Nanak, am no better than others; others are no worse than I; what the Lord wills, Nanak will honour and obey.' [Mehervan: *Janam Sakhi*]

It was, however, clear that the time of decision was at hand.

Nanak's days were spent in noting down receipts and expenses. At the end of the day he added up the totals to make sure they tallied with the accounts. He often had to work late into the night adding up his figures under the light of the lamp. One night he got angry with himself and threw away his pen and account books. He asked himself, 'Why have I got involved in these affairs and forgotten my Maker? Am I destined to spend my days and nights writing accounts? It is a vast net in which I find myself caught; if I let the days go by, the noose will close tighter around me. If I have to burn the midnight oil, it should be for something worthwhile.'

Nanak pondered over these things late into the night and, instead of returning home, went to the stream to bathe. He prayed, 'Lord send me a guru, a guide who will show me the path that leads to Thy mansion.'

That very night God revealed Himself to Nanak. Nanak prayed fervently and begged the Lord to forgive him and remove him from the world which had so ensnared him. The Lord asked Nanak, 'Why are you so agitated? You have done no wrong.'

'I have let my mind turn from Thee,' replied Nanak, 'to the petty trifles of the world.'

'Your errors have I forgiven. The *maya* that you complain of is also a part of Me. What you see is but its shadow.'

'Lord destroy in me the longing for worldly gain.'

'Nanak you shall no more crave for worldly gain. I am pleased with you. On you be My blessing.' [Mehervan: *Janam Sakhi*]

The mystic experience that finally made Nanak take up his mission is put at different times and is variously described. The incident took place in August 1507 on the third night before the full moon.

The moon had set, [says the *Janam Sakhi*] but it was dark and the stars still twinkled in the sky when Nanak, followed by his servant, went to the river. Nanak took off his *kurta* and *dhoti* and stepped into the stream.

He closed his nostrils and ducked into the water. He did not come up. The servant waited a while and then, panicking, ran up and down the river bank crying for Nanak. A strange voice rose from the waters saying, 'Do not lose patience.'

Mardana, however, ran back to Sultanpur and sobbed out his story. A great commotion took place in the town because Nanak was loved by all—Hindus and Muslims, the rich and the poor. When Daulat Khan Lodhi heard of the mishap, he was most distressed. 'Friends,' he said, 'Nanak was a man of God. Let us dredge the river and rescue his corpse.'

While the people of Sultanpur were dredging the river, Nanak was conducted into the presence of God.

The Almighty gave him a bowl of milk. 'Nanak, drink this bowl,' He commanded. 'It is not milk as it may seem; this is nectar (amrit). It will give thee power of prayer, love of worship, truth and contentment.'

Nanak drank the nectar and was overcome. He made another obeisance. The Almighty then blessed him. 'I release thee from the cycle of birth, death and rebirth; he that sets his eyes on you with faith will be saved; he that hears your words with conviction will be helped by Me; he that you forgive will be forgiven by Me. I grant thee salvation. Nanak go back to the evil world and teach men and women to pray (*nam*), to give in charity (*dan*) and to live cleanly (*isnan*). Do good to the world and redeem it in the age of sin (*Kaliyuga*).' [Mehervan: *Janam Sakhi*]

At dawn, three days later, on the full moon in August, Nanak re-emerged from the Bein. Nanak was thirty-six years old and now a changed and determined man. While the people clamoured around him acclaiming him as a new messiah, he paid no heed. 'What have I to do with men like these!' he said to himself. He gave away all he had to the poor. He even cast off his clothes, keeping for himself only a loin-cloth. He left his home and joined a band of hermits.

Soon people began expressing themselves loudly. 'Nanak was a sensible man,' some said, 'but now he has lost his head.' 'He is stricken with the fear of the Lord,' said others, 'and is no longer himself.' 'Something in the river has bitten him,' the rest were convinced, and took to calling him 'mad, bewitched.'

'It is the Lord who has possessed me and made me mad,' explained Nanak. If I find merit in the eyes of my Lord, then will I have justified my waywardness.'

'Nanak, you are a different person today from what you were,' the people exclaimed. 'Tell us the path you intend to take. We only know of two ways; one of the Hindus and the other of the Mussalmans.'

'There is no Hindu, there is no Mussalman, replied Nanak.

'You talk in cryptic language,' they said. 'In this world we understand the two ways—of Hinduism and of Islam.'

'There are no Mussalmans, there are no Hindus,' repeated Nanak. [Mehervan: *Janam Sakhi*]

Nanak spent another two years in and around Sultanpur before he forsook the habitations of men and took to the forests and solitude. The faithful Mardana was his sole companion. He took on a strange dress: a cloth cap (*seli topee*), a long cloak worn by Muslim mendicants, a beggar's bowl, staff and prayer mat. When asked why he wore this outlandish garb, Nanak replied, 'I am dressed like a clown for the amusement of my Master. If my apparel pleases Him, I will be happy.'

Nanak's first journey took him eastwards to Hindu centres of pilgrimage. His biographies have fabricated many incidents based on Nanak's hymns—many of which depict the Guru's love for nature.

One day, says Mehervan's *Janam Sakhi*, Nanak and Mardana, while travelling, espied a flock of swans flying overhead. Nanak was bewitched and began to run after them with his eyes fixed on the birds. Mardana followed him. The flock descended in a field and let Nanak approach them without showing any sign of fear—for Nanak was a man of God, who harmed no one. Nanak admired the birds; their long slender necks, their luminous dark eyes and their sliver-white plumage. He wondered whether these birds—who spanned the heavens—had ever cast their eyes on their Maker. Why, he asked himself, should such beautiful birds wander restlessly across the continents—from Khorasan in Central Asia to Hindustan and back again to Khorasan? He blessed the swans and bade them godspeed on their journey.

Another hymn illustrates the political and social conditions of the time through picturing an incident that occurred in the suburbs of the capital city, Delhi.

The city was at the time ruled by a bloodthirsty Pathan king (Ibrahim Lodhi). Nanak's fame had preceded him and large crowds of citizens, sightseers and seekers after truth, Muslims as will as Hindus, came to see him. Near Nanak's camp was a place where beggars and mendicants were fed free of charge by the wicked king. The people told Nanak of their king's evil ways and how he expiated his sins by feeding beggars.

Nanak spoke to them, 'Listen ye children of God! This charity of the king is of no consequence; it is the act of a blind man stumbling in the dark. He is worse than a blind man because even if his eyes lose their light, a blind man can hear and speak and comprehend, but one who has lost his mind has lost all. What avail is the giving of alms to one who sins by day and gives in charity at night? A stone dam can hold the flood but if the dam bursts you cannot repair the breach by plastering mud. Evil is like the flood, the stone dam like faith. If faith weakens, the dam will give way and the flood will sweep all before it. Its force is then so great that no boat nor boatman dare embark on it to save its victims. Then nothing abides save the Name of the Lord.' [Mehervan: *Janam Sakhi*]

We do not know how long Nanak stayed in Delhi. He proceeded to Hardwar on the Ganges. It was apparently at a time of some religious festival when large crowds had turned up to bathe in the 'holy' river. Mardana was very impressed with the sight and said to Nanak: 'What a lot of good people there are in the world! They must be genuinely desirous of improving themselves that is why they come on a pilgrimage.'

Nanak was not so impressed by the sight of the people "washing away their sins" by the ritual of bathing. 'Only a bullion dealer can tell the difference between the genuine and the counterfeit,' he replied, 'and at this place there is no bullion dealer.'

Nanak and Mardana stayed at Hardwar for some time in order to be present at the *Baisakhi* (March-April) fair. It was on this occasion that an incident, that made Nanak famous, took place.

There was a large crowd bathing in the river. Nanak saw them face eastwards and throw palmfuls of water to the sun. Nanak entered the stream and started throwing water westwards.

'In the name of Rama!' exclaimed the shocked pilgrims, 'who is this man who throws water to the west? He is either mad or a Mussalman.' They approached Nanak and asked him why he offered water in the wrong direction. Nanak asked them why they threw it eastwards to the sun.

'We offer it to our dead ancestors,' they replied

'Where are your dead ancestors?'

'With the gods in heaven.'

'How far is the abode of the gods?'

'49 *crore kos* from here.'

'Does the water get that far?'

'Without doubt! But why do you throw it westwards?'

Nanak replied, 'My home and lands are near Lahore. It has rained everywhere except on my land. I am therefore watering my fields.'

'Man of God, how can you water your fields near Lahore from this place?'

'If you can send it 49 crore *kos* to the abode of the gods, why can't I send it to Lahore which is only a couple of hundred *kos* away!'

The people were abashed at this reply. 'He is not mad,' they said, 'he is surely a great seer.' [Mehervan: *Janam Sakhi*]

A large number of Hindu pilgrims who had foregathered at Hardwar became disciples of the guru. He stayed on there after the *Baisakhi* festival preaching to the people:

The most precious gift of God is human birth because it is by reason and responsible action as human beings that we can get out of the vicious circle of life, death and rebirth and attain salvation. One must abolish duality in order to be a complete devotee.'

'And how does one overcome duality?' they asked.

'By faith in the One; by hearing and speaking of the One; by never abandoning belief in Him. By austerity, truth, restraint in his heart.' [Mehervan: *Janam Sakhi*]

From Hardwar, Nanak and Mardana proceeded to Prayag (modern Allahabad) where the rivers Jamuna and the Saraswati join the Ganges. From Prayag, the guru went to Banaras, the centre of Hindu learning and orthodoxy. The *Adi Granth* describes the many encounters Guru Nanak had with pandits who chided him for his unorthodoxy and probed his knowledge of the sacred texts.

'It matters not how many cartloads of learning you have nor what learned company you keep; it matters not how many boat-loads of books you carry nor the tree of knowledge; it matters not how many years or months you spend in study nor with what passion and single-mindedness you pursue knowledge. Only one thing really matters, the rest is but a whirlwind of the ego.'

'And what is the one thing that matters?' they asked.

Nanak replied—'There are a hundred falsehoods, but this one sovereign truth—that unless truth enters the soul all service and study is false.'

Nanak was equally forthright about the pandits' fetish of the purity of their cooking vessels and kitchens. He decided to draw their attention to this in his usual manner of highlighting the incongruous aspects.

Nanak went with them and saw with what care they bathed, scrubbed their utensils, swept the ground near the hearth, washed the vegetables and cooked the food. When one plate was laid before Nanak, he refused to eat from it. 'I am not satisfied with the purity of the food you offer me. It is prepared by one who is full of sin and sins cannot be cleansed by washing the body.'

The pandits did not fully comprehend the import of Nanak's words and prepared the meal afresh. This time they dug up the earth and re-plastered it; they even washed the logs of wood before kindling them. Again Nanak refused to partake of the meal and continued his sermon. 'You err in believing that purity can be gained by scrubbing and washing. That does not apply even to inanimate things like wood, dung-fuel or water, much less to a human being. Man is unclean when his heart is tainted with greed, his tongue coated with falsehood, his eyes envious of the beauty of another's wife or his wealth, his ears dirty with slander. All these can only be cleansed by knowledge. Basically all men are good but often they pursue a predetermined path to hell.'

Nanak was questioned on his attitude towards the sacred texts of the Hindus: 'The Vedas say one thing and you another. People who read the Vedas do not follow their teachings and now you confuse them more than ever. Why don't you either combine your teaching with that of the Vedas or separate them more distinctly?'

Nanak replied, 'The Vedas tell you of the difference between good and evil. Sin is the seed of hell; chastity the seed of paradise. Knowledge and the teaching of the Vedas complement each other; they are to one another as merchandise to the merchant.'

It would appear that by this time Nanak had decided that his faith was to be an eclectic one for he sang hymns of Namdev, Kabir, Ravi Das, Sain and Beni.

His new disciples tried to persuade Nanak to settle down in Banaras. Nanak refused to do so. 'I pursue the one and only path of devotion to God.' he replied, 'Your learning and religion do not appeal to me and I have no interest in trade other than the name of God for God Himself has extinguished the desire for acquisition in me.'

Piecing together evidence from other sources we find that the first journey apparently took the guru as far east as Bengal and Assam. On his way back to the Punjab, he spent some days at Jagannath Puri. He travelled round the Punjab and visited the Sufi headquarters at Pak Pattan before he set out on his second long voyage—this time southwards. He is said to have travelled through Tamil Nadu, Kerala, Konkan and Rajasthan—though there is little evidence to show that he did so.

Nanak sojourned in the Himalayas for some time before he set out on his last and longest journey. This was westwards to the Muslims' holy cities Mecca and Medina as far as Baghdad. It was on this journey that another incident took place. He was staying in a mosque and fell asleep with his feet towards the Ka'ba—an act considered of grave disrespect to the house of God. When the mullah came to say his prayers, he shook Nanak rudely and said: O servant of God, thou hast thy feet towards Ka'ba, the house of God; why hast thou done such a thing?'

Nanak replied: 'Then turn my feet towards some direction where there is no God nor the Ka'ba.'

By the time Nanak returned home, the Mughal Babar had invaded the Punjab. The Guru was at Saidpur when the town was sacked by the invaders. Nanak makes many references to the havoc caused by this invasion.

Nanak was by this time too old to undertake any more strenuous journeys. He settled in the village Kartarpur where he spent the last years of his life preaching to the people. His disciples came to be known as Sikhs (from the Sanskrit *shishya* or Pali *sikkha*). He built a *dharamshala* (abode of faith) whose inmates followed a strict code of discipline: rising well before dawn, bathing and then foregathering in the *dharamshala* for prayer and hymn-singing.

They went about their daily chores and met again for the evening service. At the *dharamshala* was the *guru-ka-langar* (the guru's kitchen) where all who came were obliged to break bread without distinction of caste or religion.

Among Nanak's disciples was a man called Lehna whom Nanak chose in preference to his sons as his successor. Said Nanak to Lehna: 'Thou art Angad, a part of my body,' and asked another disciple to daub Angad's forehead with saffron and proclaim him the second guru.

Nanak died in the early hours of the morning of 22 September 1539. He was a poet and lover of nature to the last. As he lay on his deathbed he recalled the scenes of his childhood. 'The tamarisk must be in flower now; the pampas grass must be waving its woolly head in the breeze; the cicadas must be calling in the lonely glades,' he said before he closed his eyes in eternal sleep.

Mehervan's *Janam Sakhi* records the manner his body was laid to rest. Said the Mussalmans: 'we will bury him', the Hindus: 'we will cremate him'. Nanak said: You place flowers on either side, Hindus on my right, Muslims on my left. Those whose flowers remain fresh tomorrow will have their way.' He asked them to pray. When the prayer was over, Nanak pulled the sheet over him and went to eternal sleep. Next morning when they raised the sheet they found nothing. The flowers of both communities were fresh. The Hindus took theirs; the Muslims took those that they had placed.

It is little wonder that Nanak came to be revered as the king or shah of the holy men, the guru of the Hindus and the *peer* of the Mussalmans:

Baba Nanak Shah Fakeer
Hindu ka Guru, Mussalman ka Peer

TRANSLATIONS

"Good Keertan continued, as it does to this day, to touch my emotional chords."

Some Hymns of Guru Nanak

From Var Majh

Pahley pahrey rain key vanjariya mitra
(Sri Raga Pahrey)

In the first watch of night, my trader-friend,
By order Eternal
You found yourself in the womb;
Upside down like a yogi in penance you were,
  my trader-friend!
Praying to the Lord, meditating thus head below and feet
above
Naked did you come into the world of *Kaliyuga*
Naked will you depart when your time comes.
As the eternal pen hath flown
So has your fate been writ on your forehead.
Sayeth Nanak by divine Ordinance
Does life begin in the womb.

In the second watch of night, my trader-friend,
You forget your past meditation.
You bounced from one lap to another,
  my trader-friend.
As Krishna sporting in the hands of Yashodhara
You bounced from one lap to another,
Your mother saying 'This is my son,'

O stupid and thoughtless soul of mine!
Knowest not thou that in the end
You will have nothing to call your own?
Of Him who gave you birth
You have no knowledge in your heart.
Sayeth Nanak, in the second watch
Man forgets his past meditation.

In the third watch of night, my trader-friend,
Your mind is obsessed with wealth and youth.
You think not of the Name of God,
     my trader-friend,
You are concerned only with profit.
My soul, you think not of the Name of Hari
Because you are agitated in the pursuit of wealth!
In the search for gold,
Drunk with the wine of youth
You made no truck with faith
Nor espoused good deeds as your friends.
Sayeth Nanak, in the third watch
The mind is obsessed with wealth and youth.

In the fourth watch of night, my trader-friend,
The Reaper came to your field.
Who sent Death the Reaper?
That secret no one has found, my trader-friend,
That unravelled secret is in the breast of God.
God sends forth death on its task.
False lamentation will break forth all around thee
In a trice will you become a stranger.
All that you loved will be acquired by others.
Sayeth Nanak, O my soul, in the fourth watch
The Reaper reaps the field.

From Raga Suhi

Jog na khintha, jog na dandey, jog na bhasam chadhaeeai
(Raga Suhi)

Religion lieth not in the patched coat the yogi wears,
Not in the staff he bears,
Nor in the ashes on his body.
Religion lieth not in rings in the ears,
Not in a shaven head,
Nor in the blowing of the conch-shell.
If thou must the path of true religion see,
Among the world's impurities, be of impurities free.

Not by talk can you achieve union
He who sees all mankind as equals
Can be deemed to be a yogi.

Religion 'ieth not in visiting tombs
Nor in visiting places where they burn the dead
Not in sitting entranced in contemplation
Nor in wandering in the countryside or foreign lands
Nor in bathing at places of pilgrimage.
If thou must the path of true religion see,
Among the world's impurities, be of impurities free.

When a man meets the true guru
His doubts are dispelled
And his mind ceases its wanderings;
Drops of nectar pour down on him like rain.
His ears catch strains of *Sahaj's* celestial music
And his mind is lit up with knowledge divine.
If thou must the path of true religion see,
Among the world's impurities, be of impurities free.

Sayeth Nanak, if thou must be a real yogi,
Be in the world but be dead to its tinsel values.
When the lute strikes notes without being touched
Know then that thou hast conquered fear.
It thou must the path of true religion see,
Among the world's impurities, be of impurities free.

From Raga Vadhans

Mori run jhun laya, Bhainey savan aya

(Raga Vadhans)

Sweet sound of water gurgling down the water-spout
(The peacock's shrill, exultant cry)
Sister, it's *savan*, the month of rain!
Beloved Thine eyes bind me in a spell
(They pierce through me like daggers)
They fill my heart with greed and longing;
For one glimpse of thee I'll give my life
For Thy Name may I be a sacrifice.
When Thou art mine, my heart fills with pride,
What can I be proud of if Thou art not with me?
Woman, smash thy bangles on the bedstead
Break thy arms, break the arms of the couch;
Thy adornments hold no charms
Thy Lord is in another's arms.

The Lord likes not thy bangle-seller
Thy bracelets and glass bangles He doth spurn
Arms that do not the Lord's neck embrace
With anguish shall forever burn.
All my friends have gone to their lovers
I feel wretched, whose door shall I seek?
Friends, of proven virtue and fair am I
Lord, does nothing about me find favour in Thine eye?

I plaited my tresses,
With vermilion daubed the parting of my hair
And went to Him
But with me He would not lie.
My heart is grief-stricken, I could die.
I wept, and the world wept with me

Even birds of the forest cried,
Only my soul torn out of my body shed not a tear,
Nay, my soul which separated me from my Beloved shed not a
tear
In a dream He came to me
(I woke) and he was gone.

I wept a flood of tears.
Beloved I cannot come to Thee,
No messenger will take my message;
Blessed sleep come thou back to me,
That in my dreams my Lover I again may see!
Nanak, what wilt thou give the messenger
Who brings thee a message from thy Master?
I'll sever my head to make a seat for him;
Headless though I be, I'll continue to serve him.
Why then do I not die? Why not give away my life?
My Husband is estranged from me and has
taken another wife!

Jalao aisee reet jit mai pyara veesrai

(Vadhans-di-Var)

Ritual that makes me forget my Beloved Lord shall I burn.
O Nanak that love is best that in the Lord's
eyes doth merit earn.
The body is like a wife in her home,
When her Lord is away
She pines for him.

If her intentions are pure, she'll be re-united
any time any day

O Nanak, unless there be love,
False and futile is all talk.
Man who calculates good
In the spirit of give and take
Even for the good he does
He doth its virtue vitiate.

From ASA-DI-VAR

Daya kapah santokh soot jat gandhi sat vat

When making the sacred thread, the *Janeau*,
See that following rules you pursue
Out of the cotton of compassion
Spin the thread of tranquillity
Let continence be the knot
And virtue the twist thereon.

O pandit, if such a sacred thread there be
Around our neck, we shall wear it willingly.

A thread so made will not break
It will not get dirty, be burnt or lost.
O Nanak, thou shall see
Those who wear this shall blessed be.

For four cowrie shells this thread is bought
A square is marked for the ceremony.
The Brahmin whispers a *mantra* in the ear
And thus becomes the guru and teacher.
But when the wearer dies, cast away is his thread
And threadless he goes on his voyage ahead.

The Story of Umrao Jan Ada

What story will more absorbing be
How fared the world in which I lived
Or what fate hath held in store for me?

Mirza Ruswa, why do you provoke me and try to wheedle out of me the facts of my life? What interest can you possibly have in the life-story of a woman like me? An unhappy wretch who has drifted through life without any mooring; a homeless vagrant who has brought shame upon her family; a woman whose name will be as disgraced in the world to come as it is in the world today. However, if you insist, I will tell you.

What would I gain by boasting of my ancestry? The truth is that I do not even remember the names of my parents or grandparents. All I can recollect is that my home was in a locality somewhere in the outskirts of the city of Faizabad. It was a brick house surrounded by the thatched roof mud-huts of our neighbours who were common folk: water-carriers, barbers, washermen and other menials. Apart from our home, the only other double-storied house in' the vicinity was that of a man called Dilawar Khan.

My father was employed at the mausoleum of the Bahu Begum (wife of Nawab Shuja-ud-dauwla of Oudh). I do not remember what he did nor what he was paid; but I do remember that people used to address him as *jemadar*.

I used to play with my little brother the whole day long. He was so attached to me that he would not leave my side for a moment. I cannot tell you how happy we used to be in the evenings when my father returned from work. I would fling my arms round his waist. My brother would run up shouting "Daddy, Daddy" and cling to the lapel of his coat. Father's face would light up with a broad smile. He would caress me and pat me on the back. He would take my brother in his arms and kiss him. He never came home empty-handed. Sometimes he brought sticks of sugarcane; sometimes sesamum candy or other sweets in a cup of leaves. We would get down to dividing them. And how we used to quarrel! He would grab the sugarcane, I would go for the leaf-cup full of sweets. Mother would be watching it all the while as she cooked the evening meal. It used to be such fun. And my poor father would hardly have time to sit down before I would start nagging him: "Daddy, why haven't you brought me a doll? See how my slippers have worn away! You don't even care. The goldsmith hasn't made my necklace yet and my baby cousin's weaning ceremony is to take place soon; what will I wear for the occasion? And I don't care what happens, I must have a new dress for *Eid*. I simply must."

When mother had finished cooking, she would call out to me. I fetched the basket of bread and the casserole of curry. A white sheet would be spread on the carpet. Mama would serve the food and we would fall on it together. After we had finished, we gave our thanks to God. Father said the prayer for the night and we went to bed. He rose early to say his morning prayers. I would jump out of bed and start asking for things all over again. "Daddy, don't forget to bring me a doll today. And Daddy, get a lot of guavas and tangerines…"

After the morning prayer, father told his beads. Then he went up on the roof, unlatched the pigeon-loft and fed the birds. He made them fly and wheel round in the sky a couple of times. Meanwhile mother would finish the sweeping and cleaning and get the food ready, as father had to leave quite early to get to his job. Then mother would sit down with her sewing and mending. I would take my little brother and go out in the lanes; or leave him under the tamarind tree which stood in front of the house, and play with boys and girls. What wonderful days those where! I did not have a care in the world. I ate the best of food and wore the best of clothes. I was better off than any of the boys and girls I played with. I asked for no more as I did not know that there was anything better to be had. In the neighbourhood where we lived there was no house higher than ours. It had wide verandahs on either side and lots of rooms. All my playmates lived in little hovels. We had more cooking utensils and crockery than we needed. We also had carpets and white sheets to spread over them. Our neighbours used to come to us to borrow these things. We had a water-carrier to bring water to the house; other women had to fetch it themselves from the well. When my father stepped out of the house in his uniform, people bowed low to greet him. When my mother went calling, she rode in a palanquin; women of the neighbourhood had to trudge the streets on foot.

I was also better looking than my companions. Although I was never a beauty, I was not as plain as I am now. My complexion was a shade fairer than that of the yellow champak flower. I had a high forehead and large eyes. My cheeks were full and round as children's cheeks are, and my nose, though not exactly aquiline, was neither flat nor snub. My figure was fairly good for my age and I never was, nor indeed am now, either delicate or fragile. With that figure I wore tight-fitting red silk pyjamas with a waist-band of twill. My blouse was made of *nainsook* and my *dupatta* of fine muslin. I wore three silver bangles on each arm, a gold necklace round my neck, and a gold ring in the nose. (Other girls wore silver nose-rings.) My ears had just been pierced and had blue thread strung through the lobes. An order for gold ear-rings had been placed with the goldsmith.

I was only nine when I was engaged to my father's sister's son: his parents were better off than us and owned a lot of land in Nawabganj. Before my engagement I had visited them several times with my mother. Their style of living was altogether different from ours. Although their house was not made of brick or stone, it was an enormous affair with thatched roofs and large gates. Their cattle-sheds were full of cows, bullocks and buffaloes and there was milk and butter in plenty. They had huge mounds of grain in their godowns and, during the maize season, corn cobs were brought in basket-loads. In the winter months sugarcane was stacked in large heaps.

My fiancé's parents were eager to fix a date for the wedding. I had seen my husband to be. As a matter of fact, we had played together.

My father had bought everything for my dowry. He only needed a little more money for the wedding which had been fixed for *Rajab*, the seventh month of the year.

At night, when my parents discussed the wedding arrangements, I used to eavesdrop and feel pleased with what I overheard. I was proud of my fiancé. He was far handsomer than the fiancé of my friend Kareeman, the *carder's* daughter. Kareeman's fiancé was black; mine was fair. Kareeman's fiancé's face was covered with a thick bushy beard; mine had barely grown a moustache. Hers went about in a dirty dhoti and a green vest; mine was always well dressed. I remember how smart he looked when he came to visit us on *Eid* day. He wore silk pyjamas and velvet slippers on his feet. He wore a cap with lace-work on his head, and had a cloak of green calico about his shoulders. Kareeman's fiancé had a piece of cloth wrapped untidily about his head and went about barefooted.

I was happy. I could not believe anyone was luckier than I. It seemed that all my dreams would soon be fulfilled.

As long as I lived with my parents, I do not remember having known any sorrow. Only once while playing blind-man's buff I lost a ring. It was only a silver one—not worth more than an *anna* at the most. But I was too young to realise that and cried so much that my eyes got red and swollen. I did not tell my mother about it. When she noticed my finger bare, she questioned me about it and I had to tell. She gave me a hard slap on my face. I began to shriek and howl and went on sobbing for a long time. Then my father came home. He scolded my mother and made a fuss of me. Thus I was consoled. My father was always fonder of me than my mother was. He never punished me; Mama chastised me on the slightest pretext. Her favourite was my little brother. I was often beaten because of him, yet I loved him dearly. At times I refused to look after him just to spite my mother. But as soon as her back was turned I would pick him up, kiss him and clasp him to me. If I saw Mama coming, I put him down quickly and he would begin to yell. Mama believed that I had made him cry and would start scolding me all over again. In spite of all this she would be beside herself if even my little finger was scratched. She would forget to eat or drink. She got no sleep at night. She would run about asking people for medicines or charms to make me well again.

To make my dowry, my mother had her bracelets and necklaces melted and refashioned with a little more silver added to them. She had some of her other jewellery polished for the same purpose. She kept only a few of the cooking utensils for her household and had the others freshly tinned to be given to me. When my father asked her to keep a few things for her own use, she would reply: "Never mind about me. Your sister, who is the wife of a big landowner, ought not to feel that you didn't give your daughter anything worthwhile. She may be your sister, but she will also be our daughter's mother-in-law, and you know how critical in-laws are! If our daughter goes to her new home empty handed, they will taunt us!"

I have often heard people say that girls who are born in the homes of prostitutes have little chance of improving their lot and one should only expect the worst from them. They are brought up amongst people who talk of nothing except sex and fornication. And whosoever they turn to, be it their mothers or sisters, they only have examples of degradation. That is not the case with girls who are born of respectable parents. If they run away from their homes and take to the path of evil, they have no excuse whatsoever and deserve to be slaughtered like sheep—but without even the drops of water to slake their thirst before their throats are cut. "

If I did not explain the circumstances which made me take up the profession of a courtesan, people would believe that, as in the case of other girls with my background, it could only be the physical compulsions of inherent wantonness. They would think that the delay in fixing the date of my wedding had made me impatient; that I cast my eye on some other man and ran away with him; and when that someone dropped me, I picked up another; and, when even that affair did not turn out well, with yet another man, and so gradually slipped into the profession. I would not blame them for coming to that conclusion because this is exactly how it often happens. In my lifetime I have seen and heard of many a respectable wife or daughter going astray and I know the circumstances which lead to their downfall. First is the parents' inability to marry off their daughters in good time after they have attained puberty. Second is the marrying off of girls to someone without their consent; parents do not give thought to matters like the disparity of age, looks or temperament and throw their daughters into the arms of any man they can find. As soon as the girl finds that she cannot get on with her husband, she leaves him. Yet other instances are of girls who have the misfortune to be widowed in their youth and who find a widow's lot unbearable; if they are lucky they take on another husband; if they are not and get into bad company, they go on the streets. But none of these things happened to me. I was just born unlucky. The buffetings of fate and chance left me stranded in a wilderness. There was no way out except by the path of evil.

Dilawar Khan, whose house was a short distance from ours, was in league with dacoits. He had spent many years in jail at Lucknow. At the time I am speaking of, he had just secured his release by getting someone to intercede on his behalf.

Dilawar Khan had a strong grouse against my father.

When he was arrested in Faizabad, people of our locality were summoned to testify to his character. My father was amongst them. He was a simple and honest person. And the Queen's magistrate had placed the Holy Koran in his hand and asked: "Well, *jemadar*, tell me the absolute truth; what sort of man is Dilawar Khan?" My father stated truthfully all he knew about him. It was on his testimony that Dilawar Khan was sent to prison. He nursed this grievance in his heart and when he came out of jail, he decided to take his revenge. To spite my father, he bought a flock of pigeons and got his flock to capture one of my father's birds. My father offered four annas for it; he demanded eight.

One evening, before my father had returned from his work, I happened to go out of the house and saw Dilawar Khan standing under the tamarind tree. "Come, child! Your father has settled the matter of money with me," he said to me. "You can take back your pigeon." I walked into the trap. I went with him to his house. As soon as I entered, he bolted the door from the inside. I wanted to scream but he gagged my mouth by thrusting an old rag in it. He tied my hands with a scarf and threw me on the floor. He opened the back-door and called for one Peer Bakhsh. The two men picked me up, put me in a bullock-cart and drove off. The bullocks flew apace.

I was a helpless victim in the clutches of the devil. Dilawar Khan had me pinned under his knees and I could hardly breathe. He had a knife in his hand and there was murder in his bloodshot eyes. I was petrified.

The twilight sank into night and it became dark all around. A strong bleak wind began to blow. I was chilled to the marrow and began to shiver with cold. Images of my home came crowding before my eyes. Tears welled up and ran down my cheeks, hot and unceasing. I thought of my father back from work looking for me everywhere; of my mother beating her breast in distraction and my little brother playing, oblivious of the awful plight of his sister. Mama, father, brother, the house with its verandah, courtyard and kitchen—all flashed before my eyes. And there was Dilawar Khan threatening me with his knife every few minutes. I was terrified that any moment he would plunge it in my bosom. Although my mouth was no longer gagged, I could not utter a sound. While I was in this plight, Dilawar Khan and Peer Bakhsh talked and laughed all the time and were obviously pleased with themselves. They cursed me and my parents in foul language.

"It is said that a brave man's son will avenge a wrong even after twelve years," said Dilawar Khan. "You see, brother Peer Bakhsh, I have now proved the truth of that saying. How that son of a ... must suffer now!"

"Indeed you have proved the proverb," replied Peer Bakhsh. "It would be just about twelve years since you were sentenced, isn't it?"

"Exactly twelve. Brother, what hardships I had to go through in the jail at Lucknow! However, now it is that ...'s turn to suffer. He will rue it for many a day. And this is only my first move. I mean to murder him."

"You don't say so!"

"What do you take me for? If I do not kill him I am a bastard and not the true son of a Pathan."

"I know you are true to your word."

"Just wait and see."

"What do you propose doing with this girl?" asked Peer Bakhsh.

"Kill her and dump her in a gutter. And get back home before the night is over."

When I heard these words, I had no doubt that my end was near. The tears dried up in my eyes, my heart felt a sudden jolt, my limbs became lifeless and my neck fell back as it does at the time of death. But there wasn't the slightest trace of pity on the face of the monster. On the contrary, he gave me a hard blow on my chest. I doubled up with pain and nearly fell off the cart.

"If you kill the girl," asked Peer Bakhsh, "how will you pay me?"

"I will pay you to the last penny."

"Where will you get the money? I thought you meant to do something else."

"If I can't raise it in any other way, I'll sell the pigeons and pay you."

"You are stupid. Why should you sell the pigeons? Shall I tell you of another way?"

"Speak."

"Old chap, let us take the girl to Lucknow and sell her."

The fear of death had affected my sense of hearing and the voices of these villains were like a hubbub in a nightmare. But I caught Peer Bakhsh's words and blessed him in my heart. But what would the other cut-throat want to do?

"All right, we will see when the time comes. Let's get a move on."

"Let's stop here awhile. There is a fire under that tree ahead of us. I will get some charcoal for our hookah." When Peer Bakhsh went away to get the charcoal, I began to wonder whether Dilawar would put an end to my life before he returned. I became hysterical and shrieked at the top of my voice. Dilawar Khan turned on me with savage fury and hit me hard in the face. "Shut up, you little bastard," he yelled, "or I'll stick this knife in you." Then followed a string of filthy abuse.

Peer Bakhsh had not gone very far. He shouted to Dilawar Khan to hold his hand. "Don't do that, brother."

"All right, all right," assured Dilawar Khan. "Go and get the charcoal."

A little later Peer Bakhsh returned with a few pieces of live charcoal, prepared the hookah and handed it to his companion. Dilawar Khan took a pull at the hookah and asked: "How much do you think she will fetch? Who will arrange the sale? I hope we don't get into trouble."

"What are you scared of, old man? No one will catch us. In Lucknow such deals are made all the time. You leave it to me; I will manage the transaction. Do you know my wife's brother?"

"Karim?"

"The same. It is his means of livelihood. He has abducted scores of boys and girls and made money on them."

"Where is he these days?"

"Where could he be except in Lucknow! His father-in-law's house is across the river Gomti. He is bound to be there."

"How much is a boy or a girl worth?" asked Dilawar Khan after some time.

"Depends on their looks."

"How much do you think this one will fetch?"

"A hundred, or, with luck, a hundred and fifty."

"You've got a hope, brother. She has no looks to speak of. A hundred would be too much for her."

"There is no harm in trying. What would you get if you killed her?"

We travelled all through the night. It is said that sleep can come to a condemned man even as he awaits death on the stake. So it was with me. Although death hovered in front of my eyes, after a short while they closed in slumber. Peer Bakhsh took pity on me and covered me with the blanket meant for his bullocks. I woke up several times, but I lay still without uttering a sound. Then I moved the blanket off my face. I was alone in the cart. I raised the flap on the side and saw a row of huts and a grocer's shop. Dilawar Khan and Peer Bakhsh were buying something. The bullocks had been un-yoked and were munching fodder under a banyan tree. Some villagers were sitting round a fire warming their hands and smoking a *chillum*. Peer Bakhsh came back and gave me some roasted gram. I had eaten nothing all night and was famished. I devoured it greedily. Then he brought me a jug of water. I drank a little and lay down quietly.

After a long rest Peer Bakhsh got up and yoked the bullocks. Dilawar Khan filled his hookah and came and sat beside me. And we were on the move again. That day he was not so hard on me. He did not brandish his knife, nor smack nor shout at me. They stopped at several places to refill their hookah and chatted and sang all the way. Their talk often turned into abuse. They would roll up their sleeves, tighten their waist-bands and leap off the cart. Then something would make them cool off and the quarrel would be over. There would be a reconciliation. They would start talking in such a friendly manner that it was hard to believe that there had ever been any misunderstanding between them. "How can there be any question of our falling out?" one would ask.

"None whatsoever," would come the reply.

"All right, let bygones be bygones."

"Let bygones be bygones."

You have already heard of the first night in captivity. I still wonder how I ever lived through it. I will not forget the utter helplessness to my dying day. It must have been hard for my soul not to have given up.

As for Dilawar Khan, he got the punishment he deserved. But it did not quench the fires of hate in my heart. I would not have had any compunction in seeing him cut up into small pieces and his flesh fed to the crows and kites. I am certain that even in hell he is flogged with burning faggots night and day and if God is just, a worse fate awaits him on the day of judgment.

It would have been better if Dilawar Khan had killed me. A handful of dust would have covered my virtue and my evil deeds would not have tarnished the fair name of my parents. I would also have been spared the blackening of my face in front of man and God.

I met my mother once again. But that was a long time ago. God alone knows whether she is still alive. I have heard that my younger brother has a son who, by the grace of Allah, is now fourteen or fifteen years old. He has also two daughters. I have a strong desire to see them all. They live in Faizabad which is not very far. One wretched rupee could get me there . . But my hands are tied.

Those days there were no railway trains and it used to take four days to travel from Faizabad to Lucknow. But Dilawar Khan, fearing lest my father pursue him, took a round-about route through the wilderness and it took us eight days to reach Lucknow. How would a useless creature like me know where Lucknow was? It was from the talk between Dilawar Khan and Peer Bakhsh that I gathered it was there that they were taking me. I had heard people at home talk of Lucknow because my mother's father worked there as a gate-keeper in some Nawab's mansion. Once he came to visit us at Faizabad and brought lots of sweets and toys for me. I never forgot him.

Dilawar Khan and Peer Bakhsh took me across the Gomti to the home of Karim's father-in-law which was a dingy mud hovel. Karim's mother-in-law was an old hag who looked like a bather of corpses. She took me inside and locked me up in a cell and kept me locked up all morning and afternoon. Then a youngish woman (who I later learnt was Karim's wife) came in and brought me three *chapatties*, a spoonful of lentil soup in a saucer of clay and some water in an earthen jug. Even this simple fare was like a feast for me, because for one whole week, fate had deprived me of home-cooked food; on the journey I was given nothing but roasted gram or powdered corn. I ate all I was given and drank up half the jug of water. I stretched myself on the floor and fell fast asleep. Heaven alone knows how long I slept because in the cell one could not tell night from day. I woke up several times in the complete dark and since there was no one around, I covered my face with my *dupatta* and went back to sleep. Then the old hag, Karim's mother-in-law, came in muttering and jabbering.

"Her ladyship does like to sleep, doesn't she? Shout yourself hoarse and she will not turn a hair; shake her for all you are worth and she will slumber on. I think a snake must have sniffed at her. Ah! her ladyship is awake at last."

I kept quiet and she went on jabbering till she had exhausted herself. "Where is the cup?" she demanded. I gave it to her and she went out. The door was locked again. A little later Karim's woman came in. She unlatched a window and took me out through it to a tumble-down courtyard. It did my heart good to see the open sky even though it was for a short time. I was taken back and locked up in the same dark dungeon and as on the previous day I was given lentil soup and a bowl of maize porridge to eat.

So passed another two days. On the third, a girl, perhaps a year or two older than me, was brought and locked up in the same cell. God alone knows from where Karim had enticed her! The poor thing was crying her heart out. Her arrival was a blessing for me. When she stopped crying, we started talking to each other in whispers.

She told me that her name was Ram Dei, the daughter of a Hindu trader of a village near Sitapur. I could not see her face in the dark, but next day when the window was opened, we had a good look at each other. She was fair and petite and her features were lovely.

Ram Dei was taken away on the fourth day and I had to spend another two days in that dark hole in utter loneliness. On the third night Dilawar Khan and Peer Bakhsh came and took me out with them. It was a moonlit night. We went across some open ground and then through a street till we came to a bridge. The river was in flood and a sharp breeze was blowing. I began to shiver with cold. A little later we found ourselves in another street and then we went through a very long and narrow lane. I had to walk its entire length and my feet ached. We came to another bazaar which was so crowded that we found it difficult to get through. At long last we came to the entrance of a house.

Mirza Ruswa, can you guess what this place was? It was here that I was to trade my honour for money, for this was the Chowk, the prostitutes' quarter. And I was at the house where I was to get whatever was due to me from the world—honour and disgrace, fame and notoriety, failure and success. It was the establishment of Madame Khanum Jan, and its doors were open. We went in and up a staircase, through the courtyard to a verandah where she was sitting. Khanum was nearly fifty, but what a grand old lady she was! I have never seen another woman with a more dignified bearing nor one as well dressed as her. The hair about her temples had gone snow-white and neatly framed her dark face. She wore a pair of loose pyjamas made of gold thread and had a *dupatta* of finely crinkled white muslin over her head. She had big bracelets of solid gold on her arms; her plain ear-rings became her beautiful face. Her daughter Bismillah Jan had exactly the same complexion and features but lacked that something, *je ne sais quoi,* which made the mother so much more fascinating. I have never forgotten the impression she created on me that day. She was sitting on a low settee covered with a carpet. The room was lit by a lamp with a glass globe shaped like a lotus flower. A large and richly engraved paan-leaf casket lay open in front of her. She was smoking a hookah through a long winding stem. Her daughter, the dusky Bismillah Jan was dancing. As soon as we entered, the dancing stopped and those present left the room. The deal had apparently been settled earlier. Madame Khanum looked up and asked: "Is this the girl?"

"Yes Madam," replied Dilawar Khan.

She beckoned me to her side, put her arm round my shoulder and made me sit down beside her. She tilted up my face and looked closely. "Very well," she said at last, "I stand by my offer for this one. What about the other girl?"

"She has already been disposed of," answered Peer Bakhsh.

"How much did you get for her?"

"Two hundred rupees."

"Well, then, that's settled," she commented and then asked: "Who did you sell her to?"

"A begum bought her for her son."

"She wasn't too bad to look at; I would have paid as much. You were hasty."

"What was I to do? I did my best but my wife's brother would not listen to me."

"This girl also has a nice face," interrupted Dilawar Khan, "you are the best judge."

"She will do," conceded Khanum, "at least she is human."

"Well, she is yours for the taking," replied Dilawar Khan.

"You are a stubborn lot," said Khanum. She called for one, Husaini. A dark, buxom woman of middle age came in. "Bring the cash box," ordered Khanum. Husaini went and fetched the cash box. Khanum opened it and put a lot of money in front of Dilawar Khan.

I came to know later that she paid a hundred and twenty-five rupees for me. Of these, Peer Bakhsh counted out some and tied them up in his kerchief. (I was told he got fifty). The accursed Dilawar Khan put the rest in his pouch. Both of them salaamed and took their leave. I was left with Khanum and the maid-servant, Husaini. Khanum spoke to her maid-servant: "Husaini, this girl does not seem too dear for the price we have paid."

"Dear? I would say you got her very cheap."

"On no, not so very cheap either," exclaimed Khanum. "However, she has an innocent face. I wonder whose child she is. And what a state her parents must be in! Don't these rascals have any fear of God when they abduct these girls, Husaini? Don't you agree we are absolutely blameless? It is they who will have to answer before God for deeds such as this. If I had not bought her, she would have been sold to someone else."

"She will be much better off here," Husaini assured her. "Hasn't Madam heard how these slave girls are treated by mistresses of respectable homes?"

"Of course I have heard! Only the other day, I was told that Sultan Jahan Begum chanced upon her slave girl talking to her husband and had the girl branded with a red hot iron till she died."

"These women get away with murder here," sighed Husaini, "but on the Day of Judgment, those who treat their servants cruelly will have their faces blackened."

"Only have their faces blackened!" exclaimed Khanum warming up, "they will be thrashed by hell's burning faggots."

"It will serve them right," agreed the maid-servant. "That is what they really deserve." After a while Husaini asked Khanum: "Mistress, give this child to me. I will bring her up for you. She is your property, but let me look after her."

"All right, you take her," replied Khanum waving to me. Husaini, who had remained standing all this while, sat down beside me. "Where do you come from, child?" she asked me.

"From Bangla," I replied sobbing.

"Where's Bangla?" Husaini asked Khanum.

"How dunse you are! Bangla is another name for Faizabad."

"What is your father's name?" Husaini asked me.

"Jemadar."

"You are the limit," interrupted Khanum. "How can she know her father's name? She is only a child."

"What is your name?" asked Husaini, proceeding with her questions.

"Ameeran."

"I don't like the name," interrupted Khanum again. "We will call you Umrao."

"Do you hear, child?"said Husaini. "Henceforth you answer to the name of 'Umrao'. When the mistress calls 'Umrao', you reply 'Yes, Madam',"

From that day my name became Umrao. When I grew up and took my place amongst the courtesans of Lucknow, people began to call me Umrao Jan. And when I began to write poetry I added the pseudonym "Ada" and came to be known as Umrao Jan Ada. Khanum always called me Umrao; Husaini addressed me as Umrao Sahib.

Husaini took me to her room and gave me nice things to eat. She helped me to wash and change and put me in her own bed.

That night I dreamt of my home in Faizabad. I saw my little brother at play and my father come back with a leaf-cup full of sweets. He gave my brother some and asked where I was. As soon as I heard his voice, I ran up to him and flung my arms about his legs and sobbed out my story to him. I cried so much in my sleep that I began to hiccup. Husaini woke me up. The home with its wide· verandahs, my father, mother and brother had all vanished. There was only me sobbing in Husaini's lap and she wiping away my tears. In the dim light of the oil lamp I saw that Husaini's eyes were also wet.

Husaini or Auntie Husaini as I began to call her, was

indeed a noble-hearted woman. She gave me so much affection that within a few days I forgot my home and my parents. That was perhaps inevitable as I had no choice in the matter. This was an utterly different way of life. I got food the likes of which I had never tasted before. And I wore clothes the likes of which I had never even dreamed of. There were also three girls to play with: Bismillah Jan, Khurshid Jan and Ameer Jan. The days and nights were filled with dancing and singing, shows and concerts, and fairs and picnics in pleasure gardens. No form of luxury was denied to us.

Mirza Ruswa! You will probably think that I was a very callous child to have forgotten my parents so soon and taken to games and frolics. Although I was of a very tender age, as soon as I entered Khanum's house, I knew that I would have to spend the rest of my years there. I was like a bride who, when she goes to her husband's home, knows that her sojourn is not for a day or two but that she has to live there for better or worse till the end of her time, till the day of reckoning. I had also suffered so much at the hands of the villainous dacoits that Khanum's house appeared like Paradise to me. I had realised the utter improbability of seeing my parents again; and one ceases to long for something which one knows is out of reach. Although Faizabad was only forty *kos* from Lucknow, those days it seemed a long, long distance away.

Ask me not what fascination there is in reading what the Recording Angels have writ. I found my life's story all unfolded.

Mirza Sahib, when I read your manuscript on my life, I was so angry that I wanted to tear it up into tiny bits and throw it away. Hadn't I blackened my face often enough in my lifetime not to want to leave a record which people could read and cry 'shame' even when I was dead and gone? Only my indolent nature and consideration for your labours held my hand.

Last night I happened to wake up in the middle of the

night. For a long time I turned from one side to the other
hoping that sleep would come. Then I got up, lit the lamp by
my pillow and rolled myself a paan leaf. I called out to the
maid-servant and asked her to get my hookah. I lay on my bed
and smoked for a while. There were many novels and story-
books in the almirah beside the pillow. I took them up one by
one and turned over their pages. Since I had read them several
times before, I put them away. Then my hand fell on your
manuscript. I was extremely upset by it and swore to tear it up.
Then I felt the presence of someone beside me who whispered
in my ear: 'All right, Umrao Jan, let us assume that you have
torn up the manuscript and thrown it away or burnt it, what
difference will it have made? By the order of the Just and
Powerful God, the Recording Angles have already written down
a detailed account of all the incidents of your life; who can
erase one line of that?'

  This mysterious voice made me tremble from head to foot
and the manuscript nearly fell out of my hand. I abandoned the
idea of tearing it up and decided to put it back in its place.
Then without really meaning to, I began to read it. When I had
finished the first page, I turned it over and read another few
lines of the second. By then I got so absorbed in reading about
my own doings that I wanted to go on and on. I had never
enjoyed reading other stories as much because I could never
forget that they were fabrications of the mind without any truth
or substance. All the incidents that you have penned in my
biography did, in fact, come to pass. And they passed before
my eyes exactly as they had taken place. If anyone had seen
me while I was reading these pages he would have had no
doubts left about my being utterly insane. Sometimes I was
rocked helpless with laughter; then tears would course down
my cheeks. You had asked me to make the necessary changes
as I went along. And here I was, not even aware of what I was
dong. I read on till the early hours of the morning. I got up,
washed myself, said my morning prayer, and went back to bed
to get a little sleep. I woke up at about 8 o'clock and picked
up the manuscript again. I read all day and finished it by the
evening.

What I found most fascinating in the story was your dissertation on virtuous and evil women. I agree with you that the virtuous have every right to the pride they have and street women like me can do nothing about it except feel envious. But in my case, fate and circumstances had a lot to do with the particular course of my life. The primary cause of my taking the path of evil was Dilawar Khan. If he had not kidnapped me, I would not have been sold to Khanum, nor would my life have fulfilled its sordid destiny.

I have done my best to change my mode of living. I have given up doing things of whose evil nature I am convinced. I had no chance of doing so earlier as in the atmosphere that prevailed in Khanum's establishment, I could not understand their real nature. I looked upon Khanum as my mistress and my ruler and did as she told me. If I did anything against her wishes, I did it on the sly so that I might not be beaten or scolded. (Actually Khanum never beat me, but the fear that she might was always there). My life was patterned after that of the people amongst whom I was brought up. There was never any occasion to ponder over questions of ethics or morality. No one in my circumstances could be expected to do otherwise.

I had not been taught the injunctions of religion nor explained the distinction between good and evil. That is why such matters had no meaning for me. Indeed, at that time I had no religion of any kind and was content to copy other people. If I was too lazy to do the right thing or if things went wrong due to my own stupidity I promptly ascribed them to fate. My Persian reading had acquainted me with the practice of blaming the stars for everything. If any scheme went awry, or if I was hurt by anyone, I cursed the skies:

> Though I am the master of my fate,
>   the only power I have,
> Is to curse my fate when things go wrong.

When my teacher or Auntie Husaini or other older people talked of the days gone by, it seemed that those times were much better than the present, and like them, I took to praising the past at the expense of the present without any rhyme or reason. Since the days of their youth are the best days of their lives, all persons praise old times in their old age. As the Persian proverb says, "If you have zest for life, the world is alive. If you feel dead, the world also seems dead." Young people follow the old blindly and have given currency to the habit of running down present times.

When I attained my youth, attracting men by my singing became my main occupation. My happiness and sorrow depended on the measure of success or failure I achieved in competition with the other girls. I was not as good looking as them but because of my knowledge of music, poetry and literature, I did better than them and enjoyed a certain distinction amongst them. This also did me some harm. As I won acclaim, my self-esteem grew. Other courtesans did not care how they got their custom. I was stuck-up and was frequently left high and dry. They would ask any Tom, Dick or Harry for a present as was customary in our profession. I was diffident and did not like people to get familiar too soon. I felt horribly snubbed if my request was turned down. Other courtesans' only concern was to find out how much their patrons were worth and how much they could fleece them. Most of my time was spent in discovering my patrons' background and interests. I had other traits which were not whorish and marked me out as different from women in the business. They looked upon me as self-centred, moody and somewhat mad. I went my own sweet way without heeding anyone.

Then came a time when I began to look down upon my profession as immoral and decided to give it up. I refused to receive all and sundry in my apartment, and for some time only accepted long-term engagements with noblemen; then I gave up that practice as well and began to rely only on singing and dancing for my living.

When I had given up these immoral ways, I began to toy with the idea of settling down with some person. I gave up the plan because I knew that people would say: "She was a tart;

she's made sure of the undertaker's expenses." The origin of this saying is the notion that if a prostitute has passed her prime and decides to settle down with a man, her intention is to ensure that her funeral expenses are paid for, that even when she is about to die she extracts the price of her coffin. It illustrates the utterly selfish, greedy and fraudulent nature of a prostitute. Even if such a woman turned her back on her past and became extremely virtuous, no one would believe it except God. If then she fell in love with all the sincerity her heart was capable of, neither the man who was the object of her affection nor those who heard about it would place any credence in her professions. Her love would be wasted.

It is rumoured that I am a rich woman. Because of this, despite my age, quite a few men express desire for me and flatter me in many ways. Some praise my charm and my beauty despite the fact that they have had liaisons with women better-looking by far than I. Some profess to be enamoured of my singing—although they have no ear for music and cannot tell one note from another. Some go into raptures over my poems—despite the fact that they cannot recite a line correctly—not to speak of composing one. Some admire me for my learning and although they are erudite themselves, insist on calling me the most learned of scholars and seek my guidance on elementary questions of theology and ritual, like rules of fasting and prayer, as if they were my disciples. Some loudly declare their indifference to my wealth and attainments and only show concern for my health. If I sneeze, they worry so much that it gives them a headache; if my head aches, they are on the verge of death. To every sentence they speak, they add 'May Allah preserve you'. Some assume the role of benevolent advisers. They treat me like a little child too trusting and simple to be on my own in the wily world.

I am a woman of experience who has slaked her thirst at many a stream. I appear pliable and pretend to be moulded by people, when in fact it is I who am moulding them. I have a few real friends who are men of culture with a taste for poetry, literature and music and who demand nothing except good conversation. They ask for nothing more from me, nor I from them. I like them from the bottom of my heart and value their friendship because it is not demanding. And just because it asks for nothing, it has begun to mean everything to me. I find no solace except in their company. Unfortunately none of them desires to live with me permanently. So why should I hanker for it? It would be like wanting one's youth to return.

A woman's real life lasts as long as her youth. Oh, if only life could end when youth ends! Old age is bad for everyone—particularly women—and for women of my profession it can veritably be the picture of hell. If you look a little closely at the old women begging in the streets and by-lanes of Lucknow, you will find that most of them have been prostitutes in their younger days—some so beautiful that they had disdained to put their feet on the ground. They wrought havoc in men's lives, bringing ruin to thousands of prosperous homes and slaying hundreds of innocent young men. Wherever they went, men spread a carpet of their glances for them to tread upon. Now no one as much as bothers to cast a look at them. There was a time when men's hearts rejoiced in their company. Now no one is willing to suffer them. There was a time when without their having to ask, pearls were showered on them; now they beg and can't even get a crust of dry bread.

Most of these women brought ruin upon their own heads. I used to know one who had once been a famous courtesan and had earned a fortune. She was rather fond of men. When her heyday was over, she began to entertain men at her own expense. In her old age she took up residence with a young, handsome, married man who was quite obviously not in love with her. He had squared his wife by telling her the real reason for taking in the woman. The couple made much fuss over the old lady and helped her to spend her fortune. When the money ran out, they threw her out. Now she stumbles about the streets of this city.

Some stupid courtesans adopt young girls and get very attached to them. (I was bitten by the same bug). When these girls grow up, they rake in all they can, and walk off. Even if they stay, they gradually take possession of everything and reduce their benefactors to the positions of housekeepers or cooks. Abadi would certainly have done me in the eye and robbed me of all I had, if her misdeeds had not given her away earlier. In the warped world of courtesans, there is no such thing as love. No man in his senses will fall in love with a courtesan because he knows that a courtesan can belong to no one. And one courtesan cannot afford to have affection for another courtesan because inevitably there is rivalry between them. This is more so in the case of one who adopts a young girl. The younger courtesan will soon make it clear that since she does all the work, her mistress has no right to take any money from her. When a courtesan begins to lose her looks, her erstwhile admirers begin to cool off. Having been used to flattery, she cannot bear life with no one to flatter her and turns sour. This makes men avoid her all the more, and she, in turn, bears a grievance against all men.

At one time I used to listen to long tales of men's faithlessness from other courtesans and agreed with what they said without giving the subject much thought. Despite what I suffered at the hands of Gauhar Mirza and the Nawab who had claimed to have married me, I do not think men are any more faithless than women—particularly women who take to the streets. If you do not mind my saying so, in matters of love, men are often quite dense and women extremely shrewd. Most men are honest in their professions of love: most women only simulate it. Men are hasty with their declarations and get deeply involved for a little while. Women take their time and are more cautious. For this very reason, men's affections ebb quickly and women's remain constant. If the couple, or at least one of them, is sensible, they can come to a satisfactory compromise and have a pleasant life.

In matters of love, men are credulous while women are suspicious. Men succumb easily to women's wiles. Women, on the other hand, are not so easily swayed by masculine charms. I believe nature has made this difference for good reasons. Women are the weaker sex and therefore provided with other powers which compensate for it, amongst them, the inability to fall in love easily. I would go so far as to say that this is really the one quality which makes up for their many weaknesses. The same situation prevails in the animal kingdom. Weaker animals are endowed with the ability to deceive in order to preserve themselves.

Most men think that women are beautiful. I do not agree with this opinion. As a matter of fact neither men nor women are beautiful by themselves. Each sex has been given the sort of beauty which appeals to the other. Although every good-looking person evokes admiration, the real judge of a man's looks is a woman, and of a woman's, a man. To a woman, the most beautiful woman is no more than a lovely flower without fragrance; and men whom other men find ugly perhaps quite enchanting.

Both men and women fail to grasp the subtle emotions which lead to love because their approach to the subject is entirely different. The qualities a man looks for in a woman are not those a woman looks for in a man.

Only men who serve women of wealth or who, being themselves young, enjoy the affections of older women, get some inkling of what love means to womankind.

It is undoubtedly true that women prefer younger men to older ones. But even in this preference it is not so much the charm or handsomeness of the young men which attracts them, but, being weak themselves, they wish to provide themselves with protectors. Young men, being able-bodied, can be relied on more than old men in times of trouble. Since looks usually go with youth, the combination becomes irresistible.

To a man, the pursuit of love is a quest of pleasure. To a woman, the pursuit of love is the quest of pleasure as well as of security. Since it is believed that love can only be true when it has no motive, women, because they seek security, try to conceal its existence.

If only people pondered over these matters, they would avoid a lot of bickering in their lives. If men and women knew their proper places and what precisely they wanted, they would be able to save themselves from many unpleasant situations. The trouble is that if one offers advice, there is the stock reply: "That which is written in one's fate is bound to happen." This really amounts to asking people to mind their own business and leave them with the liberty to do what they like. Since everything they do is ordained by fate, they feel they are not responsible for the consequences of their acts. Everything is ascribed to God—may He forgive us. This sort of stupidity perhaps made sense in olden times when things could change in a trice but not now. This reminds me of a story of the days of the Kings of Oudh.

One day, it is said, a soldier was sleeping on a platform near the gate of the Pearl Palace. Being poor, he was in rags. As fate would have it, the King passed by that way on his morning stroll. He was unattended. One doesn't know what came into his mind, but he woke up the soldier. The soldier got up rubbing his eyes. When he saw the King, he got very flustered. Then he collected his wits, remembered his sorry state and promptly presented his sword to the sovereign. The sword was old and rusty and was drawn out of the scabbard with some difficulty. The monarch accepted the weapon, examined it carefully and praised its excellence. He put it back in the scabbard and fixed it in the royal belt. He took off his own Damascene sword which had a gold handle and presented it to the soldier along with the belt which was inlaid with gold. At that moment, the Grand Vazier of Oudh, Huzoor Alam Ali Naqi Khan, arrived on the scene. His Majesty commended the soldier and his sword: "See how handsome the youth is! And what a fine sword he has given me!" He took out the sword from his side and showed it to the Vazier. "Just look at it!"

"Allah be praised," exclaimed the Vazier, "Lord of the Universe, one has to be a connoisseur of jewels like you to find such a man and such a sword,"

"But the sword I've given isn't at all bad either!" exclaimed the King.

"Shadow of God—how could your sword be anything but good!" replied the Vazier.

"His dress is not befitting," said the King nodding towards the young man. By then courtiers, servants, mace-bearers, and the bearers of arms arrived on the scene and there was quite a crowed to witness the goings-on.

"His Majesty is quite right," agreed the Vazier.

"Let us see how he looks in our clothes," said the King. The courtiers took the hint. They ran to the palace and brought back tray-loads of royal garments. The King took off his robes and the pearls and diamonds he was wearing and presented them to the soldier. When the soldier had changed into royal dress the King commented: "Now look at him!"

"Indeed, he looks a different person," said the Vazier. The courtiers also began to praise the soldier. The King's carriage arrived and he left to take the air.

The soldier came home full of joy. Jewellers, money-lenders and brokers followed hard on his heels. They valued the gifts at over fifty thousand rupees.

The young man had been a sepoy in Najib's platoon drawing a measly salary of Rs. 3 per month. The previous night he had had words with his wife over the dinner she had served. He had walked out of the home and spent the night wandering in the streets till he was worn out with fatigue. He had sat down by the gate of the Pearl Palace and fallen asleep. Then the miracle took place. Dame Fortune woke him up in the morning and smiled on him. In one breath he was changed from a pauper to a prince.

Such things used to take place quite often during the monarchy. Indeed they were only possible under a system in which the reins of government were in the hands of only one person, who was above the law and who looked upon the country as his fief and the public treasury as his private property. Under British rule there is no room for such waste. It is considered wrong to give someone a large sum of money without any reason or justification. Under the present system, everyone from the King down to the beggar is bound by the rule of law. If the law made any exceptions or recognised any privileges, it would break down. Fate has been rendered powerless; now one only succeeds by endeavour.

Let me tell you about what happened to Nawab Chabban who disappeared from the pages of my biography. It is a fact that he went to the river and plunged into the stream with no intention of ever coming up again. But life is precious to everyone. When he ran out of breath, he decided to come up to take one more last breath. Then quite involuntarily he began to thrash the water with his legs and arms. He went under the water once again and came up to the surface for the same reason. By this time, he had floated down the river up to Chattar Manzil. By a fortunate coincidence, the heir-apparent to the royal throne happened to be out on a barge with his courtiers. His eyes fell on the drowning man and he ordered his boatmen to go to his help at once. Nawab Chabban did his best to get away but the rescuers overpowered him and brought him ashore. The Prince discovered that the young man was of aristocratic birth. He gave him a change of clothes and took him to his palace.

Nawab Chabban was handsome, well-mannered and knew how to deport himself. He had refined tastes, a subtle sense of humour and was in every way the right man to be a companion to a prince. He was engaged as a courtier at a handsome salary. Money was advanced to him to buy the necessities for his station in life. He was given servants, attendants, carriages and began to live in greater style than before. Now when he passed through the chowk, he was on an elephant with a posse of fifty footmen with lackeys running ahead. Bismillah Jan and I saw him with our own unbelieving eyes and got the whole story from Makhdum Bakhsh who was in Nawab Chabban's train. After this change of fortune, the uncle made up with Chabban and the marriage took place as arranged. We were invited to attend. Madam Khanum was presented with a lovely shawl and a scarf. But Nawab Chabban never came to our establishment again as he had sworn not to have anything more to do with Bismillah Jan.

This sort of thing could only happen during the monarchy. Nothing of the sort happens under English rule: the days of carefree abandon are over and gone. We have been told that wealth is blind. It appears that by some miracle of optical surgery, her sight has been restored and she can now tell the difference between the foolish and the deserving.

During the monarchy, morons who did not know the first letter of the alphabet were appointed to high posts. One wonders how they did any work. Even more laughable were the appointments of eunuchs as commanders of platoons and cavalry. In the end fate outplayed its hand and brain won the day. Now it is personal merit that counts. Since merit is largely a matter of reputation, it often happens that men of ability and learning are ignored because no one knows about them.

For a long time, I was puzzled by the conflict between fate and free will. Then I came to the conclusion that people used the word 'fate' quite wrongly. If it were meant to imply that God knows our fates from the very start, there could be no objection; only a disbeliever would question this contention. But people (May Allah pardon them) usually ascribe the results of all their evil deeds to fate. This casts a slur on the divine power of God and is sheer heresy.

It is a great pity that I did not know of these things earlier. There was no one to tell me and I was not sagacious enough to learn them myself. The little that the Maulvi Sahib taught me was of great help to me. (May Allah raise his status in Heaven). At the time I did not fully appreciate their real worth. My only concern was to have a good time and to live in comfort. Moreover, I had so many admirers that I had little time to be by myself. When they began to drop out of my life, one by one, and since I had nothing better to do, I developed a taste for books.

If I had not acquired this taste for reading, I would not have been able to live very long. I would have killed myself moping over my lost youth and brooding over the loss of old admirers. At first I whiled away the time reading works of fiction. One day I took out my old books to put them out in the sun. Among them was the *Gulistan* which the Maulvi Sahib had taught me. I began to turn over its pages. I remembered that as a child I had disliked the book because I had started my education with it and the text had seemed very difficult. And since I was ignorant, I had failed to understand it. Now I read it over and over again from cover to cover. Each phrase went deep into my heart. Then I heard someone praise *Akhlaq-i-Nasiri* and got a copy from him. It is a difficult book to understand because it has a large number of Arabic words. I read a little at a time and took many months to finish it. Thereafter I started on the *Danish Nama Ghyas Mansur* which had just then been published by the Nawal Kishore Press. I followed this up by two books on logic, the *Sughra* and the *Kubra*. What I did not understand myself, I asked other people to explain. As I read these books I felt as if the mysteries of the world were being revealed to me. After these, I read many books in Urdu and Persian on my own and so enriched my mind. I glanced through the Persian *Quaseedas* (Songs of Praise) by Anwari and Khakani. They did not attract me as I had no use for false praise; so I put them away on the bookshelf.

I get many newspapers and keep in touch with what is going on in the world. My thrifty ways have given me enough savings to last me to the end of my days; Allah will take care of me in the life to come. I have been a true repentant, and, as far as possible, I observe my fasts and say my prayers. I do not wear a veil nor live a cloistered life (Allah can punish me for this if He will). But I do bless those who observe the injunction of the veil from the bottom of my heart. May God preserve their husbands and their homes and may their chastity remain untarnished until the end of the world.

Before I end I would like to say a few words to women of my profession: they should have them engraved on their hearts. O foolish women, never be under the delusion that anyone will ever love you truly. Your lovers who today forswear their lives for you will walk out on you after a while. They will never remain constant because you do not deserve constancy. The rewards of true love are for women who only see the face of one man. God will never grant the gift of true love to a whore.

I have lived my life; now I await its end. I will breathe the air of this world for as long as it is ordained. I am reconciled to my fate. All my wishes have been fulfilled and I ask for nothing more although desire is a devil that will not be exorcised till the last breath is out of the body. I hope this tale of my life will do some good to some people. I will finish with this couplet and hope that the reader will pray for me:

My day comes to a close, death draws nigh
And I have drunk of life to the dregs.

BIBLIOGRAPHY

NONFICTION :

The Sikhs. London : Allen & Unwin, 1953; New York : Macmillan, 1953; Delhi : Lustre Press, 1984.

The Unending Trail. Delhi : Rajkamal, 1957.

The Sikhs Today : Their Religion, History, Culture, Customs, and Way of Life, edited by Rahul Singh. Bombay: Orient Longman, 1959; London : Sangam, 1985.

The Fall of the Kingdom of the Punjab. Bombay: Orient Longman, 1962; London: Sangam, 1979.

A History of the Sikhs. Vol. 1: 1469-1839. Princeton, N.J.: Princeton University Press, 1963; London: Oxford University Press, 1963; Delhi: Oxford University Press, 1977. *Vol. 2: 1839-1964.* Princeton, N.J.: Princeton University Press, 1966; London: Oxford University Press, 1966; Delhi: Oxford University Press, 1977.

Ranjit Singh : Maharajah of the Punjab, 1780-1839. London: Allen & Unwin, 1962.

Not Wanted in Pakistan. Delhi : Rajkamal, 1965.

Ghadar, 1915 : India's First Armed Revolution, with Satindra Singh. New Delhi : R & K, 1966.

Guru Gobind Singh -- the Saviour. Bombay, 1977

Homage to Guru Gobind Singh, with Suneet Vir Singh. Bombay: Jaico, 1966; East Glastonbury, Conn.: Ind-US, 1970.

Shri Ram: A Biography, with Arun Joshi. London and New York: Asia Publishing House, 1968.

Religion of the Sikhs. Madras: University of Madras, 1968.

Khushwant Singh's India: A Mirror for its Monsters and Monstrosities (essays), edited by Rahul Singh. Bombay: India Book House, 1970.

Khushwant Singh's View of India: Lectures on India's People, Religions, History, and Contemporary Affairs, edited by Rahul Singh. Bombay: India Book House, 1974.

Khushwant Singh on War and Peace in India, Pakistan, and Bangladesh, edited by Mala Singh. Delhi: Hind Pocket Books, 1976.

Good People, Bad People, edited by Rahul Singh. New Delhi: Orient Paperback, 1977.

Khushwant Singh's India without Humbug, edited by Rahul Singh. Bombay: India Book House, 1977.

Around the World with Khushwant Singh, edited by Rahul Singh. New Delhi: Orient Paperbacks, 1978.

Indira Gandhi Returns. New Delhi: Vision, 1979.

Two Essays on Prof. S. Chandrasekhar. New Delhi, 1970.

Khushwant Singh's Editor's Page (editorials), edited by Rahul Singh. Bombay: India Book House, 1981.

We Indians. Delhi: Orient Paperbacks, 1982.

Delhi: A Portrait (photographs by Raghu Rai). Delhi: Delhi Tourism Development Corp., 1983; Oxford: Oxford University Press, 1983.

Tragedy of Punjab: Operation Bluestar and After, with Kuldip Nayar. New Delhi: Vision, 1984.

Three Contemporary Novelists : Criticism and Interpretation. Bombay, 1985

Many Faces of Communalism, with Bipan Chandra. Chandigarh. Indian Centre for Research in Rural and Industrial Development, 1985.

Malicious Gossip, edited by Rohini Singh. New Delhi: Konark Publishers, 1987.

More Malicious Gossip, edited by Rohini Singh. New Delhi: Konarak Publishers, 1988.

Many Moods, Many Faces, edited by Rohini Singh. New Delhi: Rupa & Co. 1989.

Need for a New Religion in India and other Essays, edited by Rohini Singh. New Delhi : UBSPD, 1991.

Nature Watch. New Delhi: Lustre Press, 1990.

Khushwant Singh's Joke Book -- Vol. I; Khushwant Singh's Joke Book -- Vol. II; Khushwant Singh's Joke Book -- Vol. III New Delhi: Vision Books, 1990, 1991 & 1992 respectively.

Punjab's Tragic Story. New Delhi: UBSPD, 1992.

The Best of Khushwant Singh, edited by Nandini Mehta. New Delhi: Penguin India, 1992.

FICTION:

The Mark of Vishnu and Other Stories. London: Saturn Press, 1950.

Train to Pakistan. London: Chatto & Windus, 1956; New York: Grove Press, 1961; also published as *Mano Majra.* New York: Grove Press, 1956. India: Ravi Dayal Publisher.

The Voice of God and Other Stories. Bombay: Jaico, 1957.

I Shall Not Hear the Nightingale. London: J. Calder, 1959, New York: Grove Press, 1959.

A Bride for the Sahib and Other Stories. Delhi: Hind Pocket Books, 1967, East Glastonbury, Conn.: Ind-US, 1967.

Black Jasmine (short stories). Bombay: Jaico, 1971.

Stories from India. New Delhi, 1974.

Collected Short Stories. New Delhi: Ravi Dayal Publisher, 1990.

Delhi -- a novel. New Delhi: Viking India, 1990.

TRANSLATOR OF:

Jupji: The Sikh Morning Prayer, by Guru Nanak, London: Probsthain, 1959.

Umrao Jaan Ada: Courtesan of Lucknow, by Mirza Mohammad Hadi Ruswa, translated with M.A. Husaini. Bombay: Orient Longman, 1961; also published as *The Courtesan of Lucknow (Umrao Jaan Ada).* Delhi: Hind Pocket Books, 1970; East Glastonbury, Conn.: Ind-US, 1970.

The Skeleton and Other Writings, by Amrita Pritam. Bombay: Jaico, 1964.

I Take This Woman, by Rajindar Singh Bedi, Delhi: Hind Pocket Books, 1967; East Glastonbury, Conn.: Ind-US, 1967.

Hymns of Guru Nanak. New Delhi: Orient Longman, 1969; Columbia, Mo.: South Asia Books, 1978.

Selected Poems, by Amrita Pritam, edited by Pritish Nandy, translated with others. Calcutta: Dialogue Calcutta, 1970.

Dreams in Debris: A Collection of Punjabi Short Stories, by Satindra Singh. Bombay: Jaico, 1972.

Sacred Writings of the Sikhs. London: Allen & Unwin, 1974.

Shikwa and Jawab-i-Shikwa, -- *Complaint and Answer* Iqbal's Dialogue with Allah, by Muhammad Iqbal. Delhi and Oxford: Oxford University Press, 1981.

EDITOR OF:

A Note, edited by Peter Russell and Khushwant Singh, on G. V. Desani's *All about H. Hatterr* and *Hali* London. Szeben, 1952.

Land of the Five Rivers: Stories from the Punjab, with Jaya Thadani. Bombay: Jaico, 1965.

Sunset of the Sikh Empire, by Sita Ram Kohli. Bombay: Orient Longman, 1967; Port Washington, N.Y.: Kennikat/Associated Faculty Press, 1987.

I Believe. Delhi: Hind Pocket Books, 1971.

Love and Friendship. New Delhi: Sterling, 1973.

Stories from India, with Qurratulain Hyder. New Delhi: Sterling, 1974.

Gurus, Godmen, and Good People. Bombay: Orient Longman, 1975; London: Sangam, 1979.

ALSO BY KHUSHWANT SINGH

Need For a New Religion in India & Other Essays

This book is a collection of essays on a wide range of subjects--
The Language of Love and Lust, The Monsoon in Literature, Ghosts
and Life Hereafter and Other Laughing Matters. There is an in-
formative piece introducing the Quran and a hitherto unpublished
title essay setting out a brilliant blueprint for a new, practical,
ritual-free religion, more relevant perhaps in today's times than
ever before. If you are one of the enlightened Indians "with the
courage to think for yourself", you cannot afford to ignore it.

The second half of the book should be of particular interest to
students of literature and readers who wish to know more about
some of the greatest authors of our times, some of whom Khushwant Singh has known personally, Nirad C. Chaudhuri, Aldous
Huxley, Dylan Thomas, Oscar Wilde, Belloc. Singh writes about
them, their lives, works and times.

Though thematically diverse, all the essays in this collection have
one thing in common--the distinctive, irrepressible Khushwant
stamp. Written in the author's familiar readable, easily compre-
hensible style, the author brings to each subject a wealth of
knowledge and information.